Cast of Characters

Mr. Cliffordson. The genial, warmhearted headmaster of the Hillmaston Co-educational Day School, a truly progressive institution.

Miss Gretta Cliffordson. His daughter, the junior music mistress, as shallow as she is pretty.

Miss Calma Ferris. The arithmetic mistress, a meek, thoroughly inoffensive woman who takes great happiness in her employment at Hillmaston.

Mrs. Alceste Boyle. A widow and former actress, she's the senior English mistress and has, for many years, been secretly having an affair with

Mr. Frederick Hampstead, the senior music master, whose unfortunate wife has long been incarcerated in a home for female inebriates.

Miss Camden. The senior gymnastics mistress, disliked by almost everyone.

Camden. Her pet pupil, who is a fiercely competitive netball player.

Mr. Donald Smith. The art master, who is secretly in love with Alceste Boyle.

Francis Henry Hurstwood. A sixth-form student, brilliant, restless, and ambitious, with a hopeless crush on Miss Cliffordson.

Moira Malloy. A scholarship student, who is smitten with Mr. Smith.

Mrs. (Madame) Berotti. An aged former actress and exacting critic who does the makeup for the school's theatrical productions.

Miss Lincallow. Miss Ferris's aunt, who runs a boarding house in Bognor Regis.

Miss Ellen Sooley. Her friend, who helps her run the boardinghouse.

Mr. Helm. A commercial traveler who boards with Miss Lincallow.

Mrs. Beatrice Adele Lestrange Bradley. A noted psychoanalyst and private detective. She's old, eccentric, and as kind as she is intelligent.

The Reverend Noel Wells. A young curate and friend to Mrs. Bradley, who presses him into service as her bodyguard.

George Bryan Cutler. An acquitted wife murderer.

Susie Cozens. An opportunistic young woman who was once fired by Miss Lincallow for making too free with the gentlemen guests.

Plus assorted faculty, students, friends, innkeepers, servants, family members, and townspeople.

Death at the Opera

(Death in the Wet)
by Gladys Mitchell

Introduction by Tom & Enid Schantz

Rue Morgue Press
Lyons / Boulder

To
Florence H. Brace

The Rue Morgue Press
P.O. Box 4119
Boulder, CO 80306
800-699-6214
www.ruemorguepress.com

Printed by
Johnson Printing

PRINTED IN THE UNITED STATES OF AMERICA

Gladys Mitchell and Mrs. Bradley

When Lawrence Block's Matt Scudder novel, *Eight Million Ways to Die,* was turned into a movie, the author wryly commented that he could enjoy the film on the same level as the rest of the audience, since he had no idea what was going to happen in it either. Having made so many changes, one wonders why the producers bothered to buy the book in the first place. Much the same can be said for *Death at the Opera,* one of five books by Gladys Mitchell filmed for the BBC's *Mrs. Bradley Mysteries*. If you've seen that stylish television program—shown here in the United States on *Mystery*—rest assured that you're about to enjoy a completely different story here.

Other than the title, the identity of the first victim and the staging of a faculty-student production of *The Mikado*, the television version went in a completely different direction from the book. The school in the book is not Mrs. Bradley's *alma mater* but a progressive coeducational school run by an enlightened and thoroughly delightful headmaster. The school in the television version is a very traditional all-girls school run by an odious prig. Nor are the suspects or the motives behind the murders the same. George, Mrs. Bradley's chauffeur, while a regular in many of the books, is given far more screen time in the film than he ever got in any of the sixty-seven Mrs. Bradley books. In fact, he's entirely absent from the book version of *Death at the Opera*. But Mrs. Bradley is there, the essence of her character—though not her physical appearance—perfectly captured by Diana Rigg.

Beatrice Adela Lestrange Bradley is a brilliant woman who doesn't suffer fools gladly but is capable of showing great kindness to others, whether it be an aging village woman, reluctant witnesses or the grandson she obviously adores. She is far more understanding of murderers than the police or other fictional detectives of the Golden Age (1913-1947), partly because as a psychiatrist she takes the time to understand their motives. This may explain why many of her murderers escape the gallows or long prison terms. Her moral values are her own, not society's. She considers rape, because of its long-lasting psychologically damage, a far more serious offense than a murder committed in the heat of the moment. Indeed, she has even been driven to commit murder herself, obviously getting away with it. She certainly shows more sympathy than we would to the murderer in *Death at the Opera* whose motive—well, that would be telling.

Educated at several universities and holding a degree in medicine, she operates a clinic and is a consultant to the Home Office. She is the author of several books, including *A Small Handbook of Psychoanalysis*. Specializing in the psychology of crime, she also works as a private detective, though it is not always clear if she collects a fee for those services. "Her detecting methods," as Michele Slung so aptly put it in *Twentieth Century Crime and Mystery Writers*, "combine hocopocus and Freud, seasoned with sarcasm and the patience of a predator toying with its intended victim." Mitchell herself admitted that she was not surprised that Mrs. Bradley "annoys people," since "she is never wrong…she has a godlike quality of being much larger than life, and of being so much superior to ordinary people." She is also surprisingly skilled at a number of physical activities, from billiards to knife-throwing, and, on one occasion, when a cellist was unable to perform, Mrs. Bradley stepped in and played flawlessly, "smirking" at the audience's enthralled appreciation "like a satisfied boa-constrictor." She became a Dame of the British Empire in 1955.

As one of the most famous women in England, Mrs. Bradley's reputation almost always precedes her to a crime scene. While at times this puts witnesses on guard—eventually Mrs. Bradley's persuasive powers allow her to break through their reserve—it also prompts others to open up to her, partly because she has an extremely mellifluous voice. However, she is known to frequently cackle in delight, especially at her own brilliance.

Her voice may be the only attractive thing about her. Her reptilian, almost repulsive appearance combined with a bizarre fashion sense would make her a formidable subject for one of those extreme makeover programs so popular on television today. Mitchell based Mrs. Bradley's looks on "two delightful and most intelligent women I knew in my youth." She is frequently compared to a lizard ("dry without being shrivelled") or to a "dreadful bald-headed bird." One character went so far as to liken her to a pterodactyl. Her limbs were considered especially striking. "She possessed nasty, dry, clawlike hands, and her arms, yellow and curiously repulsive, suggested the plucked wing of a fowl." Given her interest in the paranormal, Mrs. Bradley would probably be amused to hear herself described as "witch-like."

Born in the 1870s, Mrs. Bradley is already in her mid-fifties when the series began with *Speedy Death* in 1929. If Mitchell had paid any attention to chronology, Mrs. Bradley would have been nearly 110 when *The Crozier Pharaohs*, the sixty-seventh and last book, appeared in 1984. Golden Age writers, however, felt no compunction to watch the calendar. Just as Ellery Queen (with one notable exception) remained frozen at the age of 35 in the books published from 1940 on, Mrs. Bradley reached her mix-sixties and stayed there. Others of Mitchell's characters would age or not, depending on the demands of the plot. Modern writers of mystery series go to great lengths to develop and age their characters, making it almost a necessity to read their books in order. Golden Age writers were perhaps a bit wiser. For the most part, each of their books could be read independent of the others. The suspension of disbelief is, after all, one of the primary requirements asked of the mystery reader.

Mrs. Bradley's closest personal relationships are with Ferdinand Lestrange, a superb criminal defense attorney as well as her son, and with his wife, Caroline, and small son, Derek (and later two further children, Sebastian and Sally, who, like their parents, age far more rapidly than their grandmother). She had at least one other son from another marriage (she was married and widowed three times in all, though absolutely no information is ever give about one husband) but he emigrates to India and is really never mentioned again. George, her chauffeur, appears in many of her books but she doesn't acquire the Watson needed by every Great Detective until the arrival of her secretary, the attractive Laura Menzies, in the early 1940s.

When she died in 1983, Mitchell may well have been the last of the British Golden Agers still working at her craft. She was an early member of Britain's famed Detection Club. Sponsored by Anthony Berkeley and Helen Simpson, she was inducted by G. K. Chesterton. Founded by Dorothy L. Sayers, it wasn't an easy club to get into. When Mitchell joined their ranks in 1933, there were only thirty-one members. Club members took an oath to play fair with clues, to avoid sinister Chinamen, not to steal each other's plots, and never to eat peas with a knife or put their feet up on the dinner table at club meetings. Mitchell's favorite writers included many fellow members, including Sayers, Agatha Christie, Edmund Crispin "(that delightful boy")", and especially Ngaio Marsh. She had little use for the works of Margery Allingham and Michael Innes. The only American writer she enjoyed was, oddly enough (his books being so very different from hers), Hilary Waugh. Contemporary critics lumped her with Christie and Sayers among England's "big three" women mystery writers but in fact less than a third of her prodigious output was published in the United States during her lifetime, whereas Marsh, Allingham, Josephine Tey, and Georgette Heyer were far better known.

Indeed, Mitchell earned her living not as a writer but as a teacher for most of her life. Following her graduation from the University of London in 1921 (she later earned an external diploma in history from University College, London, in 1926), Mitchell taught at a number of private (called public in England) schools until she retired in 1950. She returned to teaching in 1953 before retiring for good in 1961 at the age of 60, and no doubt this explains why she so often used schools in her books. She taught English, history and games. Her lifelong interest in athletics earned her membership in the British Olympic Association. Her first attempts at fiction in 1923 were rejected. She also wrote a number of books as by Malcolm Torrie and Stephen Hockaby. Born in Crowley, Oxfordshire, April 19, 1901, she never married (any knowledge of romance and sex in my books was purely academic, she explained). She died on July 27, 1983.

Most of our introductions to the books in this vintage reprint series are carved from original sources. With Gladys Mitchell we were privy to a wealth of information gathered by abler hands. We borrowed freely from essays by B.A. Pike, Andrew Osmond, Nicolas Fuller, William A.S. Sargeant, and Jason Hall, the latter of whom maintains a remarkable website devoted to Mitchell (www.gladysmitchell.com). What is good in this essay is due solely to their efforts and any errors belong exclusively to us.

Tom and Enid Schantz
Lyons, Colorado
August 2005

CHAPTER I
DISPERSAL

I

The headmaster shook his head and smiled ruefully.

"There is nothing for it but Shakespeare," he said.

"Dull," suggested the senior science master.

"Quite," the headmaster agreed meekly, and waited for further suggestions.

"The parents won't come," said the junior music mistress, sadly. She liked lots and lots of the parents to come. She waylaid them in corridors and places where parents get lost, and guiding them to the main hall, booked orders for their offspring to take extra music. The fees for extra music were heavy, and the junior music mistress received twenty percent of them. "I'm sure they'll think Shakespeare too boring."

The senior history master did not agree. The parents would come, whatever the Musical, Operatic and Dramatic Society produced, he thought. The parents would come to see the children act and to hear them sing. The parents did not care whether it was Shakespeare or a revue.

At this point, the senior mathematics master wanted to know whether they could not produce a revue. Surely, with so much talent on the staff . . .?

The headmaster replied cordially that if the staff thought they could collaborate in the production of a revue, he should be delighted to assist them by any means in his power. A brisk discussion followed, but the idea was dropped. As the junior English master put it, "it sounded something like work."

"What about another comic opera?" suggested the arithmetic mistress. "I am sure everybody enjoyed *The Gondoliers.* "

"I think that was the head's point, wasn't it, sir?" said the junior English master, blending carefully the deference due to the headmaster with a certain amount of youthful contempt for the arithmetic mistress. "We can't afford to tackle another opera this year."

"We lost thirty pounds, one shilling and ninepence on *The Gondoliers*," said the headmaster, "and that in spite of the fact that we had a full house."

"I would put up the money," said the arithmetic mistress. She spoke breathlessly, out of nervousness. All eyes were upon her. She was shabbily dressed, heavy-faced and almost inarticulate except in the classroom. She taught the lower forms only.

The school was an expensive experiment in coeducation. It was a private concern, and the headmaster, who had spent a fortune on it, was chairman of the board of directors. None of the staff held shares, and it was against the terms of their engagement for them to do so. They were well paid, and were expected to be something more than merely efficient teachers, for the social side of school life was catered to as carefully and thoroughly as the educational. Games for the girls and boys were of secondary importance to hobbies. There was no prefect system. English was the most important subject. In short, it was a freak school. The staff came to weep, and remained—wondering at themselves as they did so—to rejoice. All the senior members of the staff, both men and women, were married, although the headmaster was a bachelor. There were the usual friendships and enmities, but nearly everyone united in tolerating the arithmetic mistress, for she was the mildest and most inoffensive of persons: self-effacing, meek, quietly contented with her lot. All looked at her in surprise, and some in alarm, however, as she made the offer to finance the production of a comic opera. The head broke the pause.

"But, really, you know, Miss Ferris—" he said. The arithmetic mistress interrupted him.

"I know how much it would cost," she said. "I could afford it, Mr. Cliffordson. I should like it to be a little present to the school. I have been"—she gulped, and her dull eyes filled suddenly—"I have been so happy here."

There was an awkward pause, then the headmaster cleared his throat and pronounced his benediction on the scheme.

"In that case—a present to the school—very kind indeed of you. Well, now, what about parts? We ought to decide them before the holidays, I think, and then we can get on with the rehearsals next term. Any suggestions? Let me see—what are the parts?"

"Hadn't we better settle what opera we are going to do?" inquired the junior music mistress demurely. She was very young and very pretty, and happened to be the headmaster's niece.

"Which opera? Oh, that's settled. We must do *The Mikado*, mustn't we?" said the headmaster. "I've wanted to do it for years."

There was applause.

"Yourself the Pooh-Bah, sir, of course," said the junior English master.

"I think I should like to attempt it," replied the headmaster. He patted his waistcoat affectionately, imagining a Japanese silk sash.

"Miss Cliffordson will do Yum-Yum, I take it," the junior English master continued.

"I should think so. Oh, yes," the headmaster agreed, smiling at his niece. "And the funny little chap—the Lord High Executioner—what's-his-name? Oh, you know——"

"Ko-Ko," said the junior English master.

"Ko-Ko, certainly. Mr. Poole's part, I think," said the headmaster.

The mathematics master, a spry, black-haired, good-humored little man, laughed and began to hum under his breath.

"Let me see, who else is there?" asked the headmaster.

"Well, there's the Mikado himself, sir," said the art master. "You know—the name-part. The only part I ever remember in Gilbert and Sullivan, as a matter of fact. Sings a jolly good song or something, doesn't he?"

"Ah, your part, Smith. Your part, without a doubt," said the headmaster. The art master grinned. "And isn't there a redoubtable lady related to him? I seem to remember——Of course, it's years since I saw the thing done . . ."

"Katisha," said several voices.

"Ah!" The headmaster looked at the large semicircle, and came to a sudden decision.

"Do you sing, Miss Ferris?" he inquired of the arithmetic mistress. The arithmetic mistress blushed and fumbled with her handkerchief. She had never been in the limelight since she had first come before the board of governors at her interview, when she was engaged to teach arithmetic to the lower forms. She had been longing for years to be offered a part in one of the school productions. Now that she was actually being offered one, her nerve failed her.

"It isn't a long part," said the junior music mistress, who, now that her own part was settled, was perfectly willing to help settle the other women's parts, and had some reasons of her own for wishing to spite the physical training mistress, who was the obvious choice for the part of Katisha. "It doesn't really start until the second act."

"Katisha makes an important appearance, and a very effective entrance, toward the end of the first act, Miss Cliffordson," contradicted the junior science master, who was in love with the physical training mistress, although she was four years his senior and called him to his face a precocious little boy.

"Yes, but the bulk of the part is in Act Two," the junior music mistress insisted. "And I do think," she continued, taking full advantage of her position as niece of the headmaster, "that we owe Miss Ferris the refusal of the part. After all, if she is financing us it seems only fair…"

There was polite applause. Miss Ferris, astonished at herself, accepted the part. She glanced stealthily at the physical training mistress. That lady, part of whose training had consisted in learning to smile most sweetly when she was most bitterly defeated, smiled sweetly and frankly at her. Miss Ferris, taking the smile at its face value, smiled in return.

"Then there are the other Little Maids, sir," said the junior English master abruptly.

"Little Maids? Ah, yes. Well, what about Miss Freely for one?" said the headmaster, smiling at the youngest member of the staff.

The junior geography mistress was really as pretty as Miss Cliffordson, and was far more popular with the girls and with the women members of the staff. She said simply:

"Ah! good. Bags I Pitti-Sing, please."

Everybody laughed, and the headmaster wrote it down. Miss Ferris, who happened to be sitting next to her, whispered, "Good! How nice!"

"What about the youngsters?" said the senior history master.

"I do think we might have a boy for Nanki-Poo," said Miss Cliffordson. "What about Hurstwood? He was in the *Gondoliers*, and did awfully well."

"Hurstwood for Nanki-Poo? A very good idea," said the headmaster, writing it down. "And what about Moira Malley for the third Little Maid? And now, does that settle it?"

"Certainly. Peep-Bo, yes."

"Except for the rather small part of Pish-Tush," said the junior English master, who wanted the part for himself and was about to say so when the headmaster forestalled him with:

"Ah, yes. What about you, Mr. Kemball?"

The senior history master bowed.

"Charmed, Headmaster. And the youngsters, I presume, will form the chorus of Japanese nobles and girls?"

"Yes, oh, yes. They'll enjoy that. There's a lot of chorus work. Good for them, and not too much responsibility."

"We must have Tony Sen Ho Wen for the headman's boy," said Miss Cliffordson, referring to a little Chinese lad who had lately come to live in the district, and who was the pet of all the women.

"I doubt whether Wen would consent to take part in a Japanese play," said the senior English mistress, smiling. "I think Peter Cecil would be better."

"Talking of Cecil, did I tell you . . ." began the junior geography mistress, her face alight with amusement.

"Shop!" bawled everybody, including the headmaster. The geography mistress produced a shilling from her handbag and placed it meekly on a corner of the headmaster's big desk. Discipline was almost nonexistent for the children, but was strict for the staff.

II

Miss Ferris—Calma to her friends and intimates, if she had had any—spent the next day in checking arithmetic stock, and in reconsidering her summer holiday plans, for it was with the money she had been saving toward the cost of a holiday that she proposed to finance the school production of *The Mikado*.

"Somewhere cheap," her brain repeated over and over again. "Somewhere cheap." It was not until she lay in bed in her lodgings that night, her blunt nose just above the turned-down edge of the sheet, her dull eyes fixed on the blind which covered the window, that she decided where to go. She had an aunt who kept a boardinghouse in Bognor Regis. Bognor was a nice place; a healthy place; the sands were good; one could find pleasant walks; the buses went everywhere from

Bognor; there were the Downs . . . Sussex . . . Sussex was so nice. Sussex was literary, too. One would be able to return to school, and explain, if one were asked, that one had been "doing" the Sheila Kaye-Smith country, or the Belloc country, or the "Puck of Pook's Hill" country. Rather nice, that. She began imaginary conversations at school. She could see the whole staff, half-envious, half-admiring, as she cast new light on vexed questions of this, and cleared up disputed points in connection with that. She fell asleep and dreamed that she climbed up a steep hill and stood looking down on Bognor Regis, and the physical training mistress came behind and pushed her over the edge. Falling, she woke, and it took her some little time to get to sleep again.

On the following evening she wrote to her aunt, enclosing a stamped addressed envelope, but by the time the school closed for the long summer vacation of nearly nine weeks she had received no reply. So she arranged to remain at her lodgings.

III

Miss Ferris' aunt was showing Miss Ferris' letter to her second-in-command.

"Wants a cheap holiday, I suppose," she said, with a snort. "Spent all her money on foreign tours, and now that it's too expensive, with the pound and everything going off gold, to go abroad, she wants to know what I can do for her. Best room at the cheapest rate, I suppose! That's relations all over. Never come to see you, and when they do come, expect the very best of everything! She can have Number Eight at the inclusive, less ten percent for staying the full six weeks. I couldn't do more for a Permanent."

"I'm sure she wouldn't expect more," said Miss Sooley, who was plump, sentimental and inclined toward hysteria when she became excited. "But, Miss Lincallow, there's something else. It's that new maid, Susie Cozens."

"Her with the London manners!" snorted Miss Lincallow. "Too free with the gentlemen! She'll have to go."

"It's really Mr. Helm's fault. He encourages her. I found her in his room this morning, going through his things."

"Then she can just go through her own, and take herself off," said the head of the establishment, decidedly. "Theft, as likely as not! She came here with no character, never having been in a regular situation before. I can't have a girl who can't control her curiosity. People would never put up with it. Give her her wages instead of notice, and send her off."

"What about a character?"

"I'll write her a character. 'Honest and industrious' ought to be enough. She can make up her own reason for leaving us. I'll write it now, at the same time as I write to my niece."

On the following morning Miss Ferris received a cordially worded letter from her aunt, offering her a bed-sitting room with full board and attendance for six weeks at an inclusive charge for the whole period. The money was even more reasonable than Miss Ferris had anticipated, so she sent off a telegram advising her aunt to expect her on the following Monday afternoon, and went to the public library to look up a train.

She felt contented, and although she had been prepared to feel no particular enthusiasm for her six-weeks' holiday, she found herself now looking forward to a visit to the seaside, and she found also that the warm tone of her aunt's letter had given her a feeling of cheerfulness and well-being to which, on holidays, she had often been a stranger.

Her trunk was already packed. She went by taxi to the station, caught her train with a quarter of an hour to spare, and arrived at her aunt's boardinghouse in time for afternoon tea. Her aunt received her very cordially, and showed her her room. Miss Ferris unpacked, wrote a postcard to her landlady at Hillmaston, announcing her safe arrival, and went down to tea. After tea she went for a stroll along the esplanade, and encountered Hurstwood, of the sixth form. He raised his hat, and Miss Ferris bowed and smiled nervously. She went in deadly terror of all the upper forms, because she never taught them. Hurstwood was wearing a boater and his school blazer. She was surprised at the boater. Most young men went bareheaded in the summer. She could not know that Hurstwood's father, a man of peculiar theories, believed that a straw hat protected the brain.

Dinner was at seven. She would have enjoyed it but for the fact that a handsome man of early middle age sat opposite her at table, and every time she looked up she caught his eye. The first time this happened she blushed, and looked down at her plate. The second time, the man said:

"Isn't the fish always so nice here?"

The third time, he said:

"Don't you think the air here makes one extraordinarily hungry?"

After dinner Miss Ferris asked her aunt whether her seat at table could not be changed. Her aunt, humoring her, changed it and put her at a larger table, with a married couple and their three children. The middle-aged man, whose name was Helm, did not come into contact with Miss Ferris again for more than three weeks, but toward the middle of the fourth week of her stay they became acquainted under romantic circumstances in the form of an attempted burglary.

She had gone to bed later than usual one night, because she had been to the theater, where a good repertory company was doing a play which had had a successful run in London, and which she thought she would enjoy. She did enjoy it, and after she had retired to bed she continued to think over the story and to visualize herself in the character of the heroine. Thus, at a quarter to twelve, she was completely wide awake, and was suddenly conscious of the sound of a cough which seemed to come from the balcony outside her bedroom window. She was not particularly alarmed, for her physical courage was of a reasonably high order, and she raised herself in bed and listened. There was no further sound of coughing, but she thought that she could distinguish a slight scraping noise. Curiously enough, the thought of burglars did not immediately occur to her, but her sense of duty caused her to get out of bed and proceed cautiously to the window. She peered out, but could see nothing, and the scraping noise continued. She could hear it distinctly. This time she did think of burglars. Like most teachers who take any of the games—and she sometimes coached netball with the junior forms to relieve the physical training mistress—she always carried a whistle in her handbag. She moved quietly toward the dressing table, where her handbag lay, and was about to open it when there came three quiet but distinct taps upon her bedroom door. Miss Ferris started with surprise, but she put down the handbag, pulled her dressing gown about her and opened the door. A man pushed past her without ceremony, opened her window wide, climbed on to the balcony, and apparently, from the sounds, dropped into the garden below. Miss Ferris took the whistle from her handbag, leaned out of the wide-open window and blew three shrill blasts. There was a rush of feet, a warning shout, and the sound of a motor horn from the front of the house. Below Miss Ferris' eye level a dark object appeared. Miss Ferris shouted:

"Stop, or I'll fire!"

"It's me," said the voice of the handsome middle-aged man. "They've got away."

By this time the sounds of an awakened household reached their ears. Lights were being switched on. They could hear voices.

"Go back," said Miss Ferris. "You can't use my room again."

The dark man, however, climbed back again and closed the window. Miss Ferris opened the bedroom door, to find Miss Sooley and her aunt upon the threshold.

"They've got away," she said to her aunt.

Nothing, upon investigation, proved to have been stolen. The cough which had first attracted Miss Ferris' attention had been the undoing of the burglars, who were in the act of forcing an entrance. But Miss Ferris and Mr. Helm were the heroine and hero respectively of the boardinghouse, Miss Ferris' aunt, who was deeply shocked, excluded. Mr. Helm was leaving at the end of the week, but they became sufficiently well acquainted for him to propose marriage to Miss Ferris, and to be refused. Calma Ferris was under no illusion as to her attraction for a man of Mr. Helm's appearance and character.

"I fancy he thought I might have expectations," she confided to her landlady when she got back. "And so I have," she added. She so seldom confided in anybody that it was a relief to have this woman to talk to. "My aunt who keeps the boardinghouse is making me the principal beneficiary under her will. It's rather exciting, isn't it? I've to give up teaching and carry on the boardinghouse; but I should like to do that, I think. It would be a change; and, anyhow, I hope my dear aunt has many years of life before her yet."

IV

Hurstwood was feeling decidedly ill-used. He was just eighteen, and his father had decided to leave him at school another six months, so that he might work for a Balliol scholarship. Hurstwood, a brilliant, restless, ambitious boy nearly at the top of his form, would not have been ill-pleased at this arrangement had events pursued their normal course, but events had not seen fit to do so. The disadvantage of making games a matter of secondary instead of primary importance in the school world is that it is exceedingly difficult, especially in the case of adolescent boys, to find anything quite to take their place. Hurstwood, temperamentally incapable of absorbing himself in a hobby, and possessing all the instability of character common to one type of clever boy, had occupied the whole of the previous term in falling in love. His love was sincere, painful and apparent. He had fallen in love with the junior music mistress, who, in her flighty way, was touched, flattered and embarrassed. The poor youth had had to content himself, through shyness, with a kind of silent worship, but he had managed to dance with her three times at the end-of-term social, and his mental state was obvious. His work suffered, and his end-of-term report had been sufficiently coolly worded for his father to cancel the motor tour which he had proposed to his son earlier in the year and condemn the boy to eight weeks of sea air coupled with mild exercise. Mr. Hurstwood, a mild-mannered but obstinate man, was convinced that his boy had been overworking; hence not only Bognor but also the straw hat.

To complete young Hurstwood's irritation, whom should he encounter during the first week of the holiday but Miss Ferris. The thought that, if any member of the staff had to spend a holiday at the same place as his father had chosen, it might just as easily have been Miss Cliffordson, caused him to grind his teeth with disappointment. He used to stay out of bed for hours, far into the night, and gaze at the sea and think long, long, agonizing thoughts about Miss Cliffordson and of how utterly unattainable she was. He was exceedingly unhappy, and looked it. His father was extremely worried, and even wrote to the school to suggest that he should be let off work at the midday until half-term, to see if that would do him any good. The letter was forwarded to Mr. Cliffordson at Aix-les-Bains, and was thrown by him jovially into the wastepaper basket. He wanted to forget school. Time enough to be bothered when the new term began.

Miss Cliffordson was not spending the vacation with her uncle. She was cruising in northern waters, and more evenings than not she danced with the officers, and thought how pleasant they were, and how nice it would be to marry one if only they were better paid. She had been engaged twice before in her short life, and had enjoyed the experience. She was not entirely heartless, but she had weighed life in the balance, like most of her generation, found it wanting, and was out for as easy a journey through it as was to be obtained.

There was another besides Hurstwood who thought a good deal about her, however, and that was young Mr. Browning, the junior English master. He was spending his holiday fishing, and had plenty of time for thought. Unlike Hurstwood, he was not unhappy; he was determined.

He was twenty-seven, and had his eye on the headship of a small grammar-school in the Midlands. He was also a novelist, so far unpublished, and was optimistic on the subject of his own future, both as a pedagogue and a man of letters. He had decided views on marriage and considered it the duty of every schoolmaster to embark upon the joys and responsibilities of matrimony as early in his career as was compatible with earning sufficient money to keep a wife and family. He spent a pleasant, restful, health-giving holiday, and in the seventh week of it wrote to the headmaster at Aix-les-Bains for a testimonial. The headmaster, who wanted to forget school, threw the letter into the wastepaper basket and hummed a lively tune.

Mr. Smith, the art master, and little Mr. Poole, the mathematics master, were spending the holiday on a cargo boat which went as far eastward as the Piræus. Mr. Smith painted and sketched and smoked and talked; Mr. Poole helped in the engine room and won a good deal of money at poker. Neither of them thought about school. At Marseilles a French sailor knifed Mr. Smith in the arm, and Mr. Poole, displaying a side of his character which his colleagues would not have recognized, sailed into the man and laid him out. They escaped to their ship, guided by a woman of the town who had been the original cause of the dispute, and were cursed heartily by the captain, who was a quarter of an hour late in getting away.

The history master took lodgings in London, in order to get in six weeks' reading at the British Museum for a school textbook he was writing. At the end of the six weeks he took his wife and two children to Ramsgate for the duration of the holiday.

The junior geography mistress, Miss Freely, went hiking with a woman friend. They worked their way along the south coast from Hastings to Bournemouth, trekked through part of the New Forest, returned to London by way of Oxford, and stayed in the woman friend's flat in Shepherd's Bush for the remainder of the vacation.

There was only one member of the proposed cast for *The Mikado* who had no holiday at all. That was the schoolgirl, Moira Malley. She, poor child, took a job as private governess to two little children. It was the only means she had of getting to the seaside.

The senior English mistress, Mrs. Alceste Boyle, and the senior music master, Mr. Frederick Hampstead, who were the producer and conductor respectively of the opera, were living in sin in Paris. They were enjoying themselves. Mr. Boyle was dead. Mrs. Hampstead was in a home for female inebriates. Both Mrs. Boyle and Mr. Hampstead, therefore, decided that they had a right to enjoy themselves, and as they had been in love with one another for longer than they could remember, they spent all their holidays together, but kept this fact a closely guarded secret. It was their custom to choose always a very large and usually a foreign town, so that should they be unlucky enough to be seen in one another's company by any other member of the staff, it could be assumed that they had encountered one another by accident. Thus they had lived together in London, New York, Barcelona, Vienna, Lisbon, Rome, Oslo, and other European and American cities, for more than a dozen summer holidays. Christmas they always spent together in London, and Easter in Seville or Rome. Their wants, except for the continual need of one another's companionship both of body and mind, were infinitesimal. They had managed to keep their secret so carefully that only one person on the staff guessed it. That was Calma Ferris, who, having no friends, had the more opportunity for observing the friendships of others. Neither Mrs. Boyle nor Mr. Hampstead had the slightest notion that Miss Ferris knew their secret. They were usually very careful at school, and, so far as they knew, had never betrayed themselves to a soul. They would have been horrified and amazed had they been permitted to read a certain page of Miss Ferris' diary, which referred to Mr. Hampstead as "Mr. Rochester."

The knowledge that Hampstead's wife was in some sort of mental institution had leaked out and was a subject of staff room gossip when the senior members of the common room were not present. Hampstead was temperamental and really musical. Under Alceste Boyle's inspiration and an assumed name he had published several minor works and a full symphony. The money he made, however, apart from his teaching, was negligible, and one of the most important reasons which he and Alceste shared for wishing to keep their illicit relationship secret was the fear of losing their posts. To do Mr. Cliffordson justice, he would never have dreamed of asking the board of governors to dismiss either of them. He neither approved nor disapproved of free love in itself, but he was a man who held strong views on the right of every human being to form his own code of behavior, and as long as that code did not impair efficiency or act prejudicially to health and happiness, he would tolerate it gladly. Hampstead and Mrs. Boyle did not realize this. Perhaps, too, there was a certain charm about the secrecy of the whole thing. It was hidden treasure; the more valuable in their eyes simply because it had to remain hidden.

The person who ought to have been in the cast, but had had to give place to the mild and unassuming Miss Ferris, was the physical training mistress. She had departed for Montreux in a very bad temper, stayed in Switzerland a fortnight, crossed into Italy and stayed on the shores of Lake Lugano, left because Lugano was full of elementary schoolteachers, and went to Monte Carlo, where she lost heavily at the tables. She then wired her father for the money to return home, and spent the rest of the holiday writing letters and sulking in the garden of the vicarage in Shropshire where her parents lived. She returned to school in a worse temper than that in which she had left at the end of term.

CHAPTER II
REHEARSAL

I

The autumn term took its usual course until the dress rehearsal of *The Mikado*, or, more exactly, until the day upon which the dress rehearsal was to take place. On that day Miss Ferris began badly by being late for school. She could not remember ever having been late before, but there was a certain amount of excuse which a more self-indulgent person might have made for herself. On the previous evening her landlady had given her fish for supper. It was not fresh, and Miss Ferris had been kept awake the better part of the night by severe abdominal pains. She took some aspirin tablets—two, in point of fact—and toward morning she fell asleep. She was a person who liked between seven and eight hours' sleep at night, and although, presumably, her alarm clock ran down at the usual time, it did not wake her, so it was past eight o'clock when her landlady knocked at the door to inform her that breakfast had been on the table upwards of ten minutes. The consequence of all this was that Miss Ferris was hurrying into school at five minutes past nine, knowing that she was due for a severe attack of indigestion because she had bolted a breakfast consisting chiefly of sausages, and knowing also that she would consider it her duty to seek out the headmaster and apologize for her unpunctuality. Mr. Cliffordson was urbane and sympathetic, but that did not comfort Miss Ferris, who was almost morbidly conscientious in all matters concerning school and her work there. She went to her first class feeling thoroughly out of tune with the day. Unfortunately, her first class was the upper third commercial.

It often happens in a school that different children react upon different teachers in very different ways. On the whole, Miss Ferris escaped being ragged. She was sensible, kindly, had a strong parental instinct, and was sufficiently interested herself in her special subject to make it interesting and intelligible to the children. But in the upper third commercial, which was a form of thirteen-year-olds, there was a girl whom Miss Ferris disliked. She was an unpleasantly ferret-faced damsel, Cartnell by name, with stringy fair hair, impertinent gray eyes, a keen mind for which, so far, school work had provided little stimulus, and a flair for gymnastics. Miss Ferris, who occasionally coached the younger girls in the game, would have been prepared to take an interest in the girl because of her almost uncanny proficiency at netball, but her behavior in form was such that, beyond recommending her to the notice of the gymnasium mistress (who immediately gave her a place in the school second team and declared that she was really good enough to play in the first), Miss Ferris ignored her when it was possible, reprimanded her when it was not, and, on this fateful Tuesday, the day of the dress rehearsal of *The Mikado*, kept her in.

On any other day two things would have been certain. One was that Miss Ferris would not have kept her in, because any kind of punishment was against the tradition of the school; and, under Mr. Cliffordson's rule—he happened to be a genius in managing adolescent girls and boys—it is only fair to state that punishment was seldom necessary. The other thing was that it would not have mattered quite so much if she *had* kept her in, but this particular Tuesday was the day of the semifinal of the school's netball league, and the first-term attacking center was absent with a broken arm, consequently the girl Cartnell had been chosen by Miss Camden to fill the vacant position.

"And, between you and me," Miss Camden had told the headmaster, "we shall do better with Cartnell than with Poultney, for she's a far better player, although I don't agree with putting youngsters in the first team, really."

The headmaster, lacking interest in the subject, agreed absently.

To do Miss Ferris justice, she was not aware that the girl had been chosen to play in the match that day, but, having announced her decision, she declined to depart from it in spite of the victim's tearful reproaches. The rest of the lesson passed off in silence, Miss Ferris gloomily aware that she had put herself in a very delicate position but determined that she would not give way, the form—even the boys—oppressed by the atmosphere of misery, and the girl Cartnell moodily drawing on the outside cover of her pencilwork book and praying for Miss Ferris to be smitten of God. At the end of the lesson the child went straight to Miss Camden and informed that belligerent lady that she could not play in the match that afternoon.

"Why not?" demanded Miss Camden.

"Please, Miss Camden, I'm staying in for Miss Ferris until five o'clock."

"Rubbish," said Miss Camden, unwisely. "I'll speak to Miss Ferris. Go along now. I shall expect to see you at the school gate at three-thirty."

The girl Cartnell went back to her class, which was prepared to take a geography lesson from Miss Freely, and managed to get a note passed round the form which ran thus:

"Fuzzy Ferris is going to get it in the neck from Cammy for trying to keep me in. What do you bet I play after all?"

She did not play after all. Miss Ferris, with a forcefulness which surprised herself, defended her position even when the case was taken before the headmaster. The headmaster, who thought the gymnastic mistress far too much interested in games to allow full scope to the ideals of the school, which might be summed up: "The individual first, the team spirit afterwards," took the side of Miss Ferris, sent for the girl Cartnell, admonished her, sent for her arithmetic book, admonished her again when he had seen it, and kept her in his room from two o'clock until five doing arithmetic.

Miss Camden took the netball team to play their match. They lost by twelve goals to seven, and so had no chance to play in the final and gain the handsome trophy which was offered to the winning school. Miss Camden was furious in a way and to an extent which can only be understood and sympathized with by persons who habitually put all their eggs into one basket and then drop the lot. She was a hard, narrow-minded, egotistical young woman who lived entirely for success with the school games, and had dreams of breaking down the headmaster's slightly antagonistic attitude toward her subject and making the girls of the school foremost in England in gymnastic competitions and in games.

Poor Miss Ferris, worn out with argument, nervous strain, indigestion and loss of sleep, went home to tea at five and came back at half-past six for the dress rehearsal of *The Mikado*. She was the most complete, but not the only, failure that night. Hurstwood, who was nervous, sang his first song half-a-tone flat and his second entirely out of tune. Moira Malley was exceedingly nervous and *gauche*, and owing to their united fumbling, the first act was a fiasco. Alceste Boyle was furious, young Mr. Browning, the prompter, was in despair, Frederick Hampstead, the conductor, was laughing. Poor Miss Ferris was almost and Moira Malley was quite in tears. Miss Cliffordson was cold to poor Hurstwood during the interval and colder at the end of the performance, and he was in the depths of despair. The headmaster was soothing. Everything, he was sure, would be splendid on the night. Nobody believed him. It was a most disastrous evening. It was nine-thirty by the time they had finished, but Alceste Boyle was determined to do the first act again.

"And, look here, Miss Ferris," she said, suddenly getting back her temper, and smiling kindly at the wilting Katisha, hideous with the makeup which little Mrs. Berotti, the professional, had so liberally plastered on her ordinarily plain but not unpleasing countenance, "when Katisha says the bit beginning, 'None whatever. On the contrary, I was going to marry him—yet he fled!'—you remember?—I think perhaps it wants a little more—"

"Do it, Alceste," said Mr. Smith, the Mikado himself, grinning.

"Yes, go on, do!" said a number of other voices. Miss Ferris, humility itself before the great Alceste, added timidly but with evident sincerity, "It would be so good of you."

"Start at the beginning of Act Two," suggested the headmaster, "and we'll all play up to you. Pitch it high. It will pull us out."

The little ex-actress, Mrs. Berotti, came from behind the scenes to watch.

"But it is magnificent," she replied, in response to a whispered question from Frederick Hampstead. There was a spontaneous burst of applause at the conclusion of the "Tit-Willow" song, but it was less for Mr. Poole, good though he was, than for Alceste. She laughed, her good humor completely restored, and then commanded that the first act should be commenced before it was too late to get through it.

Calma Ferris' first entrance did not come until almost the end of the first act, and, still very much upset by her own mishandling of the part, but valiantly determined to copy Alceste's wonderful rendering to the life, she wandered into the nearest classroom, which happened to be the art room, and, knowing that at least an hour must pass before she would be wanted, she switched on the lights and began looking at the pictures. On a stand about four feet high, opposite the door, was an object covered with a cloth. Miss Ferris, wondering what was the nature of the work of art thus chastely hidden from view, walked over to it. It was intended, apparently, to be covered completely by the cloth, but the covering had been done so carelessly that a darkish-colored lump was visible. Miss Ferris was not an abnormally inquisitive woman. Had none of the object been visible the probability is that she would not have dreamed of uncovering it; but the sight of part of what was obviously a piece of modeling in clay, and therefore something upon which she felt herself to be an authority, for she had trained for primary school teaching, proved to be too stimulating to her curiosity to be ignored. She began to withdraw the rest of the covering. To her horror, the whole model fell to the ground, and in trying to save it she damaged it badly. She could have wept with remorse. She was ordinarily so careful of other people's property and so meticulously scrupulous about minding her own business that it was a piece of very bad luck that such a misfortune should have occurred. She realized too late, when she tried to assess the extent of the damage she had done, that this was not the work of a boy or girl in the school. It could be nothing other than the art master's own model upon which he had been working for weeks past, ready to make a plaster cast from it, so that it was not, in one sense, finished work. Nevertheless, it was, even to her untutored sense, a particularly fine model; and it was something which she could do nothing to replace. Distressed beyond measure, she switched off the lights, and, wandering out again, found a chair at the side of the stage but below the stage level, and there she sat, waiting for her cue, a somewhat curious sight with her neat eyeglasses adorning the fearful countenance of Katisha.

The particular place she had chosen was in a rather dark corner. She sat there for a long time listening to the rehearsal, which seemed to be going rather better, she thought, and she was almost forgetting her worries in absorbing herself in the now-familiar lines and songs, when her attention was distracted by the sound of voices close at hand. The first was Miss Cliffordson's voice. The second she could not place for a moment, and then she realized that it could belong only to Hurstwood, the youthful Nanki-Poo.

"My dear boy," Miss Cliffordson was saying in tones low enough not to disturb what was being done on the stage, "I'm old enough to be—well, your aunt, anyway! Do be sensible."

"I can't, any more," responded the boy.

"Well, for goodness' sake, come in here, then, and talk," said Miss Cliffordson, half annoyed and half tenderly.

There was the sound of a classroom door being opened, and they went into the art room from which Miss Ferris had lately emerged. She rose abruptly, and walked in after them. They had not closed the door, and the embroidered Japanese slippers she was wearing happened to be soundless as she walked. Her purpose, subconscious, not expressed even to herself, was to prevent anybody seeing the damage she had done to Mr. Smith's model. As she got to the door, however, she paused, for Miss Cliffordson's voice, low and urgent, was saying:

"Harry, you idiot, you *can't!*"

There was a scuffling noise, and Hurstwood's voice, muffled and with a note of agony, said, almost on a sob:

"I must! I must! I can't stick it any longer!"

"No!" said Miss Cliffordson, breathlessly this time. "You're not to be . . ."

The sentence trailed off. There was the sound of kisses and heavy breathing, and then Miss Cliffordson said in a frightened tone, "My dear, you can't go on like this! It isn't—it isn't right!"

Then the boy's voice, full of pain, replied, "It is! It is! Oh, God, how it hurts! Oh, God, how I love you!"

At this point, and not entirely of her own volition, for her finger had been on the switch for some moments and the pressure she suddenly exerted was nervous rather than wilful, Miss Ferris turned on the light. There was an exclamation. A heap of brilliant coloring in the middle of the space in front of the teacher's desk sorted itself into a youth and a girl, both in Japanese costume. Miss Cliffordson said with nervous hilarity:

"What ho! Here's your Katisha come for you, my lad!"

Miss Ferris managed to say:

"I thought I had left my fan in here just now. Were you rehearsing your bit?"

Hurstwood, with the usual defenselessness of youth, stood tongue-tied. Miss Cliffordson laughed, and then the two of them followed Miss Ferris into the wings, and no more was said. Hurstwood determinedly escorted Miss Cliffordson to her home when the rehearsal was over. He was so silent and gloomy that she rallied him, trying to appear more at ease with him than she actually was. She was a shallow but not a cruel or heartless girl, and, so far as it was in her nature to be sorry for anyone, she was sorry for this boy. She told herself that it was calf-love, that he would get over it, that he would soon be leaving and would find new friends, new interests, and that the evening's episode, together with everything which it stood for and illuminated, would soon be forgotten by the boy; but in spite of these assurances she was conscious of having behaved very badly. She had known for nearly two years what this poor lad had been thinking and feeling, and at first she had encouraged him. Then, when, during the previous term, the thing looked like getting out of hand and becoming uncomfortable instead of pretty, she had tried to ignore him. This did not prove to be a solution. It merely put him off his work instead of causing him to work better (the first effect she had had on him), and it did nothing to quench his love. She was in an exceedingly difficult and uncomfortable position, and was well aware of the fact. It was lucky, she reflected, that it was only the good-natured, obtuse and self-contained Miss Ferris who had found them. She went hot and cold by turns as she thought of all the other members of the staff, both male and female, who might just as easily have walked into the art room that evening.

Hurstwood said suddenly, as they walked down the deserted street toward Miss Cliffordson's home:

"Do you think she'll split?"

Startled, she replied:

"Whom do you mean?"

"Ferris."

"Of course not."

"She split to the old man today about a kid in the Upper Third."

"Oh, but that was a staff row."

"Well, wouldn't *you* be a staff row?"

Miss Cliffordson laughed, but not very convincingly. Her uncle, she knew, was not a narrow-minded man, but she felt uncertain as to his reaction if he were informed by another member of the staff that one of the sixth form boys had kissed her. "The boy," she imagined her uncle saying, "must have received some sort of encouragement, my dear Gretta, must he not?"

She could not construct any reply which would at once fit the facts as reported by Miss Ferris, who, she reminded herself, was unfashionably conscientious and suffered from an overdeveloped sense of duty, let out Hurstwood—she had genuinely sporting qualities, and hated the idea of getting the boy into trouble—and cover herself. It was all very difficult and embarrassing.

Arrived at the gate of her home, she took her attache-case from Hurstwood with a hasty word of thanks, bade him good-night and almost ran up the garden path to the front door. Hurstwood stood there, school cap in hand, for about three minutes; then he turned, put on his cap and walked slowly homewards. It remained to get through supper and the family conversation, go up to bed as soon as possible, and recreate, with additional details, the crazy but wonderful evening.

II

Miss Ferris found herself again unable to sleep. She could think of nothing but Mr. Smith's model, which she was certain she had ruined. If, by any chance, her mind did leave this wretchedly perturbing subject, it persisted in reminding her of the unpleasant time she would have for the rest of the term with Miss Camden, who would neither forgive nor forget the netball incident. True, there was no proof that the school team would have won with the assistance of the girl Cartnell, but the fact that it had lost without her would be sufficient justification, in Miss Camden's opinion, to be as unfriendly as possible. Poor Miss Ferris, who was well-disposed toward everybody, and a lover of peace and concord if ever there was one, dreaded the thought that she had provoked the ill-will of a young woman whom she knew to be narrow-mindedly unscrupulous. There was no petty annoyance which Miss Camden would not inflict upon her in order to be revenged for what she chose to consider a personal injury and affront. At the back of Miss Ferris' mind there was also a third consideration. It nagged like an aching tooth. This was the remembrance of the—to her—extraordinary and shocking scene which she had been instrumental in interrupting and terminating. It seemed to her that she ought to inform the headmaster. Miss Cliffordson obviously had no control over the boy and his emotions, and it appeared to Miss Ferris that she, as an older woman, ought to lay the facts of the case before Mr. Cliffordson, whom she knew to be a man of great kindness of heart and very wide experience, and leave him to deal with them as he saw fit. On the other hand, she wondered whether, in fairness to Miss Cliffordson, she ought not to have a word with her first. Hurstwood, she felt, had better be left alone. In any case she seriously doubted her own fitness to talk to a boy about his first love affair.

One after the other, this triumvirate of morbid, melancholy thoughts chased one another through her mind. She fell asleep at last, dreamed horribly, and woke unrefreshed, heavy-headed and heavyhearted. One thing, and one thing only, she had settled to her satisfaction. She had made up her mind to go to Mr. Smith before school began, explain what she had done to his model, and accept humbly whatever blistering words of reproach he might choose to hurl at her. She only hoped he would not swear. She really did hope he would not swear at her.

She arrived at the school gate at twenty-five minutes past eight, and went straight to the art room. Mr. Smith was not there, but a couple of boys were rearranging the desks, so she sent one of them up to the masters' common room to find out whether Mr. Smith had arrived at school. In less than three minutes the boy returned with Mr. Smith.

The senior art master was a tall, dark-faced, melancholy-looking man whose whole expression altered when he smiled. It was easy enough, thought Calma Ferris, to imagine that most women would be greatly attracted by him. He looked inquiringly at Calma before ordering the boys out of the room, and then invited her to sit down. She was far too agitated to accept the offer. She said, plunging headlong into the subject and speaking much too fast and rather breathlessly:

"Mr. Smith, I don't know what you'll say, and, really, I deserve anything for my clumsiness, but I came in here last night, and I knocked your clay modelling—the covered one there—off the stand, and I've damaged it. I really am most terribly sorry. I can't think how I came to be so clumsy." She thought wildly, "He's so dreadfully immoral! I do hope he won't actually swear at me."

Mr. Smith walked slowly over to the tall stand upon which his model was placed, pulled off the cloth and looked at the damaged figure. It was ruined irretrievably.

"H'm!" he said. "That's done for, I'm afraid." He began to whistle.

Miss Ferris began again to apologize, but he stopped her.

"Please," he said. "It really can't be helped. I'd rather you didn't distress yourself."

Then he suddenly threw the little model on the ground, and solemnly stamped it flat and shapeless. Even when the figure was quite unrecognizable, he went on methodically stamping and stamping and stamping, getting clay on his shoes and clay all over that part of the floor. Miss Ferris stood aghast. She was stricken with grief and horror. Reproaches she could have borne. Even if he had turned and struck her in the face she would have taken the blow as a just reprisal for her carelessness and ungoverned curiosity. Even if he *had* sworn at her, she believed she would have borne it. But this steady stamping sound, without a word being said, and as though the artist himself had become oblivious of what he was doing, was too terrible to be contemplated. She turned and ran blindly to the mistresses' common room and clutched Alceste Boyle. She had immense faith in the senior English mistress, and thought her the best person to deal with the situation. Smith, she knew, was hopelessly in love with Alceste, who mothered him with humorous strictness.

"Oh, come with me! Come quickly!" she said. Amazed, Alceste followed her.

"In there!" Miss Ferris cried, turning when they got to the art room door. "It's dreadful! I can't bear it! I had no idea . . ."

They went in. Mr. Smith had finished his work. He was scraping bits of clay off his shoes with a palette-knife. His fine hands were quite steady. He rose when they came in, dusted the knees of his trousers, smiled at them and said:

"That's that."

Alceste Boyle gave an exclamation of horror.

"Oh, Donald! Not your Psyche, surely?" She turned to Calma Ferris. Calma was white.

"I spoilt it. I knocked it down," she said.

"You shouldn't have done it at school, you know, Donald," said Alceste to Mr. Smith. Then she said to Calma Ferris, "I know you couldn't help it. I know he's careless. I don't suppose for one single instant that you intended to ruin his work, but go away, *now*, before I do anything I shall be sorry for!"

Later in the day she said to Calma:

"I'm sorry I spoke to you like that. He shouldn't have used school time. I told him no good would come of it. Don't worry yourself, Miss

Ferris. Accidents will happen." She smiled kindly and sincerely at Calma Ferris.

Calma answered:

"I ought never to have touched the model. It is unforgivable to have ruined it."

To this Alceste Boyle made no reply, and after a pause Miss Ferris suddenly said:

"I can't understand all this. I thought it was Mr. Hampstead you were . . . you . . . I mean, I understood that you and Mr. Hampstead . . . I mean, it *is* Mr. Hampstead, and not Mr. Smith, isn't it?"

Mrs. Boyle gave a little moan, and then said, "How do you know that?"

Her voice was quiet, but it frightened Miss Ferris. She mumbled something and walked away.

III

The world of a school is so narrow that any disturbance, however unimportant, or any trouble, however transitory, assumes an air of portent out of all proportion to its true significance. The day upon which the dress rehearsal had taken place was a Tuesday, and the following day was that on which Miss Ferris had the disturbing experience of watching Mr. Smith stamping on his ruined work. On the following day, the Thursday, the day before the performance of *The Mikado*, a last rehearsal was held. Miss Ferris found herself dreading this rehearsal. She dreaded coming into contact with Mr. Smith again; she dreaded having to encounter the hostile looks of Alceste Boyle, and she felt certain that Alceste would have told Mr. Hampstead that the secret of their attachment for one another was a secret no longer, so she dreaded meeting him too. The actual rehearsal would not have been so bad, but it had been arranged that the whole cast was to have tea in the headmaster's room, at his invitation, so there would be the terror of having to meet socially the people whom she felt she had wronged. Also, every time she set eyes either on the boy Hurstwood or on the headmaster's niece, her conscience began to plague her again. Ought she to tell, or ought she to let events take their course? Surely she ought to allow Miss Cliffordson the right to manage her own affairs? And yet, if she was managing them so badly that she could not prevent one of the big boys mauling her about and kissing her—the whole expression was Miss Ferris' own—ought not some older person to make it her business to interfere and get the situation under control? Surely it could not be good for the school tone—Miss Ferris and the headmaster probably had different ideas as to what was likely to jeopardize the school tone—that boys should fall in love with the junior mistresses? Miss Cliffordson was notably feckless and irresponsible. Miss Ferris, who had never been either, was conscious—for she was a woman with a very nice and exact sense of justice—of a feeling of slight jealousy. Fecklessness and irresponsibility were, in her mind, to be classed among life's luxuries, and were not to be indulged in by persons who had their living to earn. The headmaster's niece might be able to afford them, but Miss Ferris, with not even a degree to lend weight to her teaching certificate, could not, and felt the poorer because she could not.

The tea and the rehearsal both went off better than she could have hoped. Hurstwood sat as far from Miss Cliffordson as he could manage, and to Miss Ferris, unversed in the idiosyncrasies and shynesses of lovelorn adolescence, this was a sign of grace. If Hurstwood was beginning to see the error of his ways, perhaps it would be unnecessary for her to inform the headmaster of what she had seen. The last thing she wanted was to get anybody into trouble, especially Hurstwood, who was attractively tall and fair and slight, with a sensitive mouth, a classically-modeled nose, gray eyes and a rather charming smile. She had heard, too, that he was a very clever boy, and that his father was proud of him and had great ambitions for his future. It would be a thousand pities to interfere with a career so promising, she reflected.

Miss Cliffordson was talking animatedly to the junior English master, teasing him, and being saucy and provocative. She looked very pretty, Miss Ferris thought, and absurdly young. Perhaps—she glanced again at Hurstwood, who was eating cake in a furtive, reticent manner—perhaps, after all, it would not be necessary to say anything to Mr. Cliffordson. She must think about it again before deciding.

Mr. Smith spoke to nobody. He was never very sociable at staff gatherings—he was an atheist with a slightly epicurean bent and a keen appetite for good food; but Miss Ferris did not remember this. She felt certain that he was brooding over his ruined Psyche. She scarcely dared to look at him for fear that she should catch his eye and be compelled to meet the reproach in it.

Alceste Boyle was pouring out the tea. She spoke when she had to, but otherwise preserved a motherly silence which was quite companionable. One of her gifts was to be with a crowd of people, not to say anything, and yet to appear sociable and friendly. Frederick Hampstead laughed and joked, chiefly with Moira Malley, who was nervous but amused, and with Miss Freely, who was just a jolly girl, not long enough out of college to have acquired the hallmarks of her profession; perhaps too simple-hearted and human ever to acquire them. She seemed to be the only person present—except for Mr. Poole, who ate an enormous tea, and recited, between-whiles, the most atrocious limericks—who was wholeheartedly enjoying the party. Even the headmaster seemed *distrait*, and Mr. Kemball, the History-master, was downright morose, ate scarcely anything, refused a second cup of tea, and lighted his pipe without asking permission and before anybody else had finished eating. It was revealed later that his wife was expecting her third child. It was a joke among the men's staff that Kemball regarded his children as visitations of the wrath of God, refused to accept any personal responsibility for their appearance in the world, grumbled continuously at the provision he had to make for them, but spoke of children in general with self-conscious sentimentality, chiefly to curry favor with the head.

The rehearsal, which was to be carried out in ordinary dress, and without makeup, began at half-past five. The second act was taken first, and, whether from nervous excitement or some other cause, Calma Ferris did exceptionally well. Her songs were good, and she spoke her lines better than she had ever done. Moira Malley, too, was successful that night, and when the act was finished and Alceste Boyle suggested that the whole opera should be run through just once, if they all felt that there was time to do it, the company unanimously resolved to stay until eleven o'clock, if necessary. The whole thing went through without a hitch. Alceste Boyle affected to the headmaster to be superstitiously inclined.

"Too good by half," she said, laughing, as the players collected properties and cleared the stage. "Something is sure to go wrong tomorrow night! Or so Madame Berotti would say! Have you ever seen her act? She's old, of course, but *what* an artist!"

Calma Ferris, so delighted with her own successful performance that she forgot, for the time, her little nagging difficulties of the past day or two, had not the slightest premonition of disaster. She sat down before she went to bed, late though it was when she reached her lodgings, and recorded in her diary her pious hope that she would do as well on the morrow in her part as she had done that evening. Having blotted the entry carefully, she went to bed, and rose early in the morning to commence her last day on earth. As a matter of historical accuracy, when dawned the Friday morning, the day of the performance, there were at least six people in school more perturbed than Calma Ferris. Hurstwood thought, "I wonder if she'll split today? She keeps looking at me. I wonder whether she's made up her mind yet? I wonder whether the old man will split to the governor if she splits to him? I wonder whether Gretta would care much if I got turfed out? Suppose the old man won't let me sit for the Schol.? Wish I had the guts to tackle Ferris and see what she means to do! I won't stick this much longer. Every time I look at Gretta now, or speak to her, I shall imagine that fool of a woman is sticking round, listening and snooping."

Miss Cliffordson thought: "Uncle will never stand it. Out I shall go, and I couldn't stick teaching in any school but this. It's only just bearable here, and I do it frightfully badly, anyway. I don't believe any woman would have me on the staff for more than a fortnight. I wonder whether I'd better marry Tommy Browning and put myself out of pain? Besides, there's poor little Harry! Oh, hell and blast! What did she want to come poking round for, anyway? I suppose she's on the vigilance committee somewhere—or something!"

Mr. Smith thought: "Six months' work! Commissioned, too! How the devil am I going to pay Atkinson now? Serves me right for pinching school time, I suppose. If I'd done the stuff at home this couldn't have happened. Blast the woman, all the same! I couldn't have done it at home, anyway. The girl wouldn't have come."

Miss Camden thought: "Just wait until I get the chance to pay you out, Ferris, my love! That's all! And I've *slaved* over the school netball. *Slaved* over it."

Frederick Hampstead thought: "I suppose the head will give me a testimonial before he sacks me. Or won't he? Better ask for it now, before that condemned female blows the gaff, I think. I'll see him during first lesson, when I haven't a class. He can't refuse if she hasn't said anything yet. Perhaps she'll keep her mouth shut, but I don't think I can stay. It'll be so difficult now."

Alceste Boyle thought: "Why worry? She doesn't *know* anything, and, anyway, I think she's a good sort. It will damage Fred, not me, in any case. Thank God for widowhood! But I wish she didn't know. It makes it, in a way, less wonderful, now someone knows."

CHAPTER III
DEATH

I

By half-past ten on the Friday morning Calma Ferris had something to think about other than school difficulties and problems. A telegram was handed in, which ran thus:

"BEWARE HELM WIDOWER SUSPICIOUS CIRCUMSTANCES ASKED SCHOOL."

Several years of coping with arithmetical problems had sharpened Miss Ferris' wits, and a message which, to less well-trained senses, might have suggested the babblings of lunacy, resolved itself for her into the following perturbing set of ideas:

"Beware of the Mr. Helm from whose table you asked to be moved at the commencement of your summer holiday at your aunt's boarding-house. He is undoubtedly an imitator, if not an actual reincarnation, of George Joseph Smith, who was charged in the year 1915 for drowning three brides in the bath, and he has asked for the address of your school."

The telegram bore her aunt's surname. Miss Ferris, who had lived the narrowest, safest and most sheltered of lives, was seriously upset by the message. Advice she felt she must have, and therefore five pairs of interested and four pairs of anxious eyes noted that at recess, instead of taking coffee and biscuits in the staff room, according to the time-honored and civilized custom of the staff, she repaired to the headmaster's study.

"So she's going to split," thought Miss Cliffordson. "Oh, well!"

She meant to say something to Hurstwood when she got the chance. She wondered whether it would be compatible with her dignity as a member of the staff to suggest to the boy that they should both deny Miss Ferris' story, and rather reluctantly decided that it would not do. In less than three minutes, however, Miss Ferris returned to the staff room. The headmaster was engaged, and could not see her.

"So she's going to, but hasn't yet," thought Frederick Hampstead. He shrugged. After all, what did she know? He and Alceste had always been so very careful. True, there had been those two mad evenings in

35

the women's common room, but surely nobody knew anything about those! And it had been unbearable that long, long autumn term, and there had been only the short Christmas holiday together at the end of it! And even that had been cut short by his having to go and see poor Marion in that ghastly private asylum which drained his resources so thoroughly. The remembrance of those two mad evenings worried him. They had flung caution to the winds on each occasion. They had been crazy. *Could* anybody have found out? A school was such a peculiar institution, and the staff had to be like Cæsar's wife—above reproach. He had said to Smith on one occasion that it was a pity people did not fall into ornamental lakes when such were provided. There was an ornamental lake in the grounds of the asylum. . . . He regretted the ironic jest immediately he had made it and sincerely hoped that Smith would not refer to it again.

At any other time Miss Ferris might have shown the telegram to Alceste Boyle instead of to Mr. Cliffordson, but at the recollection of Alceste's words and look at the mention of Frederick Hampstead, she felt she did not dare to seek her sympathy or advice. No, she must wait until the headmaster was less busy. During the next hour she could set a class to work some arithmetic examples, and perhaps go and see him. She felt, for the first time in her life, alone and unprotected. She had not forgotten Helm's invasion of her room on the night the burglars came, nor his subsequent impudent proposal of marriage.

She went to Mr. Cliffordson at about a quarter to twelve, and received advice and reassurance. Nobody saw her go, and Mr. Cliffordson did not mention to anybody at that time that she had visited him. He asked for, and received, a description of Mr. Helm, and when Miss Ferris had gone he chuckled. She seemed so extremely hardboiled a virgin to be dreading unwelcome attentions from a man of the type he judged Helm to be.

The performance of *The Mikado* was timed to begin at half-past seven, and soon after seven the school hall was beginning to fill up. Masters and mistresses who were not in the opera were acting as stewards, and Alceste Boyle, as senior mistress and producer, was combining the delicate duties of welcoming the guests of importance and darting behind the scenes to make certain that all was going smoothly in readiness for the rise of the curtain. Apart from the fusing of an electric wire which caused a five-minutes' delay in making up the women principals, nothing out of the ordinary happened until halfway through Act

One. Alceste Boyle, who had decided not to add to the onerous office of producer the slighter one of callboy, was informed by her small deputy, a child from the fourth form, that the Katisha was nowhere to be found. "She was dabbing her face in the water lobby, but it's dark in there now." Concluding, naturally enough, that she had gone to the W. C., which was at the end of a long corridor which led from the classroom where the women principals were dressing to the school netball court, Alceste sat down in the dressing room, and, because she was tired and because Calma Ferris' remark of the previous day had compelled her to face a fact which, for the sake of her sanity, she managed to ignore for the greater part of each term—namely that Frederick Hampstead never would and never could be hers unless his wife died, for he was a Catholic and even an amendment of the divorce laws would have had no significance for him—she began to brood. Five minutes went by, and there was no sign of Calma Ferris. The child came back and reported that she was still missing. Alceste had a sudden vision of her having been taken ill. She hastened down the corridor and pushed open the door of the lavatory (beyond which again was the W.C.). She called softly, but loudly enough for anyone inside to hear:

"Are you all right, Miss Ferris?"

There was no answer. She switched off the lavatory light, but no answering beam of light shone under the door of the toilet. She knocked on the door to make certain that no one was there, called again, opened the door and switched on the light, but the place was empty. Puzzled, she switched off the light again and went back to the dressing rooms. There was still no sign of Calma. The only other player who had not yet been on the stage, and who, as a matter of fact, was not due to make his first entrance until Act Two, was the Mikado himself, the senior art master, Mr. Smith. It occurred to Alceste Boyle that the two might be conversing, and that Calma might even now be on the opposite side of the stage, ready to make her entrance. A short transverse corridor made it possible to get to the other side of the school without crossing in front of the stage or going out of doors, so she slipped along this, and presently came upon Mr. Smith, who was enjoying a cigarette in the corridor and was talking to the electrician. She admonished him with a smile and in a whisper, for they were very near the stage, told him he would cough when he began to sing, and then asked him whether he had seen Miss Ferris anywhere.

He had not, and so, feeling irritated and worried, Alceste found a couple of chorus people and sent them to assist in the search, while she herself hastily made her way into the darkened hall, found Miss Camden, who should have had the part of Katisha had not Calma Ferris financed the production of the opera, took her into the women principals' dressing room and asked her to take the part. Miss Camden declared she could not possibly go on like that at a moment's notice, and begged to be excused. Alceste let her return to the auditorium, collared the biggest girl in the chorus, borrowed her costume, got Madame Berotti to make her up very quickly for the part of Katisha, and, Calma Ferris having failed to materialize, went on at the end of the first act, and, being by that time in a state of high nervous tension, justified her Irish blood by rising magnificently to the occasion and taking the part as poor Calma Ferris might have taken it in dreams but could never have managed to take it in reality.

The curtain fell to tremendous applause. Alceste had herself made up a little more carefully during the interval, and to all Miss Cliffordson's questioning she would only reply:

"Whatever has happened, she can't go on now. I shall have to finish."

"But what on earth can have happened to the woman?" Miss Cliffordson persisted. Alceste, sacrificing her own good looks with every touch of greasepaint, in order to create successfully the illusion of Katisha's hideous Japanese countenance, shrugged one shapely shoulder, stood motionless while the last smears were added, and then went out to round up the chorus.

It was not only behind the scenes that Calma Ferris' absence was causing comment. Her landlady, and Frederick Hampstead, the conductor, together with those members of the staff who were on duty as stewards, and those members of the school who were seated in a solid and appreciative phalanx at the back of the hall, wondered audibly, during the interval, why Miss Ferris was out of the cast. Various conjectures were rife, from the landlady's "Taken bad with the excitement, poor thing" to the school's almost unanimous "Old Boiler blew up because the Ferret was so rotten at rehearsal, so Ferret's gone off in a bate and left Boiler stranded," which went to prove, if proof were needed, that children are not the infallible judges of character which sentimental persons would have us believe they are.

The second act was a great success. Hurstwood, who had begun very badly in Act One, had gradually regained his self-confidence, and toward the end of the act was singing and acting almost hysterically, as though carried along by overmastering excitement. During the second act he controlled this excitement sufficiently to give a very good performance. Alceste Boyle was magnificent, and Mr. Smith, as the Mikado, assisted her in bringing the house down. In fact, in spite of the comparatively lifeless show put up by Moira Malley, and the fact that she was in tears at the fall of the curtain, the production of *The Mikado* was the most outstandingly successful production the school Musical, Operatic and Dramatic Society had ever staged.

"Thank heaven that's over!" observed Miss Freely, wiping off makeup in the women principals' dressing room. "Nothing will ever induce me to take part in a school performance again."

"Oh, I don't know," said Miss Cliffordson, ravishingly pretty in a pale pink negligee, as she sat on a school chair and put on her stockings. "You were very good, you know."

It was so palpably a baited hook that Miss Freely perversely decided not to rise to it. She was good nature itself, but Miss Cliffordson was rather too certain that Miss Cliffordson was the prettiest, the best-dressed, the most interesting, the most temperamental and the most talented member of the staff.

"Donald Smith was better than usual, don't you think?" she said.

"Oh, I always think Smith rises to the occasion," replied Miss Cliffordson. "He's lazy, like all real artists, and he won't rehearse, but on the night he always comes up to scratch."

At this point Madame Berotti, who had been gently removing the more outrageous portions of Alceste's hideous makeup, patted her on the shoulder and said good-night.

"*She's* pleased, anyway," remarked Miss Freely, looking after the slender, upright figure of the old ex-actress who carried her eighty years so gallantly. "She thought you were marvelous, Mrs. Boyle. And so you were," she added. "Absolutely great! I don't know how you do it."

Alceste, who was tired, said ungraciously, "I wish I knew why Miss Ferris did it! I can't imagine what's the matter with her. It isn't like her to have left us all in the lurch like that."

"Must have been taken ill," said Miss Cliffordson. "I expect she looked for you and couldn't find you. But I think it was too mean of Miss Camden not to take the part when she was asked. Knows every word of it, too, because she did it for the Hillmaston Players last season."

"Well, she was awfully sore, you know, when Mr. Cliffordson handed it straight to Miss Ferris like that, without a suggestion that anyone else might do it better," said Miss Freely. "And, after all, she would have done it better—tons better. Although not a patch, even then, on Mrs. Boyle's rendering," she went on, glancing sidelong at Alceste's beautiful bare shoulders whence the strap of her petticoat had slipped as she bent to pick up her shoe. Alceste, flushed and laughing, said happily:

"Don't encourage me. Oh, but I loved it!"

The younger mistresses, none of whom knew why she had ever left the stage, said nothing, hoping for revelations. But none came. Instead, Alceste turned to the other occupant of the dressing room and said:

"Well, Moira? Nearly ready? I expect the others have all gone."

It was the thankless duty of those of the staff who had been acting as stewards to see the audience off the building, and then to go round to the dressing rooms and chivvy the children home. Before Moira could make any reply, there came a series of light taps at the dressing room door, and the headmaster's voice outside said:

"Gretta, how long?"

"Half a tic, Uncle," replied his niece, collecting her Japanese costume preparatory to stowing it away.

"Right. I shall be in my own room when you're ready. I've told some of the girls to wait for Moira."

He went away, and the conversation died down among the three women as they hastily concluded their dressing and tidying-up. Then Alceste Boyle, ready to go, turned again to the girl in the far corner of the room, and said, a trifle sharply:

"Come along, Moira. Surely you're ready by now!"

Moira, with a tear-stained face, came up to her, and said abruptly, because she was upset and nervous:

"Mrs. Boyle, I want to speak to you."

"Say on," replied Alceste shortly. The tears had irritated her.

"Not here," said Moira. "Will you come outside a minute? I—I think I know where Miss Ferris is."

"What?" said Alceste, while Miss Freely and Miss Cliffordson came nearer. "What do you mean, child?"

"She's dead," said Moira. "I found out—I found her—in the interval I went for a drink—I didn't like to spoil the show—I—she . . . Oh, they'll hang him! And he can't die! He can't!"

"Get out," said Alceste to the younger mistresses. "Find Mr. Cliffordson at once. See whether it's true."

The two went out, and shut the door behind them. When they had gone Alceste turned to the overwrought and frightened girl.

"Listen, Moira," she said. "Nobody is going to hang. Now don't be silly any more. I want you to pull yourself together. Stop crying. It's quite all right. That's better. Now tell me exactly what you did. Sit down in that chair. Take your time."

"I was thirsty, and I wanted a drink of water," said the girl, "so I went to the water lobby with one of the beakers out of the laboratory to get a drink. It was dark, and I tried to switch on the light, but it didn't come, so I thought if I was careful not to knock the beaker on the tap, I could manage in the dark. I felt carefully, and I touched her. I—she was all wet—I went away. I didn't know whether to tell anybody or not."

"You don't know, then, that it was Miss Ferris," said Alceste quietly, "and you don't know whether she was dead. Don't think about it any more. The others will attend to her. Go home now. Who's going with you?"

Moira mentioned the names of one or two of the girls who were in the chorus, and who went past the house where she lived in term-time, with her aunt. Alceste Boyle had just dismissed her when the headmaster came in. His face was gray. He looked, for the first time in Alceste Boyle's experience, an old man. He nodded in response to her raised eyebrows.

"I've sent Browning for a doctor," he said, "but there's no doubt of it, poor woman. I wonder what on earth was the cause!"

"But how terrible!" Alceste said. "There will have to be an inquest, I suppose?"

The words sounded banal and in rather bad taste, she thought, but the shock had been great. The headmaster nodded.

"Bad for the school," he said. "Well, you'll be wanting to get home, I know. Good-night. Don't worry about it, will you? You'd better not see her. We've done what is necessary. Don't worry."

He went back to the men principals' dressing room, to find Hampstead talking to Smith.

"Do you want us any longer, sir?" Smith asked. He was a dirty-white where he had removed his makeup, and looked ill.

"No. There's nothing to be done. I shall stay until the doctor has made his examination, of course. Good-night. Don't worry. I can't think how it happened. You'll . . . I needn't ask you—you won't discuss it outside the school at present, will you?"

He called Hampstead back as the two masters got to the door.

"Mrs. Boyle has not gone yet," he said. "You'll see her home, I expect, as usual, won't you? Impress upon her not to worry. It's a terrible affair, but we must take it that the poor woman was either the victim of sudden illness, or else that she had trouble of which none of us knew. Good-night, my dear fellow. Don't linger, or Mrs. Boyle may be gone."

Hampstead, who had been staring dumbly, went out like a sleepwalker, and in less than ten minutes young Mr. Browning returned with a doctor. Alceste had no intention of going, however, and as soon as she saw Hampstead she said:

"You'd better go, Fred. I must stay and see things through. After all, there ought to be a woman on the scene."

"The head quite expects that you will go home," Hampstead replied. "In fact, he told me to take you. This is a frightful business, Alceste. I've seen her . . ." He paused and fidgeted with the hat he was holding. "Do you think it could be suicide? She was sitting on a chair in the water lobby, on this side of the building, and her head was in a bowl of water."

Alceste said:

"I don't believe she would have committed suicide. I know my own sex thoroughly, and Miss Ferris wasn't the type. Probably religious, too. I should think she must have fainted. The child said Miss Ferris was 'dabbing her face.' I never for one moment . . . But it's queer. Has the doctor arrived yet, do you think?"

"I don't know. Shall I go and see?"

"No. I'll go. Poor woman. It will be a nuisance for the school. It's certain to get into the papers. I don't believe, after all, we'd better go. We shall probably be in the way."

Together they went to the classroom which had been used as the men principals' dressing room. It was empty, except for the headmaster. The body had been taken into the laboratory, he told them, and the doctor had made a preliminary examination, sufficient to be certain that the cause of death was drowning.

"There will have to be an inquest, of course," said Mr. Cliffordson. "The doctor is going to give orders for the body to be removed. What an awful business it is! One doesn't want to be unfeeling, but I do wish it had happened anywhere but in school. I can't think what possessed her, can you? Or could it have been an accident? The light has gone wrong in there, too. We had to get candles from the stock cupboard. I must communicate at once with her relatives, I suppose. Oh, well, don't worry. As long as it isn't one of the children, it isn't as bad as it might be. Good-night to you both. Don't worry. Poor woman. Oh dear, oh dear!"

II

The verdict which concluded the inquest upon Calma Ferris was "suicide while of unsound Mmind," this in the face of all that the dead woman's acquaintances could say on the subject of her apparent freedom from worry and ill health. The headmaster, still looking old and worn, called a staff meeting at ten o'clock on the following morning. The staff, nervously silent, guessing the subject of the meeting, came in in ones and twos, and seated themselves. When they were all present Mr. Cliffordson addressed them. His tones were dry and formal.

"I have been in consultation with the governing body of the school," he said, "and it seemed to all of us that for the sake of the boys and girls it would be wiser to appoint immediately a successor to Miss Ferris. I have been fortunate enough to secure the services of an able and distinguished lady whose qualifications happen to be a good deal higher than those required for the post, but who is anxious to obtain a firsthand impression of a coeducational day school of an advanced modern type. She will accordingly be appointed for the remainder of this term, while the governors and I are deciding upon a candidate for permanent appointment. I should be glad if you would all take pains to welcome the lady. She is elderly, and probably . . ." he smiled, and for a moment looked himself again, the lines washed from his forehead, and his eyes candid and kind—"has pronounced views which some of you may find irritating. However, I think you'll like her. Her name"— he consulted a paper before him on the big desk—"is Bradley. Mrs. Beatrice Adele Lestrange Bradley. She will commence her duties on Monday at nine."

There was a stunned silence. Then Mr. Browning said blankly:

"But—you don't mean—not *the* Mrs. Bradley, Headmaster?"

"Why not?" said Mr. Cliffordson coldly. The staff, taking its cue, rose and filed out, but the headmaster motioned Browning to remain.

When the others had gone and the door was shut, Mr. Cliffordson said:

"Mrs. Bradley is coming here to make a study of the school. She is writing a psychological treatise on adolescence, and wishes to make firsthand observations in boys', girls' and mixed schools. You understand?"

"I understand," said young Mr. Browning, meeting the headmaster's eye, "that you think Miss Ferris was murdered, and, in view of the fact that the verdict of the coroner's jury was one of suicide, I don't consider you are being fair to us, Headmaster, in getting Mrs. Bradley here like this. I wish to tender my resignation."

"And I refuse to accept it," said Mr. Cliffordson firmly. He changed his tone.

"My dear boy," he said, "pause and consider. I do believe Miss Ferris was murdered, but I don't want the school turned upside down. Mrs. Bradley will decide, quietly, whether I am justified in my conclusions, and then, if I am, some action must be taken. That is all. Last night I was convinced that poor Miss Ferris had drowned herself. Later, I discovered that the waste pipe was completely stopped up with clay. That struck me as curious. I must beg of you not to communicate these tidings to your colleagues. I hope that I am wrong. Things are quite bad enough. But there are facts which cannot be ignored, and I must face them."

"Well, Headmaster, I won't say a word, of course," said Browning, mollified by the headmaster's attitude. "But if you imagine I'm the only one to smell a rat, I think you'll find you're wrong. Everyone has heard of Mrs. Bradley. She's news, as they say in journalistic circles, and . . ."

"Enough, my boy," said Mr. Cliffordson. "I have your assurance, then?"

"Oh, I won't say anything about it," said the young man. But to himself he said, as he walked back to his room, "I wonder who the devil he suspects? Smith, I expect. That clay in the waste pipe came out of the art room, for a certainty, and she ruined his Psyche. But how on earth did he persuade her to go into the lobby in the first place? And the electric light! Someone had tampered with it so that she would not be found very quickly. Dirty work at the crossroads, undoubtedly!"

He was so interested that he forebore to remark on a pitched battle that was being waged by the male members of form lower four when he got back to the room they were in, and merely invited them, in magisterial tones, to get to their places and find page twenty-three. But his mind was not on his work, and at least nine boys and quite seventeen girls did their homework openly during what was left of the English period, while their teacher sat and brooded, and the rest of the form passed notes, flicked ink-soaked blotting-paper pellets or played noughts and crosses. At eleven o'clock Mr. Browning dismissed them, and at two minutes past eleven he was being asked in the men's common room to bet on which of his colleagues was suspected of the murder. The headmaster's ruse of passing Mrs. Bradley off as a member of the staff appeared to have failed completely.

The women's common room did not bet on the identity of the murderer, but among some members of the staff consternation held sway. Miss Freely voiced the general view by observing with a shudder, after Mrs. Bradley's advent had been discussed by seven people, all talking at once:

"Well, there's one thing I'm quite sure of! I'm not going to stay a minute after school hours, to please anybody. I'm not going to run any risks! Have any of you heard of hoodoo? Thank goodness it's only a few weeks until the end of the term!"

At the end of a twelve-minutes' break the staff had to return to their classes, so that several interrupted conversations had to be resumed at lunch. It was the custom for at least three-quarters of the school to stay for lunch, so that every day four members of the staff, two men and two women, were on duty during the dinner hour. Those who were not on duty lunched together in the big staff room.

Miss Cliffordson was the first person to tread on dangerous ground.

"You know, she wasn't a bit the kind of person to commit suicide," she said, choosing this oblique method of approaching the subject chiefly because it seemed indelicate to talk of murder.

"I don't agree." The physical training mistress flushed deeply and spoke with considerable emphasis. "She was just the sort of woman you read about in the 'Great Trials' series—you know—morbid and quiet, with all sorts of repressions and complexes. I think it's the most likely thing in the world that she knew she was going to make a fool of herself in the opera, and she couldn't face up to it."

"I can't think she would have drowned herself," said the deep voice of the physics master. "Not so easy, you know. Demands a tremendous amount of willpower to shove your head into a bowl of water and keep it there until you're dead."

"There's something in that," agreed the botany mistress. "And with a laboratory full of poisons quite handy, it seems a silly thing to attempt—drowning. No; what I think happened was that she felt faint, went for some water, found the light wouldn't switch on, and collapsed over the basin, which happened to be full of water."

"H'm!" said Mr. Poole. "Very queer she should collapse over the one basin in twenty which was not only full of water but which had had its waste pipe carefully plugged with clay so that the water could not possibly run away, wasn't it? And how do you account for the fact that she was sitting on a chair?"

"I can account for the chair being in the water lobby, anyway," said young Mr. Browning, who had, in fact, done so at the inquest. "Don't you remember, I had a boy suffer from nose bleeding in form, and I sent him out there to lean over a basin. I sent another boy with a chair for the fellow to sit down. I can't find that the chair was ever taken back to the hall, so that accounts for the chair."

"Well, it's a funny business, and I for one shan't be a bit surprised to hear that children are to be withdrawn from the school at the end of term because of it. I heard of one large semipublic school—it was residential, certainly, but I can't see that that makes any difference—where the science master cut his throat, and they lost seventy per cent of their pupils almost immediately," said the senior geography master, a mild, bald-headed man in the early forties.

"Look here, do let's drop the subject," urged young Browning, fearful lest the headmaster should suppose he had not kept his promise to refrain from suggesting that murder had been committed at the school. "Who's reffing senior football? Because it is now just turned one-ten."

"I'm taking netball," said Miss Camden crossly. Since the loss of the semifinal for the schools trophy, netball was a sore point with her. "And you'll have to ref junior," she added, turning to Miss Freely. That amiable young lady went at once to get her whistle, and Miss Camden and Mr. Hampstead followed her down.

"Look here," said Miss Camden to Mr. Hampstead, when they reached the school hall and were walking across it to the door which led out onto the school grounds, "who *is* this Mrs. Bradley? Everybody seems to have heard of her but me. Put me wise. I do hate to be out of things."

"She's a psychoanalyst," replied Hampstead. He hesitated a moment, and then went on, "I expect she has been invited to investigate the death of Miss Ferris."

"Oh, lor! Is that her job—investigating deaths?" asked Miss Camden. Hampstead hesitated again before replying.

"Well, unnatural deaths," he said.

"Oh, suicide you mean?" Miss Camden sounded relieved.

"No. Murder," replied Hampstead. He did not hesitate at all this time. His companion said in a frightened voice:

"Murder? But nobody thinks . . . I mean, there can't be . . . Well, but I mean, she wasn't murdered, was she? She committed suicide. They said so."

Hampstead laughed, a short, hard sound.

"Trust a coroner's jury to make fools of themselves," he said. "But, whether Miss Ferris was murdered or not, the headmaster thinks she was."

"Why, has he said anything?" Miss Camden asked, betraying an eagerness of which she was not aware. Hampstead shook his head.

"I don't think so. Not to me, at any rate. But this Mrs. Bradley business—I don't like it. It looks—what's the word they use in novels?—sinister. That's it. It looks decidedly sinister to me."

This conversation was but a sample of any conversation that day on the subject of Calma Ferris' death. Those of the staff—and they were very few—who did not know Mrs. Bradley by reputation were soon enlightened by the others; and by the time school was dismissed at the end of the afternoon, not only the whole staff but also most of the sixth form knew the reason for Mrs. Bradley's coming to the school.

Miss Cliffordson sought out her uncle and tackled him boldly. Mr. Cliffordson, looking worried, a sufficiently unusual state of affairs to cause his niece a certain amount of anxiety, nodded in response to her remarks.

"I wanted to keep the reason of Mrs. Bradley's appointment a secret," he said, "but murder will out, it seems."

"Well, if it really was murder, I suppose it is only right that it should come out," replied his niece. "But I think you might have left things to the coroner, Uncle. It won't do the school much good to have members of the staff murdered, you know. Even suicide is not as bad as that. You'll get all the nervous mothers taking Little Willie away before the murderer murders him, if you're not very careful."

"And if I *am* very careful, too!" said Mr. Cliffordson, ruefully. "Oh,

I've thought matters over, my dear, and, if my conscience would allow it, I would willingly leave matters as they are. But if that poor woman was murdered in my school, then it seems to me that I am responsible at any rate for seeing that her murderer is brought to justice."

"But is it really justice to hang one person for drowning another, do you think?" inquired his niece. The sixth form had debated the question of capital punishment, the headmaster remembered, at some time during the previous term. In spite of an able and thoughtful speech by Hurstwood, the motion "That capital punishment is an error on the part of the State" had been lost by seventeen votes to three. Besides Hurstwood himself, the people who had voted in favor of the motion were a boy whose hobby was woodcarving and another boy who collected beetles. The girls were vehemently in favor of capital punishment. The headmaster, who was, in effect, opposed to punishment of any kind, shook his head sadly.

"I'm not open to conviction. I am not even prepared to listen to argument," he said. "The idea that that poor, inoffensive, innocent woman was done to death in my school appalls me. I am not, as you know, an ignorant, a cowardly or a superstitious man, but I should live through the rest of my life haunted by my conscience if I allowed matters to rest where they are. You are a sensible, levelheaded, well-balanced girl, and so I will give you my reasons for asking Mrs. Bradley to make an inquiry into the circumstances of Miss Ferris' death. You have heard about the clay that was used to stop up the waste pipe so that the water could not run away?"

Miss Cliffordson nodded.

"That clay, I am morally certain, came from a big piece of modeling clay in our own art room. Now I am convinced that no person contemplating suicide would have thought of such an extraordinary method of killing herself. If she was determined to drown herself on the school premises, there is the swimming bath, there are the slipper baths in the girls' and boys' changing rooms, there are several large, deep sinks in the laboratory; there is even the school aquarium. Why choose a small basin so low down that the only way of keeping the head under water a sufficient time to be certain that death will ensue is to sit on a chair? A most extraordinary proceeding!"

"Well, but some women wash their hair like that," Miss Cliffordson pointed out.

"Do they? Oh, well, I didn't realize that. Let the chair pass, then.

But you admit that the idea of stopping up the waste pipe was fantastic on the part of a suicide, and that the swimming bath sounds a great deal more reasonable as a means of drowning oneself, don't you?"

"No. Not in December," said Miss Cliffordson, with a little shudder at the thought of the cold water.

"But we keep the swimming bath open all the year round. You know we do. The water at the present moment has a temperature of something over sixty-six degrees. But further to all this, there is something else. Would she have dressed herself in the Katisha costume, and even gone to the length of having her face made up for her part, if she intended to commit suicide?"

Miss Cliffordson wrinkled her charming nose.

"No," she said at last. "She might have put on the clothes but—not the Katisha makeup. Nobody could possibly want to look so hideous. I don't believe any woman would risk being found dead like it."

She thought deeply for another moment, and then said firmly:

"You've convinced me, Uncle. All women think about what they'll look like when they're dead, and there can't be a woman on earth who could bear to think of looking like Katisha. Miss Ferris didn't commit suicide. She was murdered. I haven't any further doubt about it."

The headmaster groaned.

"I believe I hoped that you would be able to convince me I was wrong," he said. "But I'm not wrong. She *was* murdered, poor inoffensive woman! Unless, of course, the whole thing was an accident. She had cut her face, you know, and may have gone to bathe it."

"Yes, but, in that case, why the clay in the waste pipe?" argued his niece. The headmaster shook his head hopelessly.

"Why, indeed?" he said. "Oh, you're right! You're right! Undoubtedly she was murdered. But *why?*"

CHAPTER IV
FACTS

I

When the headmaster's letter arrived at the Stone House, Wandles Parva, Mrs. Bradley was breakfasting. Out in the garden, dimly perceived through a frosted casement window, the trees were leafless and the green grass swam nebulously between the bottom of the window and the sky. There were three other letters by the side of Mrs. Bradley's plate, and, having concluded her meal except for the last half-cup of coffee, she picked up the envelopes in turn, scrutinized them, then laid aside the one which contained Mr. Cliffordson's urgent missive and dealt briefly with the others. The first envelope contained a publisher's catalogue of psychological and psychoanalytical treatises; the second was a begging letter; the third contained a check and the thanks of a grateful patient who, according to her family, had once been a candidate for a lunatic asylum, but was now, owing to Mrs. Bradley's efforts, a useful, ornamental and popular member of society. Mrs. Bradley threw everything on the fire except the check, on which she stood the sugar basin as a paperweight, and then she opened Mr. Cliffordson's envelope. She read his letter twice and then replaced it in the covering. It had been written before the inquest on Calma Ferris, and so he had not attempted to foreshadow what the verdict of the coroner's jury might be, but he stated, in a firm, pedagogic and yet scholarly hand, that he was certain the unfortunate woman was the victim of murder. He gave all his reasons for coming to this terrible conclusion; said frankly that he did not want to drag in the police unless or until it was absolutely necessary, and promised to send Mrs. Bradley a telegram as soon as the verdict at the inquest was known.

Mrs. Bradley seated herself in an armchair beside the fire, picked up a bag which contained a half-finished woolen jumper in stripes of mauve and green, and began to knit. At the end of twenty minutes she rang the bell, and her maid Celestine appeared.

"I am going away for about three weeks," said Mrs. Bradley.

"*Bien, Madame.*"

"Pack suitable raiment for a schoolmistress."

"A schoolmistress," repeated Celestine, obediently. "*Bien, Madame.*"

"Then send Henri to the vicarage with my compliments and request him to ask the vicar to lend me an arithmetic textbook of a simple kind."

"*Bien, Madame.*"

"Come back when you have done all this. I have more to say."

Celestine disappeared, and Mrs. Bradley completed three inches of jumper. Then there was a tap at the door, and the vicar entered. He drew a small clock from the pocket of his waterproof, gazed at it with an expression of puzzled inquiry, apologized and went out again. In about half an hour he returned without the clock and with an armful of battered-looking books.

"Good-morning," he said. "Er—arithmetic textbooks."

He spread out the selection on the hearthrug. Mrs. Bradley put down her knitting and bent to examine the books. Having made her choice and thanked the vicar, she said:

"On Monday I commence my duties as form mistress and arithmetic teacher at the Hillmaston Coeducational Day School."

She chuckled at his first expression of astonishment, but his face gradually cleared.

"Ah! You are going to study the psychology of coeducation," he said. "Very interesting, these modern ideas. I hope you will enjoy yourself."

"I hope so too," said Mrs. Bradley. "Go away now. I must learn some simple arithmetic."

The vicar took his leave, and when he had gone Celestine reappeared, with the little red enameled clock from the hall table in her hand and an expression of indignation upon her vivacious countenance.

"The naughty old one!" she exclaimed, displaying the clock. "Figure to yourself, Madame, his duplicity!"

"Did he pocket the clock?" inquired Mrs. Bradley.

"But certainly, Madame," replied Celestine. "He puts it into his pocket and goes to promenade himself."

Mrs. Bradley cackled harshly.

"Bless the man!" she said. "Go to the post office, Celestine, and send this telegram."

She wrote a few words in her tiny medicolegal calligrapher, and Celestine went away again. When the door was shut, Mrs. Bradley picked up an arithmetic textbook and gravely began to study the theory of long division of money.

II

Form lower three commercial, dazzled optically by Mrs. Bradley's blue-and-sulphur jumper and uncomfortably conscious that her black eyes were sharp with amused understanding of the peculiarities of the twelve-year-old human mind, decided to reserve judgment on their new form mistress, and spent a quietly strenuous first period in wrestling with a lengthy test on vulgar and decimal fractions.

Mrs. Bradley had arrived on the premises at eight-thirty-five, had inspected her colleagues collectively rather than individually, and had asked the headmaster for a program of *The Mikado* production. He had produced it without comment, but had looked inquiringly at her. Mrs. Bradley, smiling in a way that reminded him oddly of the picture of a dragon which used to alarm him when he was a child, made no remark other than a word of thanks for the program, and had been taken in tow by Miss Freely, who conducted her into the hall for prayers. After prayers, a brief, semi-military ceremony of disciplinary rather than religious significance, the headmaster had introduced her to her form, which, as it happened, took arithmetic during the first period on Monday mornings.

"Good morning, boys and girls," he said.

"Good morning, sir. Good morning, madam."

It was as meaningless and as old-fashioned as a nineteenth-century board-school greeting, Mrs. Bradley reflected. She bowed in her own precise, nineteenth-century way, and smiled her reptilian smile at the assembled children.

"This is your new form mistress. Her name is Bradley. Mrs. Bradley. B-R-A-D-L-E-Y," said the headmaster. "Who are the class monitors?"

"Kathleen Bell and I, sir," said a young boy in the front row.

"Very well. Who is responsible for cleaning the blackboard?"

"I am, sir." Another fresh-faced child rose, looking scared.

"Very good, Collins."

He walked out. Mrs. Bradley said benignly to the class at large:

"How long does this lesson last?"

Several voices informed her that it lasted until a quarter past ten. One young man was particularly emphatic. Mrs. Bradley considered him a moment. Then:

"I *hope* that you are right," she said, in her deep, rich voice. The form stirred uncomfortably. It was at that point that they decided to reserve judgment.

III

Mrs. Bradley had a free period during the afternoon, and she spent it in consultation with the headmaster. She obtained from him but little extra information, however, for, beyond reiterating his belief that Calma Ferris had been murdered, and reproducing the arguments he had collected in support of that belief, he could give her no assistance and could offer no suggestions. The only new matter which he could produce was an account of the conversation he had had with Calma Ferris on the morning of the day she met her death.

"She came to me to ask my advice," he said. "It seemed that she had received a telegram from her aunt, who keeps a small private hotel at Bognor Regis, warning her against a man named Helm whom she had met there during the summer holiday. I was not able to elicit any particular reason from Miss Ferris for her aunt's seeing fit to warn her against this man, and so all I could do was to reassure her, and to advise her to keep a lookout for the man in the neighborhood and inform me directly he importuned her. I don't see what else I could have done. Oh, I got a description of the man, of course. Here it is."

"Had she any other relatives, do you know," asked Mrs. Bradley, "besides this particular aunt?"

"I am sure she had none whatsoever. It seems a queer thing to say, perhaps, but I think she liked the school and the life here chiefly because she had nothing outside her work to interest her or engage her attention. I know she was an orphan, and I never heard of any other relatives apart from this aunt. I know, too, that she was to be the principal beneficiary under her aunt's will, although how much the older lady had to leave I could not give you the slightest idea."

"I see," said Mrs. Bradley. "By the way," she added, "I feel certain that most, if not all, of your staff know why I am here, and therefore, as the cat is out of the bag, I should prefer to give up my class teaching and devote myself to this investigation."

"I was afraid your reputation might have preceded you," the headmaster admitted. "I can easily arrange for someone to take over the form until we get a teacher appointed. You mean that you have an idea to work on?"

"Several," said Mrs. Bradley concisely. "The first is that the aunt, having warned her niece hurriedly by telegram last Friday week, would probably have followed up the telegram by an explanatory letter."

"None was produced at the inquest," said the headmaster. "And yet it is impossible to suppose that an elderly lady would have deemed a cryptically worded telegram a sufficient deterrent to prevent her niece from entangling herself with an undesirable widower."

"How was the telegram worded?" inquired Mrs. Bradley. The head-master wrinkled his brow, but his excellent memory soon produced the required sequence of words.

"Beware helm widower suspicious circumstances asked school."

"This afternoon, when school is over, I shall go to Miss Ferris' lodgings and see what I can discover," said Mrs. Bradley. "There certainly ought to be a letter to explain that telegram."

"Go now," suggested Mr. Cliffordson. "I'll go and take the class."

So at five minutes past three Mrs. Bradley, an eyesore to all and sundry in her queer but expensive garments, went briskly through the quiet streets that bordered the school and made her way to the house where Miss Ferris had lodged.

The landlady herself opened the door.

"I understand that you have rooms to let," said Mrs. Bradley, without preamble.

"Come in," said the woman. Mrs. Bradley entered the house, a small villa, and was shown into the drawing room.

"Several people have been after the rooms, but they were all these nosey-parkers who only wanted a thrill out of staying a week or so where a suicide had lived, that's all. They wouldn't have been permanent, any of them, and I didn't see having to tell them all about her, poor woman, which anybody could see with half an eye was all they wanted. But I could do with the money, unfortunately, so if you'll take the rooms I shall have to ask you not to talk about her to me, that's all."

"I see," said Mrs. Bradley.

"It's all this talk about suicide that does me down," the woman continued. "Whatever anybody says, I *knew* her, and she wasn't one to commit suicide, no matter *what* happened, and that I'll swear. A real Christian woman was Miss Ferris, and well brought up, and it's a sin and a shame for them to go and pretend she'd drowned herself just because they're afraid of finding out who did it!"

"Afraid of finding out who did it?" repeated Mrs. Bradley, affecting to misunderstand the implication.

"Well, what else can you think?"

Mrs. Bradley considered the woman. She was flushed and earnest, a smallish, careworn person, still on the right side of middle age, but prematurely gray and with a face which had known anxiety and trouble. Mrs. Bradley learned later that she was a widow with one child.

"I think you may be right," Mrs. Bradley observed. "The headmaster of the school thinks as you do. He is having the case investigated independently of the police."

"I don't take much account of other people's business as a rule," the woman continued, "because I haven't the time nor the curiosity. But I feel ever so sorry about poor Miss Ferris and the things they are saying about her. Why, even that aunt of hers, that came here the day before the inquest, told me some things that I could have turned round and told *her* weren't true, only she did genuinely seem upset about it all and I didn't like to be hard. Miss Ferris was her only niece, you see, and she was dreadfully cut up about her death."

"What did the aunt think was the cause of Miss Ferris' suicide?" asked Mrs. Bradley. "You say she believed it *was* suicide?"

"Oh, she believed it, and ought to be ashamed of herself for harboring such a wicked thought," said the woman vehemently. "And a fine tale she told me! According to her—although, take it from me that knew poor Miss Ferris far better than she did, her having lived here just on eight years, and I do miss her, too, for all she was so quiet and nice—it was a lie from beginning to end—according to her, Miss Ferris had had this man Helm in her room one night at the boardinghouse, and, thinking they had been discovered, they set up an alarm of burglars. And Miss Ferris' aunt, if you please, thinks something happened that night between them, and that Miss Ferris couldn't face the future unmarried. Anyway, rather than have her marry this Helm, she sent her a telegram, which worried poor Miss Ferris dreadfully, and me, too, for neither of us could really make head or tail of it. So Miss Ferris said she should show the headmaster and ask his advice, which hardly looks like the seventh commandment, does it?"

Mrs. Bradley concurred in this delicately expressed opinion, and then asked whether the telegram had been followed by a letter.

"There *was* a letter," the woman admitted. "It came Friday evening, by the nine o'clock post, only nobody was here to take it in, because my little girl and Miss Ferris and me were all at the concert. Of course, I got a shock when Miss Ferris didn't come on the stage, and more of a shock when she never came home that night, and the police told me she was dead. But there was the letter on the mat, and I put it in her room as usual, and there it is now, I suppose. I'll go and see."

She returned in a few moments.

"It had fallen into the hearth and slipped under the front of the fender," she said. "That's why nobody found it, I suppose. Here it is, anyway. I don't suppose it matters much who reads it now everything legal is over."

The letter was long and rambling, and beyond conveying an impression that the man Helm was a thoroughly undesirable person, gave no more help than the telegram had done. The letter did not give any clue to the whereabouts of Helm, nor any definite reason why Miss Ferris should avoid his society. The aunt had stated vaguely: "Things have come out about him which nobody suspected, but he seemed to me a bold, undesirable fellow," but she had not committed herself further, except to confess that her partner at the boardinghouse had given him Miss Ferris' school address.

Mrs. Bradley read the letter twice, made a note of the aunt's address, paid a week's rent for the rooms and returned in a very thoughtful mood. It was a quarter past four by the time she reached the school gate, and the junior forms had been dismissed and came past her in groups. One child of about twelve accosted her.

"Please, Mrs. Bradley, was Miss Ferris really murdered?"

Mrs. Bradley smiled in the manner of a well-disposed and kindly boa-constrictor, and poked her small interlocutor in the ribs.

"Go and ask your headmaster," she said. But when Moira Malley, the sixth-form girl who had taken part in the opera, stopped her outside the headmaster's room and put the same question, Mrs. Bradley was a good deal more interested.

"What is your name?" she asked. And when the girl had told her, she said, "Why, you are one of the people I want to talk to. Can you keep a secret?"

The Irish girl smiled.

"Yes, I think I can," she answered. She looked pale, Mrs. Bradley thought, but was an attractive creature, with a wide mouth, gray eyes and dark brown hair.

"Wait downstairs in my form room—you know which one?—for a quarter of an hour. If I am not with you by that time, come back here and knock for me."

Moira descended the stairs, and Mrs. Bradley tapped at the headmaster's door.

"Nothing to report," she announced, "but that your opinion is shared by Miss Ferris' landlady. The landlady knew Miss Ferris for eight years, and is certain that she would never have committed suicide. One other question arises which may be important. Was Miss Ferris pregnant, do you know? Was it suggested that that might have been a reason for her suicide?"

"She was not pregnant," replied Mr. Cliffordson. "The coroner asked the question at the inquest, and I myself heard both the question and the doctor's reply."

"Thank you," said Mrs. Bradley. She made an illegible note on a clean page of the notebook which, together with a small silver pencil on a chain, she drew from the capacious pocket of her skirt. "With your permission I am now going to have a talk with Moira Malley."

"There's something worrying that girl," said Mr. Cliffordson. "She hasn't been herself since the dress rehearsal."

"When was that?" asked Mrs. Bradley.

"On the Tuesday. It was rather a failure, you know. Poor Moira was dreadfully nervous, and hasn't been right since. I'm sorry for that child. Her mother lives in Ireland, on nothing a year, more or less, and the girl is here on a foundation scholarship. Her books and most of her clothes come out of the grant she receives, and, for the rest, an aunt with a family of her own takes her in. Last summer holiday things were in such a bad way that the girl got herself a holiday post as nursery governess, as it was not possible for her mother to send the return fare for Moira to visit her home. She is a clever girl and a very nice girl. We're going to see whether she can win the scholarship to Girton which the governing body offers, and, if she does, I am going to give her a post here later on, if she'll take it. She is a girl of excellent character and is exceedingly popular here, both with the staff and the boys and girls."

It was less than the specified quarter of an hour later when Mrs. Bradley walked into the form room of the lower third commercial. Moira Malley had switched on the lights and was reading. She put the book down, rose to her feet and smiled a little nervously as Mrs. Bradley came in. The little old woman shut the door and Moira drew forward a chair for her. Mrs. Bradley sat down, but the girl remained standing. Mrs. Bradley looked at the clock. It was ten minutes to five.

"What about your people?" she asked. Moira shrugged.

"Aunt doesn't mind. Often she doesn't know whether I'm in the house or not until suppertime. I get my own tea. The others have theirs earlier."

"I see," said Mrs. Bradley. "Well, sit down, child, and tell me what's the matter."

"What's the matter?" the girl echoed. She flushed painfully. "I don't think there's anything—"

"Why did you ask me whether Miss Ferris had been murdered?" was Mrs. Bradley's next question.

"Well, everybody from the third form upwards is saying so. And you—you're not really a mistress, are you?"

"No," said Mrs. Bradley. "I'm not. And Miss Ferris may have been murdered."

"That's what everybody says," said the girl. "John Lestrange said nobody would have sent for you if there hadn't been murder in the air."

"The graceless child!" said Mrs. Bradley, laughing. "I didn't know he was at school here. He was at Rugby when last I heard from him."

"Yes; he's only been here a term, and he's jolly sick about it," said Moira. "His mother, Lady Selina Lestrange, thought he ought to have coeducation. She'd heard a lot about it, or something, so she sent John here. His sister is an awfully nice girl, I believe, but she did not come here. Her name's Sallie."

"My niece," said Mrs. Bradley complacently.

"Oh, is she? Then John's your nephew—Oh, that's silly and obvious, isn't it?"

Mrs. Bradley, who had been out of England for some months previously and so had not kept track of Lady Selina's gyrations, was wondering what her massive sister-in-law would think when she received news that a murder had been committed at the coeducational school which had commended itself to her so heartily a few months before. Mrs. Bradley could visualize a satisfied sixteen-year-old John Lestrange returning to Rugby the following term, if the authorities there would take him back. She chuckled, and Moira Malley looked surprised.

"A mental picture," Mrs. Bradley explained. "But we must be serious. I want some help. Have you any idea when it was that you last saw Miss Ferris alive?"

The girl did not answer, and when Mrs. Bradley looked at her she saw that she was biting her bottom lip and that her hands were clenched so that the knuckles showed white.

"You need not be afraid," said Mrs. Bradley gently. "Tell me the truth, child, and don't leave anything out."

The girl remained silent.

"Very well," said Mrs. Bradley. "Please yourself, my dear. Come and show me the water lobby where the body was found."

"No!" said the girl. "I can't go round there after dark! I can't face it!"

"Very well," said Mrs. Bradley, as equably as before. There was a note of hysteria in the girl's voice, so the little old woman laid a skinny claw on her knee and said:

"I understand that on the night of the performance Miss Ferris cut herself and had to go into the water lobby to staunch the bleeding. Is that right?"

Moira began to cry.

"I promised I wouldn't tell," she said, "but as you seem to know, I suppose it doesn't matter."

She was crying so bitterly that Mrs. Bradley had some difficulty in making out the words.

"It was Mr. Smith. He came charging round a corner and knocked into Miss Ferris and broke her glasses. A bit of broken glass dug in her cheek just under the eye. It made the tiniest little mark, but it bled a good bit and she said she would go and wash it. That's the last I saw of her. The next day Mr. Smith came round to Aunt's home and said he wanted to speak to me about using our hockey pitch for a boys' match. It was Saturday"—she was regaining control over herself, and her words were becoming easier to follow—"and we hadn't a match in the afternoon. Aunt sent for me to talk to him, after he'd told her what he wanted, and when we were in the drawing room together he told me that Miss Ferris was dead, and asked me to promise not to tell about the accident to Miss Ferris' glasses. He said he had fearful wind up when he found out that somebody had seen it happen, because it made him partly responsible for her committing suicide by putting the idea of water, that is, drowning, into her head. It seemed silly to me, but, of course, if he thought she had been *murdered* . . ."

She broke off suddenly. Mrs. Bradley pursed up her mouth into a little beak, and decided that the girl was not being entirely frank with her. But what Moira was hiding, time, Mrs. Bradley's experience informed her, would probably disclose.

"At what time did the accident take place?" she asked, determined at the moment not to press the girl.

"Oh, let me see. Very near the beginning of the opera, because I was just going to make my first entrance—you know—the 'Three Little Maids from School' bit—so I couldn't stop and see to poor Miss Ferris. The other two, Yum-Yum and Peep-Bo, where already in the wings, only they are both mistresses, so I didn't like to tack on to them too closely, so neither of them saw it happen. It was only me."

"Was there the slightest possibility that anyone else could have witnessed the collision?" Mrs. Bradley asked.

"Anybody in the men principals' dressing room might have seen it, but I don't know who was there."

"And you were about to make your first entrance?" pursued Mrs. Bradley thoughtfully. "Thank you, Moira. That's all, then. Cheer up, child."

When the girl had gone, Mrs. Bradley switched off the lights in the form-room and made her way to the water lobby where the death of Calma Ferris had occurred. The school keeper was busy with a broom and a pail of damp sawdust, and politely stood aside to allow her to enter.

"You aren't superstitious, ma'am, I see," he observed, noticing that Mrs. Bradley was pressing the tap which flowed into what he had now become accustomed to refer to at the Hillmaston Arms as "the Fatal Bowl."

"Oh, is this *It?*" asked Mrs. Bradley, with a show of great interest.

"It is, ma'am. Took me an hour and ten minutes to get all that nasty messy clay out of the waste pipe, too. What with that and seeing what was wrong with the electric- ight switch, I had a busy day Sunday, I can tell you."

"I can imagine it," returned Mrs. Bradley courteously. "And what *was* wrong with the electric light switch?"

"Some of them boys had been up to their mischief, I reckon. The switch 'ad worked a bit loose, you see—I was meaning to replace it— and it was easy enough to take it off and put the wiring out of action, and put the whole thing back again. Barring that it hung a bit loose, as I said before, you wouldn't notice anything wrong, but when you actually went to switch on the light nothing wouldn't happen, ma'am. See? Them boys do it just for devilment. They done it to all the school switches one Guy Fawkes night, and the headmaster made 'em put 'em all right again. Mr. Pritchard learns 'em all the tricks. He's real clever at electricity—got the boys in his form to make the school a wireless set—ah, and it's a beauty, too!—and any of the young devils could have put that switch out of order as easy as look at it."

"Ah," said Mrs. Bradley. "The switch was not out of order on the Thursday evening, then, when you did your cleaning?"

" 'Course it wasn't," replied the school keeper. "I 'as to have the lights on every night at this time of the year, to do my work, you see. Ah, and I can go further, ma'am. It was all right on the *Friday* evening, when I cleaned up. I didn't do more than I could help, that Friday evening, as I had to get the hall ready for the concert, but I *did* happen to come in here, because I remember for why. I does the inks in this lobby and I remembered Mr. Cliffordson asking me about a gallon jar of blue-black, that had somehow got mislaid from stock, so I thought I'd just have a deck in here to see if it had got itself mixed up with the ink already in use. I knew it hadn't, but I'd got to satisfy him with what you might call an official observation and report, and it just happened to occur to me. So I know the switch was all right then, because I used it."

"I suppose Miss Ferris herself had not tampered with it?" suggested Mrs. Bradley.

"Considering the poor lady didn't know no more about electricity than to ask me to come and look at her electric iron she used in the sitting-room at her lodgings and tell her why it wouldn't heat up, when all the time one of the wires at the plug end had come right out and she'd never noticed it——" said the school keeper.

"Odd," Mrs. Bradley reflected, as she made her way to her new lodgings without having washed her hands, "that Calma Ferris should have gone into a pitch-dark lobby to wash a cut on her face. I should imagine that she did nothing of the sort. However, we shall see."

When she arrived at her lodgings she scrutinized the books on Miss Ferris' little bookshelf, took down the script of *The Mikado,* was immersed in it when the landlady brought in her tea, and was still immersed in it when the landlady brought in her supper. By the time the woman came in again to clear away, however, Mrs. Bradley had returned the book to the shelf and was okaying Patience. She grinned in her saurian fashion at the landlady and asked after her little girl.

The woman was consumed with curiosity, for she had recognized the book which Mrs. Bradley had been studying. Dozens of times had she good-naturedly held it in her hands and prompted Miss Ferris when the latter had been learning the part of Katisha. The amount of time Mrs. Bradley had spent in studying the book, and the sight of Mrs. Bradley's notebook and pencil, and the undecipherable hieroglyphics with which the only page she could see, as she set the table, had been covered, made her very anxious to talk about her late lodger, in spite of the fact that she had told Mrs. Bradley she did not want to discuss Miss Ferris. She took as long as she could over clearing the supper things away, while Mrs. Bradley, black eyes intent on the small cards, appeared to be absorbed in her game and unconscious that such a person as Calma Ferris had ever existed. At last the woman could bear it no longer.

"Have you heard anything more, Mrs. Bradley?"

Mrs. Bradley looked up.

"Yes, a little," she said. "Tell me. Did Miss Ferris always wear glasses?"

"Blind as a bat without 'em, I think," the woman answered. "At least, she always had two pairs, and I remember once when one pair was at the optician's, she mislaid the other pair one day, and quite hurt herself walking into the edge of the chest of drawers in her room, she was that short-sighted."

"So that even after she had been made up for her part she would still have worn her glasses up to the moment of going on the stage?" said Mrs. Bradley.

"I doubt whether she could see to get on to the stage up the steps at the side without them," said the woman. "She'd have handed them to someone in the wings, I shouldn't wonder, ready to put on again as she came off."

"I see," said Mrs. Bradley. "Yes. Thank you. I think I'll go to bed. Breakfast at nine o'clock, please."

"Why, but that'll make you late for school, won't it?"

"I am not teaching at the school tomorrow," replied Mrs. Bradley. She sighed. There was a boy in the lower third commercial with, she felt certain, all the psychological peculiarities of the Emperor Caligula. She would have liked to study him.

CHAPTER V
INTERROGATION

For nearly the whole of the next morning Mrs. Bradley was closeted with the headmaster, and the "Engaged" notice was hung on the outside of his study door from nine-fifteen until just after twelve.

"It seems to me," Mrs. Bradley remarked, "that the evidence in support of the theory that Miss Ferris was murdered in the lobby is sufficiently strong to warrant further investigation, but not sufficiently tangible to offer to the authorities. I have reason to believe"—she took out her notebook—"that, as the result of a collision in the corridor, Miss Ferris had her glasses broken and sustained a small deep cut just beneath one eye. She went into the water lobby to bathe the cut, and I have not found out yet that anyone went with her."

"Who collided with her?" the headmaster demanded. "The way boys rush down these narrow corridors is most dangerous."

"It does not seem to have been a boy," replied Mrs. Bradley. "It was Mr. Smith."

"Smith?" The headmaster looked astounded. "Surely not! Why, this is serious!"

Mrs. Bradley did not ask why. She fixed her twinkling black eyes on those of the headmaster and waited for enlightenment. After a moment or two, it came.

"You remember, perhaps," said Mr. Cliffordson, "the clay which was effectually stopping up the waste pipe, so that Miss Ferris' head was still immersed in water when she was discovered dead?"

Mrs. Bradley looked intelligent, and nodded.

"That clay, it was established at the inquest, came from the art room. Smith is the senior art master. Furthermore, modeling clay was used, I believe, as part of his facial makeup."

"Where is the art room?" asked Mrs. Bradley, who had not been in the school long enough to have learned all the ramifications of its ground-floor plan.

"Almost opposite the prompt side of the stage."

He drew a rough sketch on his blotting-pad, and Mrs. Bradley nodded.

"So that anybody who knew there was a lump of modeling clay in the art room could have slipped in and taken enough to stop up that waste pipe," she said. "Cheer up! Mr. Smith isn't hanged yet." She laughed. "This brings me to a particularly important point," she went on. "How many people were in a position to go into the art room and/ or into the water lobby that night? Who was allowed behind the scenes— that is to say, apart from those people who were taking part in the opera?"

The headmaster began to write on a scribbling pad which was close at hand on the desk.

"I am not going to trust entirely to my own memory," he said. "Mrs. Boyle was in charge of everything that went on behind the scenes, so in a moment, when I have made my list, we will send for her to confirm it. Now, let me see." He wrote, after two pauses for consideration, a list of six names and handed it to Mrs. Bradley. She took it, and read aloud, with a questioning note:

"Madame Berotti?"

"An ex-actress, very old and frail now, who comes to all our school entertainments and makes up the principal characters. A delightful person. An artist to her fingertips. She used to produce for us at one time."

"Mrs. Boyle?"

"Senior English mistress. The producer," said the headmaster. "An ex-actress, too, incidentally. Shakespeare, repertory—all the usual high-brow stuff."

"Mr. Hampstead?"

"He is our senior music master, and was the conductor of the orchestra. He was behind the scenes before the beginning of the opera and again during the interval."

"The electrician?"

"The lighting was important, and our homemade footlights have their disadvantages, so we had the electrician in attendance. I don't know how long he stayed behind, I'm sure. I know one of the lights went wrong—apart, I mean, from the one in the water lobby where Miss Ferris was found."

"Who found her?" asked Mrs. Bradley.

"The girl Malley, poor child. She went to get a drink, it seems, found that the switch was out of order, groped in the darkness, and touched Miss Ferris' body."

"No wonder she is in a highly nervous state, poor girl," commented Mrs. Bradley. She no longer wondered at Moira's hysterical refusal to accompany her to the water lobby on the previous evening. "The next name on the list is that of Mr. Browning," she continued.

"Yes. Our junior English master. He was acting as prompter. He would have been about behind the scenes before the commencement of the opera and during the interval, unless it proves that he left his post as prompter at any time during the performance. Otherwise he would have been seated in the wings, with the script."

"I shall have to see these people," said Mrs. Bradley, and continued to read from the list.

"The curtain operator?"

"Otherwise the school keeper," said the headmaster. "Yes. He was in position in the wings at just before the commencement of the performance, but I do not imagine that he stayed there during the whole of the first act, which, at our rate of playing the opera, lasted for about an hour and twenty minutes. He is certain to have gone away during that time. I don't know where he went. Probably to the back of the hall to watch the performance. He had been well drilled at three or four rehearsals, and knew exactly when he would be wanted. He takes great interest in everything connected with the running of the school, and is even more enthusiastic and partisan than *I* am where the boys and girls are concerned. He has been with us since the opening of the school."

"That is the last name on your list," said Mrs. Bradley. "Can we see Mrs. Boyle now?"

"Surely." The headmaster touched an electric buzzer which brought his secretary from an adjoining room.

"Ask Mrs. Boyle whether she can kindly spare me a moment," he said. He consulted the large timetable. "She is in Room K."

In less that four minutes, Alceste Boyle appeared, and Mrs. Bradley and she exchanged glances. Mrs. Bradley saw a tall, well-made woman on the threshold of middle age, with beautifully dressed dark hair, dark-blue wide-set eyes under arched eyebrows, a sweet mouth and a broad, noble forehead; it was a gracious and pleasing face, and Mrs. Bradley smiled and nodded as her eyes met those of its owner. Alceste Boyle saw a woman in the middle sixties, with sharp black eyes like those of a witch, an aristocratic nose, a thin mouth which pursed itself into a queer little birdlike beak as its owner summed her up, and, lying idle for the moment, for Mrs. Bradley had returned his scribbling tablet to the headmaster some two minutes before the entrance of Alceste Boyle, a pair of yellow, clawlike hands, the fingers of which were heavily loaded with rings. Alceste's noncommittal cardigan, jumper and dark skirt—a costume which was almost the uniform of the women members of the staff—contrasted oddly with Mrs. Bradley's outrageous color scheme of magenta, orange and blue. Notwithstanding all physical and sartorial evidence to the contrary, however, Alceste decided that the queer little old woman was attractive.

"You wanted me, Mr. Cliffordson?" she said.

"Yes. Take a seat, Mrs. Boyle. Look here." He handed her the list of names. "All those people were behind the scenes on the night of Miss

Ferris' death. Is the list complete, or can you add to it?"

Alceste scanned the list, thought for a moment, and then said:

"I had a fourth-form girl behind with me. She acted as callboy and general messenger. I sent her on one or two unimportant errands, I know, and she also helped in the search for Miss Ferris."

"Who was she?" inquired the headmaster.

"Maisie Phillips."

"Oh, I know the girl. Nobody else?"

Alceste shook her head. "Nobody else," she said. "I was very strict about not allowing unauthorized people behind the scenes. They only want to gossip and get in the way. I'm sure that was everybody, except the boys and girls in the chorus—and the principals, of course."

"Thank you." He turned to Mrs. Bradley. "Mrs. Boyle is my head assistant. I think she should be taken into our confidence."

"If you mean that you believe Miss Ferris was murdered—why, so do I," said Mrs. Boyle, surprisingly. "She was delighted—thrilled—to be taking part in the opera. It's true she made a hash of the dress rehearsal, but so did several others, and we all knew it would be different on the night. Besides, at the last rehearsal, which was not a dress rehearsal, she did ever so well. The pity is that nobody was there to see the difference. But, goodness knows, there are plenty of people who would have been pleased to see her dead! Anyway, I am certain in my mind that she was the last person to commit suicide."

"Plenty of people who would have been pleased to see her dead?" repeated the headmaster incredulously. "But surely—she was such an extraordinarily inoffensive woman. . . ."

He halted, uncertain of what to say. That Mrs. Boyle believed what she was saying, and had foundation for her belief, he had no doubt whatever.

"I think you will have to tell us everything you know," he said at last. Alceste folded her large, well-shaped hands in her lap, and nodded.

"Mrs. Bradley is here to investigate the circumstances of the death, of course," she said, "and advise us how to proceed if it proves that Calma Ferris was murdered?"

The headmaster nodded. He opened a drawer in his desk and produced a box of cigarettes.

"Excuse me one moment," said Mrs. Boyle. "My form. I'd better set them some work."

"Oh, let 'em rip," said Mr. Cliffordson easily. "Who goes in to them next? Poole? Oh, that's all right. He'll blow the flame out. They won't hurt for half an hour. Do 'em good to be on the loose for a bit!"

"They'll have the roof off," said Alceste, uneasily. She had never entirely accommodated herself to the free-and-easy methods at the school.

"My dear girl, don't worry yourself. I don't care, so why should you? Take a cigarette, and do let us hear a little more about this frightful business," said the headmaster, who firmly believed that a noisy child is a good child and that silence breeds sin.

"Well, Mr. Cliffordson," Alceste said, studying the burning tip of her cigarette, "to explain myself I shall have to tell you a story, and then throw myself on your mercy. I shall also have to refuse to answer a question which you are certain to ask me."

"Carry on," said the headmaster.

"When the school was first opened I applied for the post of English mistress, and got it," Mrs. Boyle began. "I was a childless widow, and was content. My married life, without being in the least sensational, was not an unqualified success, and when my husband, an Irish doctor, died in Limerick during an influenza epidemic there, I had no desire, I discovered, to return to the stage, so I came to England, and for some time was very happy in this school. Then I fell in love with a man who was not free to marry me. We have spent every holiday—Christmas, Easter and summer—together, and when I say 'together' I mean that we have lived in every sense—physical, mental, spiritual—as man and wife. This has been going on for the past eleven years. I was young, hopeful, headstrong, passionately in love when all this began. Now, at the end of eleven years of it—eleven years of treasuring it up, keeping it secret, looking forward, even in the dreariest term, to the coming holiday time when I could be myself and fulfil myself—I discover that it has not been a secret at all. For several years Miss Ferris knew of it. When I heard that she was dead I went to her lodgings and asked to rent her rooms, because I wanted to find her diary if I possibly could and destroy it. I communicated with the—the man, and he tried also to rent the rooms when they were refused to me. . . ."

Mrs. Bradley had a mental audition of the landlady's voice, a trifle high-pitched and peevish, saying, "Several people have been after the rooms, but they were all these nosey-parkers who only wanted a thrill out of staying a week or so where a suicide had lived. . . ."

". . . but the landlady wouldn't have him either. So I never got hold of the diary."

"Had you seen the diary previously, do you mean?" asked Mr. Cliffordson. "Had you seen it before Miss Ferris' death?"

Alceste shook her head.

"She let out by accident that she knew. It was after she had ruined Mr. Smith's clay figure on the night of the dress rehearsal."

"What?" exclaimed the headmaster. "She ruined Smith's model? Not his Psyche, surely?"

Alceste Boyle nodded.

"Wasn't it dreadful?" she said. "It was absolutely an accident, of course, and I know she was terribly distressed. But the point is that she brought me in to comfort Smith—as though one *could!*—and it was then that I learned she knew the truth about me and about my affairs. Smith isn't the man, by the way, although I believe he loves me." Her dark-blue eyes challenged the world. "Oh, and I lent him two hundred and fifty pounds to compensate for the loss of the little Psyche."

"Did Miss Ferris attempt to make capital out of her knowledge of your affairs?" inquired Mrs. Bradley, interestedly.

"Not in the least. She made the most offhand remark about them, as though she had known for ages and took it for granted that I should have a lover. She was a bit like that, you know. She was so meek and docile and colorless herself that she took it for granted that other people were different. I never had the slightest idea that *she* would make capital out of her knowledge, but as soon as she was dead I could not help wondering whether she had left some record of her discovery. I didn't want my secret to be broadcast, and she was just the type to keep an elaborately written and thoroughly indiscreet diary—indiscreet in the gossiping sense, I mean. And people are not scrupulous when they are going through dead people's belongings, are they? I was afraid of what might be said."

Mrs. Bradley had taken out her notebook and pencil and was rapidly filling a page with her own personal shorthand signs. The headmaster was leaning back in his chair, his pipe between his teeth, and his eyes fixed on the top row of volumes in his bookcase.

"Then there was Miss Camden and the netball match," Alceste went on. "I don't suggest Miss Camden killed Miss Ferris. I am sure she didn't; but she *could* have done, over the result of that match."

"What match was that?" Mr. Cliffordson inquired, for the incident of Miss Ferris, Miss Camden and the girl Cartnell had entirely faded from his mind. Mrs. Boyle reminded him of the occurrence.

"Oh, that business—yes! But, my dear Mrs. Boyle, it had no real importance. A most trivial affair!"

"Not for Miss Camden," said Alceste. "She's a tortured, warped, ambitious sort of girl, and this is the fourth year she's tried for the interschool trophy. We have never got into the semifinal before, and, with the girl Cartnell in the team, she thinks we might have figured in the final, and even won it. Considering there wasn't a netball team at all in the school when she came, I think she's worked wonders. It was very hard luck to have a team girl kept in on the day of the match."

"Well, I don't believe in competitive sports," said the headmaster heavily; "and as long as I am in command here they will be relegated to their proper place. It's a lot of nonsense, pitting teams of children one against the other, and fosters entirely the wrong spirit. And if it reacts like this upon the staff, well, the least said in its favor the better."

He was evidently riding a hobbyhorse, thought the sharp-eyed listener with the notebook, and made a note of the headmaster's prejudice against competitive sports.

"My point is this," said Mrs. Boyle, after a short pause. "Even if Miss Ferris *was* inoffensive, yet she did manage to upset one or two people rather seriously. There might be others, of whom we know nothing, and who had far more reason to bear her a grudge than had Miss Camden, Mr. Smith or myself. After all, even inoffensive people have to make some contacts, and it is quite possible that the result may be that fur will fly or sparks set fire to tinder. Don't you think so?"

Mr. Cliffordson nodded gloomily. Then he said abruptly, because he felt he was exceeding his rights as a headmaster:

"Who is the man with whom you spend your holidays?"

Alceste Boyle stubbed out the end of her cigarette on an ashtray and rose to her feet. She smiled. No wonder two men were in love with her, thought Mrs. Bradley sympathetically.

"I told you there would be a question I should not answer," Alceste said. "You need not worry about him, though. He wouldn't hurt a fly."

As soon as she had gone the headmaster said morbidly:

"Well, there's the solution, I suppose. I'm not going to do anything about it. Smith's not a murderer. He's a temperamental fellow who flew off the handle in a fit of rage. People shouldn't go about ruining other people's work. The man she's in love with is Hampstead. I've known that for years."

"You think Mr. Smith was the murderer?" asked Mrs. Bradley, innocently.

"What else can one think?" demanded Mr. Cliffordson.

"Well, I haven't seen Mr. Smith yet, except at a distance of about forty-five feet, you know," said Mrs. Bradley. "Besides, if he is as temperamental as you say, why should he wait from Tuesday until Friday to take vengeance on a Philistine? The whole trouble about temperamental people, of the kind you mean, is that they act swiftly, heedlessly, in the sudden heat and under the sudden compulsion of the moment. I should say that by Friday Mr. Smith was getting over it. But I had better see the gentleman."

The headmaster pressed the buzzer again.

"Please ask for Mr. Smith. The art room," he said to his secretary.

The first thing Mrs. Bradley noticed about Mr. Smith was that he was obviously ill at ease. He looked from the headmaster to Mrs. Bradley, and seemed inclined to turn and flee.

"You sent for me, Headmaster?" he got out, at last.

"Ah, Smith. Yes. Come in, and shut the door, my dear fellow." Mr. Cliffordson, thoroughly embarrassed, was more genial than the occasion warranted, and the wretched art master, his tie askew, his lank black hair in an untidy flop over his left eye, looked more hunted and miserable than before. He did not appear to have noticed the headmaster's suggestion, so Mrs. Bradley said gently, in her deep, full voice, "Shut the door, dear child."

Smith started, brushed the back of his hand across his eyes, and then obeyed.

"Now sit down over there," said Mrs. Bradley, pointing to a chair. "Now tell us why you wanted to kill Calma Ferris."

Smith blinked.

"Did I want to?" he said. Then his face cleared. "Oh, yes, so I did. She walked into my Psyche and shoved her on to the floor. Ruined her, of course. Yes, I was angry. But it was all right. Alceste lent me the money to pay Atkinson. I didn't care awfully for the Psyche, as a matter of fact. She was commissioned. I hate working on a commissioned figure."

"I see," said Mrs. Bradley. "So you didn't kill Miss Ferris?"

"I don't think so, you know," replied Smith. "Did Moira Malley say

I did? I like that girl. She's got a sense of perspective. More than you can say about most of these oafish kids here. You'd scarcely believe," he continued, turning to Mrs. Bradley as though he found hers a sympathetic presence, "how few of these boys and girls can draw. And I can't teach 'em. I'm a first-rate artist and a rotten teacher. I wouldn't stick it if it weren't for Alceste. She thinks I'd starve if I didn't draw a regular salary, you know, so I stay to please her. Besides"—he blinked rapidly and clawed the air—"I must be near her! I must! I must!"

"Why did you ask Moira Malley not to say anything about the way you cannoned into Miss Ferris and knocked her glasses off and cut her face?" demanded Mrs. Bradley. Smith blinked again.

"Did I say that?" he asked. "I can't remember. I remember barging into Miss Ferris round a corner. . . . Oh, yes! I know. I was afraid it was my fault she committed suicide. You see, she'd spoilt my Psyche, and I thought perhaps the sight of me, coupled with the fact that she had to go into the water lobby to bathe her face, might have given her the idea that she should drown herself, and I didn't want to be asked a lot of questions. It's just an act of lunacy to ask me questions, because I never remember things five minutes after they have happened."

"I see," said Mrs. Bradley. "Go on!"

"I've nothing more to say," said Smith. He glanced up at the portrait of a florid, self-satisfied-looking man over the table.

"You took the name-part in the opera, I think?" said Mrs. Bradley. She produced a program from her skirt pocket and flourished it at him.

"The name-part? Oh, yes. I was the Mikado," answered Smith.

"Yes. You had not to make your first entrance until the beginning of Act Two," said Mrs. Bradley. Smith nodded.

"And during the interval Miss Ferris was found dead."

"But *was* she dead?" asked the Art-master.

"Oh, yes," said the headmaster quickly, before Mrs. Bradley could speak. "You remember the medical evidence at the inquest?"

Smith shook his head.

"Oh, well, it was definitely established that Miss Ferris had met her death at least two hours before the doctor examined the body. That means that she died before the interval, you see."

"I didn't know that doctors cared to commit themselves to the extent of giving an exact time of death," protested Smith. He held up his thin long hand before either of the others could speak. There was a slight flush on his high cheekbones, but his voice did not change as he continued: "Please don't mistake me. I do know what you're driving at. You think Miss Ferris was murdered. So do I. And you think"—he turned and addressed Mrs. Bradley—"that as I had the whole of the first act with nothing to do, I filled up the time by revenging myself on Miss Ferris for damaging that clay figure of mine. You weren't joking a few moments ago when you asked me why I wanted to kill Miss Ferris. You meant that you thought I *had* killed her. Well, I didn't."

He smiled very nervously. Mrs. Bradley could see that his hands were trembling.

"Very well, Mr. Smith," said Mrs. Bradley soothingly.

"May I go, Headmaster?" asked he. Mr. Cliffordson was about to answer when Smith continued: "By the way, perhaps you would advise me. Really, I know very little about the law and crime. . . . Ought I to get into touch with a solicitor about all this? Ought I to tell him my version of the story and get him to watch proceedings, or anything?"

Mrs. Bradley grinned mirthlessly and waved a skinny claw.

"One moment, Mr. Smith. I understood you to say that you agreed with us in our belief that Miss Ferris was murdered?"

"I do believe it," said Smith.

"Can you give us any reason for your opinion?"

"Only that I'm certain she did not commit suicide," said the art master. "I think one is sensitive to that aspect in people. The only person on this staff at all likely to commit suicide, except for myself, is Miss Camden, the physical training mistress."

"Then it is merely surmise on your part that Miss Ferris was murdered?" asked the headmaster. He sounded disappointed. Mr. Smith shrugged. He appeared less nervous.

"It's the electric light going wrong," he said slowly. "Something more than coincidence, don't you think, that the electric light should go wrong in the place that houses a dead woman?"

"Indeed, yes," said Mrs. Bradley. She wrote swiftly for a moment, and then intimated that the interview was at an end by saying:

"And consult a solicitor if it will relieve your mind, but if your conscience is clear and your mind at rest, I shouldn't think you will need or want to consult anybody."

"Well," said Smith, with a wry smile, "I hope the wrong man won't get hanged."

"Stranger things than that have happened," said Mrs. Bradley, as the door closed behind the senior art master.

"I suppose you didn't see the electrician?" she asked suddenly. The headmaster shook his head.

"I can give you his address," he said. " 'The light that failed,' of course?"

"No," replied Mrs. Bradley succinctly. She drew her chair closer to the small table at which she was seated. "It comes to this," she said. "If we think that Miss Ferris was murdered, the murder could only have been committed by some person or persons"—she cackled—"who had business in that part of the building during the performance. I spent a good deal of time yesterday evening in reading the script of *The Mikado*, and, granted that the actual drowning could have been done in two minutes, we have the following interesting data:

"1. The Mikado, Mr. Smith, had the whole of the first act in which to commit the murder.

"2. The curtain-operator, who happened to be the school keeper, had almost as long.

"3. The electrician had at least as long as the curtain operator.

"4. Madame Berotti, the makeup woman, was in a similar position.

"5. Pish-Tush, Mr. Kemball, had the smallest male part, and so might have had plenty of time during his offstage periods.

"6. Mrs. Boyle, the producer, is at present a dark horse.

"7. Ko-Ko, Mr. Poole, had until his first entrance, but once he had made his first appearance he was on the stage a great deal, and may or may not have had the opportunity for murder. I should be inclined to count him out if it could be proved that Calma Ferris was alive when he first came on to the stage, because there were no stage waits, I imagine?"

"None at all. All the actors were ready on every occasion," replied Mr. Cliffordson.

"Good. That simplifies things," remarked Mrs. Bradley.

"Does it? I am glad to hear you use the word 'simplifies'! I never knew a more complicated business," said Mr. Cliffordson.

"Poo-Bah (yourself, Mr. Cliffordson) had little opportunity to commit the murder. He was on the stage a great deal during the whole of the act, with, on the whole, too short an interval between any two of his stage entrances for him to have been able to risk leaving the wings in order to kill Miss Ferris. I think we might almost count you out, you know."

She gave vent to her harsh cackle.

"Thank you," said the headmaster.

"Not at all. Nanki-Poo, Mr. Francis Henry Hurstwood, sixth-form boy, had as much opportunity, perhaps, as anybody else to commit the murder, for he had a lengthy interval after his exit just before the first entrance of Ko-Ko. Mind you, that delayed first entrance of Ko-Ko may be important. If that little man had any *motive* for killing Miss Ferris—"

"Yes, yes," said the headmaster, a trifle impatiently, "but what about this boy? You don't really imagine he could have had any hand in the affair, surely?"

"Meaning," said Mrs. Bradley shrewdly, "that you do! Come, out with it. What about the poor boy?"

"I—don't—know," said Mr. Cliffordson. "In fact, I wish you'd have a talk with the lad. Mind, I don't really imagine for one moment that he did have anything to do with Miss Ferris' death, but he is highly strung and rather unbalanced and emotional. For instance, I happen to know— although neither of them suspects that I *do* know it!—that the unfortunate lad cherishes a hopeless passion for my niece, Miss Cliffordson, the junior music mistress. You've met her, of course?"

"Yes," replied Mrs. Bradley, a vision of Miss Cliffordson's challenging prettiness coming into her mind.

"I believe Gretta is handling the thing sensibly, mind you," the headmaster added. "But these affairs are always painful for the boy and embarrassing to us. Coeducation has its drawbacks for the coeducationists, you see."

Mrs. Bradley nodded.

"The other members of the cast are not under suspicion for the moment," she said, "therefore perhaps it might be a good plan to have the boy next." Mr. Cliffordson pressed the buzzer and consulted the timetable.

"Ask Mr. Poole, in Room C, whether he will be kind enough to excuse Hurstwood for a few minutes," he said to his secretary. A little later a discreet tap at the door announced Hurstwood's arrival. The headmaster invited him in, and he stood on the threshold, tall, fair, slightly embarrassed, a likable boy, with thin hands and a broad low forehead.

"Shut the door, Hurstwood," said Mr. Cliffordson. "You remember the night of *The Mikado*?"

"Yes, sir."

"*You* weren't the person who collided with Miss Ferris and broke her glasses, were you?" asked Mrs. Bradley, before the headmaster could speak again. Hurstwood raised his eyebrows.

"I? No," he replied. "I—knew she had broken them, though, because I lent her my handkerchief to bathe a little cut she had on her face."

"When was this?" asked Mrs. Bradley. The boy considered the question and then answered:

"Very near the beginning of the opera, because I was just ready to take my cue, so I pulled out my handkerchief—I had stuck it in my sash—and shoved—er—pushed it into her hand, and in about ten seconds my cue came and I went on."

"H'm!" said the headmaster.

"Sir?" The boy's face was flushed, and he had thrust his jaw slightly forward.

"What did you do when you came off the stage the first time?" inquired Mr. Cliffordson, this time managing to forestall Mrs. Bradley.

"I went into the dressing room and had a look at my makeup, sir. Then I went round to the other side of the stage to see whether Miss Ferris had finished with my handkerchief, because it was the only one I had, sir, and I was suffering from a slight cold."

"But you must have realized it would be wet, if Miss Ferris had been bathing her face with it?"

"Oh, yes, sir, but things soon dry on the radiators. I thought I would spread it out on one so that I would soon be able to use it if I required it."

"Go on," said Mrs. Bradley, as the boy paused for a moment.

"I went into the lobby," said Hurstwood. "At least," he added, correcting himself, "I *should* have gone into it, but everything was quiet round there, and when I pressed the switch the light wouldn't act, so I thought nobody could possibly be in there, and I went back to the dressing room and found Mr. Smith and the electrician. We talked a bit, and then I had to go on again."

"You know where Miss Ferris' body was found, Hurstwood?" said Mr. Cliffordson.

"Oh, yes, sir. It almost seems as though she might have been—"
The headmaster shook his head.

"Not when you went to the lobby the *first* time," he said. "We've proved that."

"Yes, sir?"

"Yes, my boy." Mr. Cliffordson leaned forward impressively. "Miss Ferris was murdered, Hurstwood."

There was dead silence. Then the boy said simply:

"Yes, sir. I know."

Even Mrs. Bradley, although she managed not to betray the fact, was startled by this admission. The headmaster was frankly astounded.

"You *what?*" he shouted. Hurstwood remained silent. "What do you mean, boy?" demanded Mr. Cliffordson. Hurstwood cleared his throat.

"Well, sir, the modeling clay."

"What about it?"

"She—Miss Ferris wouldn't have done it, sir. Ladies don't stop up things like that. She would have used the plug. In any case, sir, why shouldn't she use running water? You—one generally does for a place that's bleeding, sir, and her face bled quite freely."

The headmaster nodded. Mrs. Bradley nodded also.

"Go back to your form, then. That's all I want to ask you," said Mr. Cliffordson.

"Yes, sir." He turned to go.

"And, by the way," said Mr. Cliffordson pleasantly, "my niece is at least seven years your senior, my boy. Remember that when you are twenty-five she will be thirty-two, and don't make a fool of yourself any longer."

The boy, who had turned as the headmaster had gone on speaking, went white. He put his hands to his head and swayed from side to side.

"Quick!" said Mrs. Bradley; but the headmaster was in time, and got to him before he actually fell.

"Silly fellow," said Mr. Cliffordson, smiling at him when he had regained his normal color and was sitting upright and looking rather foolish. "Did you think I didn't know? There! Don't worry about it, my boy. We all make fools of ourselves at your age. There's no harm in it, but don't take it too seriously."

But to his embarrassment, the lad burst into tears. Mrs. Bradley got up and went out, closing the door behind her. She detached the EN-GAGED notice from its little brass hook on the wall, and hung it from its little brass hook on the door. Then she went in again and beckoned the headmaster outside.

"I want to see Miss Camden," she said.

"It's her free time, I believe," the headmaster answered. "Come with me and we'll invade the staff room. But she wasn't in the cast, you know. A queer girl. Very enthusiastic—about all the wrong things."

"By the way," said Mrs. Bradley, "what can there be that is familiar to me in the face of the gentleman in the frame over the table?"

"Oh, I expect you saw it in the newspapers last year," replied Mr. Cliffordson. "That's Cutler, the man who was acquitted of drowning his wife. Smith painted him immediately the trial was over, and, with a humorous gesture which I confess I still do not fully appreciate, presented the portrait to me."

CHAPTER VI
DISCLOSURES

I

"I don't like it," said Mr. Cliffordson, shaking his head. "I don't like it at all. To my mind, there is something extraordinarily fishy about that boy's story. He is omitting to tell us something of vital importance."

"Well," said Mrs. Bradley, pausing at the top of the stairs, "I should not advise you to employ any third degree methods in order to coerce him. Murder will out, so let sleeping dogs lie and make hay while the sun shines."

She ended on an unearthly screech of laughter which caused the overwrought Hurstwood to raise his head and listen intently. The sound was not repeated, so he rose and walked to the window of the headmaster's study.

"Meaning?" said Mr. Cliffordson, when they reached the foot of the stairs and were walking across the large hall where the opera had been staged.

"I suggest that we interview the rest of the cast in turn before coming to any definite conclusions," said Mrs. Bradley. "I wonder whether we might speak to Miss Cliffordson next, instead of Miss Camden? I could see Miss Camden later."

"You won't get much out of Gretta," said Gretta's uncle, shaking his head.

Mrs. Bradley, who knew quite well that she would get exactly what she wanted out of Gretta, smiled amiably, like a sleepy python, and waited while the headmaster tapped at one of the form-room doors. In a few moments Miss Cliffordson, looking fresh and pretty in a white blouse, navy skirt and the inevitable cardigan, came out into the hall, and, seeing Mrs. Bradley, walked toward her.

"You wanted to see me?" she said.

"Yes, dear child. Is there an empty room where we can talk without being disturbed?"

"I believe the music room is empty at present," replied Miss Cliffordson, leading the way. The only furniture which the music room contained consisted of six pianos with their stools, so, each occupying a stool, Mrs. Bradley and the headmaster's niece sat down.

"Of course, I never for one moment believed that Miss Ferris committed suicide," remarked Miss Cliffordson, "and when Uncle told me that he had invited *you* to come down and look into the affair, I *knew* I was not mistaken."

"In what?" Mrs. Bradley politely inquired.

"In thinking that poor Miss Ferris was murdered," replied Miss Cliffordson, lowering her voice. "And, do you know, Miss Freely told me that the older girls won't stay a second after school hours now it gets dark so early, and that, for her part, she will be thankful to goodness when the Christmas holidays arrive and she can go home. She says the school gives her the creeps since the opera, and that neither for love nor money would she go into that water lobby after dark. I don't know that I should care to, either, if it comes to that."

Mrs. Bradley made noises indicative of agreement and sympathy with this feeling.

"And as for poor Moira Malley," Miss Cliffordson continued, "I wonder the poor child didn't go off her head, finding the body in the dark like that! Fancy her not telling anyone about it until after the performance, though!"

"I imagine that she was afraid of ruining the entertainment," said Mrs. Bradley. "I wonder, though, that she didn't say something to one of the other girls. Several of her form were in the women's chorus, weren't they?"

"Well, I don't really suppose she got much chance of speaking to them. She used our dressing room, you see. The chorus had another for themselves. Of course, there was nothing to prevent her going in there during the interval if she wished."

"Oh, yes. She was the only pupil to take a principal part, wasn't she?" said Mrs. Bradley carelessly.

"Well, no," replied Miss Cliffordson, rising to the delicate cast. "She was the only *girl* who had a principal part, but it was one of the boys who did so well. A rather talented boy called Hurstwood. Do you know him?"

"A tall, rather slight boy?" said Mrs. Bradley. "Oh, yes; I know him. He has an interesting face."

"He's rather clever," said Miss Cliffordson. "And . . ." she paused, and then plunged, "he's being rather difficult."

"Ah. In love with you?" said Mrs. Bradley. Miss Cliffordson laughed, frankly enough, but with a shade of embarrassment.

"It's very awkward," she confessed, "and he's so horribly sensitive that I don't like to be quite ruthless, because I'm afraid"—she laughed again, and there was no mistaking her embarrassment this time—"he might do something serious . . . even make away with himself. Oh, it sounds ridiculous, I know—"

"Not to me," said Mrs. Bradley quietly.

"Well, that's a comfort, anyhow," confessed Miss Cliffordson, "because I know you understand these things. But, tell me, please,"—she looked Mrs. Bradley full in the face—"you don't think a boy of that age could have . . . would have . . .? I'm so terribly worried!" she ended suddenly. "I lie in bed every night and I seem to see him doing it! It was such an easy way to kill anybody—especially anybody who was sitting down. You offer to help—you lend a handkerchief—you stuff the waste pipe up with clay and press the tap and talk—any kind of nervous, silly talk, so that no suspicion is excited; then, as the basin fills, you begin to press the woman's head down . . ."

"But why should the boy think of doing it?" the little old woman asked calmly.

"Oh, of course, you don't know that. Why, you see, after the dress rehearsal, Harry—Hurstwood, you know—became excited and he was quite beyond control. He told me a lot of nonsense about being in love with me, and he insisted upon kissing me—he was quite beside himself and very violent—and Miss Ferris walked herself into the middle of it! That's all."

"I see," said Mrs. Bradley. She pursed her mouth into a little beak. "And where is Hurstwood's handkerchief now?" she demanded suddenly. Miss Cliffordson fumbled and produced it.

"Any proof that it is his?" asked Mrs. Bradley, noting that the hand-kerchief had been carefully washed and ironed and bore no name, initials or laundry-mark. Miss Cliffordson shook her head.

"I suppose I did the wrong thing," she said, "but I unpicked the laundry-mark and an initial H from the corner."

"Good," said Mrs. Bradley, absently pocketing the handkerchief. "Now, as to actual proof . . ."

"Oh, but—" Miss Cliffordson began to look distressed.

"But?" prompted Mrs. Bradley.

"Well, I thought . . . I've only told you my suspicions so that you could—I mean, I thought you'd drop the inquiry if you knew who it was—in which way it was trending. You surely . . ." Her voice was rising. Soon it would be audible through the open ventilators in the two classrooms opposite, thought Mrs. Bradley—"you surely don't intend to accuse a boy of eighteen of murder!"

"I thought you were his accuser," said Mrs. Bradley mildly.

"I've only told you what I fear. I don't actually *know* anything. Harry has never said a word! Not a single word! You mustn't think he has confessed, or anything, because he certainly has not!"

"Well, don't encourage him to do so," said Mrs. Bradley, who had taken a sudden dislike to the headmaster's pretty niece. She rose, and smoothed down her violet-and-primrose jumper. "Thank you for your information," she said, in a precise, old-fashioned voice, and walked out and across the hall and up the headmaster's staircase. Miss Cliffordson, a little startled by this sudden departure of her audience, got up and went back to her class. Her uncle, who had taken her place whilst she was conversing with Mrs. Bradley, rose from the chair he was occupying, and raised his eyebrows. Miss Cliffordson shrugged her shoulders.

"I don't think she is much farther on," she said. "I've confessed about that wretched boy—"

"Hurstwood?"

"Yes. It *couldn't* have been Hurstwood's doing, Uncle, could it?"

The headmaster, who had been sitting pondering the same question, looked gloomy and said it was impossible.

"I feel so horribly responsible," Miss Cliffordson added, "if it *was* Hurstwood. Oh, but it couldn't have been! Only an utterly depraved boy would have thought of such a thing. And Harry isn't depraved."

"No," said the headmaster. "He is merely highly strung, temperamental, morbidly imaginative and sensitive. Where's Mrs. Bradley now?"

"I don't know, Uncle."

"I'll go and have a talk with her. If it *was* Hurstwood, the 'suicide' verdict will have to stand. One of the staff would have been bad enough, but a boy at the school, trained by us——And it would be impossible to keep you out of it, Gretta, you know."

He walked off, looking extremely perturbed, and found Mrs. Bradley occupying a chair at the small table in his room and writing busily and indecipherably in her notebook. Beyond cackling in a terrifying manner, she would commit herself to nothing. Hurstwood had not been in the room when she returned to it after her talk with Miss Cliffordson, she said, in response to a question from the headmaster, and in response to a second question she agreed that the said talk had been enlightening.

"But not sufficiently enlightening to please me entirely," she added. "I must have a talk with Mr. Hampstead. May I see him privately in here?"

"You mean you do not wish me to be present?" asked Mr. Cliffordson.

"I want to talk to him about his private affairs," replied Mrs. Bradley. The headmaster pressed the buzzer, sent for the senior music master, and then went out of the room.

II

Frederick Hampstead spoke first.

"I've just seen Mrs. Boyle," he said.

"Ah!" Mrs. Bradley nodded pleasantly. "Sit down, Mr. Hampstead. Why are you wasting your time teaching in a school?"

"I beg your pardon?" said Hampstead, blankly.

"Come, don't hedge," said Mrs. Bradley, grinning. "In the words of the last of the prophets, 'He who can, does; he who cannot, teaches.' What about that Second Symphony?"

Hampstead laughed.

"Are you a witch?" he asked. "I haven't even told Alceste about the Second Symphony? How did you know?"

"I didn't," confessed Mrs. Bradley. "I deduced. Do you know Maxwell Maxwell?"

"Only by his photographs in musical journals," said Hampstead, ruefully.

"Send him your work. I'll give you a letter of introduction. Now, what about this wretched murder?"

"Do *you* think that, too?" Hampstead looked genuinely amazed. "Do you know, such a thing would never have occurred to me unless I had heard other people talking about it."

"Why not?" asked Mrs. Bradley.

"Well, what had the woman to live for? No home, no intimates, no lover, no brains—nothing to work for; nothing to look forward to; no special interests . . . I should have thought she was the very type to commit suicide, you know."

"This is very illuminating," said Mrs. Bradley, drily, writing it all down. "Nevertheless, I may tell you that Miss Ferris *was* murdered, and that she was murdered before the interval. So I can cross you off my list of suspected persons, can't I?"

"But what about the police? Oughtn't they to be told?" said Hampstead doubtfully.

"It's a nice point," Mrs. Bradley admitted. "At the moment, you see, we can offer them nothing but the evidence on which the coroner's jury brought in a unanimous verdict of suicide."

"Yes, I see," said Hampstead. "Well, why not leave it at that? I mean, the poor woman is dead. It can't matter now whether it was suicide or murder, can it?"

"There speaks the unregenerate musician," said Mrs. Bradley, laughing. "The Church would tell you that it made a great deal of difference—to the woman herself, if to nobody else."

"Yes, I suppose so. I'm a Catholic, you know," he added, "but by tradition rather than conviction, I'm afraid."

"Forgive an old woman's impertinent curiosity," said Mrs. Bradley briskly, "but I suppose Mrs. Boyle is not free to marry you?"

"Other way about," said Hampstead brusquely. "She's a widow, but I've a wife living."

"I've attended your wife, then," said Mrs. Bradley surprisingly. "I thought the name was familiar. In Derbyshire, isn't she?"

Hampstead nodded.

"Fieldenfare Manor," he said.

"Yes." Mrs. Bradley nodded in her turn.

"It happened a year after our marriage," said Hampstead, staring into space. "Luckily the child died." Suddenly his grim expression softened. "I couldn't stay in a place where everybody knew me, and be stared at and pitied," he went on, "so I came here, and met Alceste."

"And that relationship was threatened by Miss Ferris' knowledge of it?" said Mrs. Bradley softly. Hampstead shook his head.

"Alceste thought so, but, after all, what could Miss Ferris do? She could tell the head, but why should she bother? She didn't dislike us; she wasn't jealous of Alceste; she didn't envy us—I can't see why she should trouble to take any action. I was worried at first, I admit, but, on thinking it over, I don't believe she would have told."

"No," said Mrs. Bradley. "And even if she had, I don't see that the headmaster could take official notice of it. There was never any scandal, I suppose?"

"I don't know of any," Hampstead answered. "Mind you, we've been fools and taken risks at times—when it got unbearable, you know. But I don't think anybody knew. In public we were always very careful. I even go to see poor Marion occasionally. Why don't you people dope the poor devils out?" he asked savagely.

"I don't know," said Mrs. Bradley truthfully. The same thought had often occurred to her. "I suppose it is partly because, as doctors, we hope to effect a cure."

The startled expression on Hampstead's face caused her to add briskly:

"Don't worry. Mrs. Hampstead's case is hopeless."

"Oh, heavens! I didn't mean that!" cried the man, genuinely distressed. "God knows, I pity her. But Alceste! I couldn't give up Alceste! I should die!"

"Somewhere behind that heartfelt statement," mused Mrs. Bradley, when the senior music master had departed, "is the motive for a murder. But not necessarily for the murder of Calma Ferris," she was compelled to admit.

III

"And now," thought Mrs. Bradley, "for Miss Camden." She returned to the hall and passed through it to the gymnasium, where the physical training mistress was taking a class. Mrs. Bradley seated herself on the edge of the platform, which held a piano, and watched the proceedings. Miss Camden, whatever her shortcomings as a human being, was

an exceedingly good teacher. Mrs. Bradley noted the enthusiastic response of the girls—a form of fourteen-year-olds—the finish displayed,
all the obvious results, in fact, of capable teaching over a long period—and nodded approvingly.

Miss Camden, aware, of course, that a visitor was present, carried
on with the lesson cheerfully, and had not the slightest objection to
showing off the prowess of the class. When the lesson was over and
the form dismissed, she came up to Mrs. Bradley with a smile and said:

"Time off?"

Mrs. Bradley smiled.

"I want to talk to you, dear child. When will it be possible?"

"Can you get it over in ten minutes?" inquired Miss Camden, glancing at the clock on the wall behind the platform. "I have a netball practice before lunch."

"Get someone else to take it," said Mrs. Bradley briskly.

The physical training mistress looked at her and smiled sardoni-
cally.

"So easy, isn't it?" she said.

"Isn't it?" said Mrs. Bradley innocently.

"Since Ferris—" Miss Camden paused. "Since Ferris' time, there's
nobody will do a hand's turn for the games except young Freely, and I
can't keep on asking her. There ought to be two of us in a school this
size, you see, only the headmaster won't be persuaded to take any interest in the physical work. The girls, anyway, are luckier than the boys.
The boys haven't even *one* qualified person. There's a 'pro' comes to
take cricket in the summer, but, unless we get an enthusiastic master,
the football goes hang. They never play any outside matches, poor kids.
I give them a bit of hockey occasionally, but I'm worked to death as it
is. It's a damn' shame for the poor little devils!"

Mrs. Bradley could see that the girl was worked to death. She could
hear it in the high-pitched, overloud voice, so different from the "professional" tones in which she had given her lesson. Her eyes were dark-
circled and she blinked them rapidly as she talked.

"I'll have a word with Mr. Cliffordson," she said.

"I wish you would," said Miss Camden. There was something about
Mrs. Bradley which forced her hearer to the conclusion that if she had
a word with the headmaster something would very likely come of it.
"Well, I must be off. I can hear the girls out there, and they are right
underneath the old man's window." She hurried away, an athletic figure in

her beautifully cut tunic, and disappeared through swing-doors at the farther end of the gymnasium. Mrs. Bradley, balked of her prey, wandered into the grounds.

It was a pleasant day for December, sharply cold, but filled with thin, pale golden sunshine which lay along the bare twigs, giving them significance and beauty. Fourteen girls, all dressed exactly alike in navy-blue tunics, white sweaters, long black stockings and white rubber-soled shoes, were passing a football up and down the length of the asphalt netball court with an ease, vigor and accuracy born of frequent practice. Miss Camden, a blazer with an impressively decorated breast-pocket distinguishing her from the players, blew occasional sharp blasts on a whistle. Mrs. Bradley, who did not understand the game, watched with considerable interest until she found herself—hatless, coatless and gloveless—becoming rather cold. She was about to reenter the building when she saw the boy Hurstwood. He was walking toward her up the long side of the school field, intently kicking a large fir-cone as he walked. Mrs. Bradley waited for him.

"Ah, child," she said. Hurstwood, who, as most young people did, had taken a liking to the queer little old lady, grinned at the nominative of address and waited for her to continue. He had himself completely in hand once more, for, upon leaving the headmaster's study, he had not returned to his form room, but had spent the rest of the lesson in walking round the field.

"Go up to the women's common room and bring me"—Mrs. Bradley checked off the items on her yellow fingers—"one coat, dark green, one hat from the same peg, one silk scarf in divers colors—"

"I bet they are!" thought Hurstwood, who had imbibed sufficient sense of color from Mr. Smith to realize that Mrs. Bradley's conception of appropriately blended hues would be gruesome in the extreme.

"—and two gloves—heaven knows where I put those, but they fit exactly"—she extended a skinny claw—"this hand."

Hurstwood, realizing that she was cold, cast sixth-form dignity to the winds and cantered off. He took the staff room stairs three at a time going up, and five at a time coming down and returned in a few moments with the required garments.

"Tell me," said Mrs. Bradley, as he helped her on with them, "do you box?"

"No," replied Hurstwood. "Like to. Never had the chance."

"I have a theory," said Mrs. Bradley, "that Mr. Poole boxes."

Hurstwood grinned.

"I don't know about boxing," he said; "but he must be a lad in a roughhouse."

"Really?" said Mrs. Bradley, pricking up her ears. "Give time, place and circumstances, child, and anything else you happen to know."

"Summer holiday, Marseilles, a row in a pub," replied Hurstwood, readily and intelligently. "He was telling us about it in form a week or two ago. Whenever we get a sticky bit of maths, we switch Poole on to his holidays. It always works. He and Smith sail a boat about nearly every summer holiday and seem to have a jolly good time. I expect Poole tells lies—well, embroiders, you know,—but, even allowing sixty percent off for that, they must have done all sorts of jolly decent things in the holidays."

"When did *you* learn to sift evidence, young man?" demanded Mrs. Bradley.

Hurstwood grinned.

"Oh, it's only historical evidence," he said. "I matricked with distinction, so old Kemball rather decently gives me extra-tu, and . . . he's pretty hot," he concluded. "I owe him the distinction, really."

"H'm!" said Mrs. Bradley. She looked at the boy curiously, and an idea came, quite unbidden, into her mind. Mrs. Bradley distrusted sudden flights of fancy, and, to do her extremely well-disciplined mind full justice, she was very seldom afflicted by them. She tried to dismiss this one, but it persisted. She said to Hurstwood suddenly:

"I wonder whether anyone at school could put my portable wireless set right? I suppose anyone with an elementary knowledge of electric lighting could do it, couldn't he?"

There was a long pause. Then Hurstwood said awkwardly:

"I daresay several of the lower fifth scientific could manage it. They've done a lot of work on electricity this term."

"Oh, yes. Thank you. The lower fifth scientific." She began to walk along the cinder track. It skirted the netball court and then wound serpent-wise round the school field. Its surface was trodden flat and hard, for it formed the school promenade except at the end of the Spring term, when it was forked over by the groundsmen in preparation for sports day.

"I say, Mrs. Bradley," said Hurstwood, when they had almost circumnavigated the field, "are the police going to be brought into this?"

Mrs. Bradley did not attempt to pretend that she did not understand him. She pursed her thin lips into a little beak and replied:

"Not at present, certainly. But at any moment, possibly. Again, possibly not. It depends partly on what we discover."

"Suppose," said Hurstwood, pursuing a train of thought which had been in his mind for some days, "a person is wrongly accused of murder?"

"Yes?" said Mrs. Bradley encouragingly.

"What chance does he stand of getting—of being acquitted?"

"Every chance in the world," said Mrs. Bradley confidently. "But why these morbid theses?"

"Oh, I don't know. My father wants me to be a barrister," said Hurstwood.

"Does he? And what is your own choice of a career?" asked Mrs. Bradley.

"Oh, I shouldn't mind. Young Lestrange says his uncle has got more murderers off than any other defending counsel in England."

"Yes. A depraved nature, Ferdinand's," said Mrs. Bradley. "Ferdinand Lestrange is my son by my first husband," she explained in response to the boy's glance of inquiry.

"Oh, really? How topping," said Hurstwood, conventionally. "Then young Lestrange is your nephew?" he added, with considerably more interest.

"He is. Younger than you, of course?"

"Yes, a good bit, I think. He's sixteen, isn't he? I'm eighteen in April. Only just within the age limit for the scholarship, in fact."

"The Balliol scholarship? What chance do you think you stand?"

"Pretty good, I believe," replied the boy. "But this death business has put me off, I think."

"These *contretemps* are bound to have some immediate effect on a sensitive nature," said Mrs. Bradley. Hurstwood grinned and invited her to refrain from pulling his leg. Having walked round the field three times in all, they returned to the building, where the bell had just been rung for lunch. Miss Camden blew her whistle to indicate that netball practice was at an end, and she, Hurstwood and Mrs. Bradley walked into the hall together.

"I'm not on duty for lunch," said Miss Camden, "so if you wanted to talk, I could finish quickly and meet you in the needlework room in a quarter of an hour from now."

IV

The physical training mistress had changed into blouse and skirt, with her blazer taking the place of the other mistresses' cardigans, when Mrs. Bradley next saw her. They closed the door of the needlework room and sat among sewing machines and trestle tables, confronted by diagrams, pinned-up paper patterns, examples of the various kinds of stitchery, and all the paraphernalia of school needlework.

"Very practical," said Mrs. Bradley, looking about her with great interest. Miss Camden, who did not know a piece of whipping from a run-and-fell seam, cautiously agreed.

"But there isn't a lot of time," she added, looking at her wristwatch and comparing it with the clock on the west wall of the room. "What do you want with me?"

"I want to know whether you know who murdered Calma Ferris," said Mrs. Bradley, with such implicit directness that Miss Camden gasped and then flushed brick red.

"I!" she said. "Oh, no, of course I don't! Whatever made you ask?"

"You agree, then, that she *was* murdered?" asked Mrs. Bradley, a little more mildly.

"Yes, I do."

"Why do you agree?"

Miss Camden considered the question, and then answered slowly:

"Well, *you're* here. That proves it. Besides, she wasn't one to commit suicide."

"Can we say that confidently about any person on this earth?" Mrs. Bradley inquired.

"Perhaps not. You know I had a row with her just before—just before the opera?" said Miss Camden, taking the plunge.

"I had heard some rumor of it. About a netball match, wasn't it?" said Mrs. Bradley. "You're the second person I've spoken to who was not behind the scenes at all during the performance, I think," she added with seeming irrelevance.

"Who is the other?" asked Miss Camden, amused.

"Mr. Hampstead. Miss Ferris was killed at some point during the first act of *The Mikado*, and he was conducting the orchestra."

"And I was in the audience, as you indicated just now. Oh, I say!"—she appeared startled, as though the thought had presented itself to her for the first time—"what a jolly good thing I didn't accept Mrs. Boyle's invitation! It was fairly pressing, too!"

"Mrs. Boyle's invitation?" echoed Mrs. Bradley. "Explain, child."

"Well, when Miss Ferris couldn't be found, Mrs. Boyle came out into the auditorium, found me, and asked me to take the part. I refused, so she took it herself."

"You didn't feel equal to taking the part at a moment's notice?" asked Mrs. Bradley. Miss Camden blinked more rapidly than ever.

"It wasn't that," she said. "The fact was—although it sounds a bit mean, perhaps,—I didn't see why I should get them out of a difficulty. I had been turned down absolutely to give Miss Ferris the part, and—well, I didn't bear the slightest ill will, but I didn't see, either, why they should expect to come wailing to me to carry on when they'd got themselves into a mess. Don't you agree?"

"Within limits, yes," said Mrs. Bradley, trying to remain strictly truthful, without this having the effect of drying up the flood of Miss Camden's remarks. It appeared that she was successful, for the physical training mistress went on, with scarcely a pause:

"Of course, I will say for Mrs. Boyle that I couldn't have done the part any better myself. She was frightfully good. I *believe* my singing might have improved matters a trifle, but then I've been trained, you see, and she hasn't. Before I took up teaching my idea was to go on the operatic stage, but Dad wouldn't hear of it. He's a clergyman, you know, and he had a fit when he heard that his only daughter wanted to be an actress. I tried to show him what I could do by staging *Carmen* in the village hall one Christmas, and taking the name-part myself, but"— she laughed, a hard, grating sound—"it just finished him off entirely. So here I am—always in hot water with the head, who doesn't care for jerks and games, and always disapproved of at home. I've got a brother, but he's in holy orders, chaplain to a bishop and marked for high preferment, and the apple of my parents' eyes."

"Poor girl! Poor child!" said Mrs. Bradley, with genuine sorrow in her beautiful voice. The young mistress looked startled.

"Heaven knows why I've been telling you all this," she said blankly. "You'd better forget it, please. What's the time? I've got a hockey practice at twenty past one."

It was not quite five minutes past one, but Mrs. Bradley did not attempt to detain her as she rose and walked toward the door. When she reached it, however, Mrs. Bradley said suddenly:

"But if the work here is so hard and the headmaster so unsympathetic, what makes you stay?"

Miss Camden turned, her hand on the doorknob, and swallowed twice.

"I couldn't get a testimonial at present," she said. "That's why."

"How long have you been here?" asked Mrs. Bradley.

"Five years. It's my first job," the girl answered.

"Come here," said Mrs. Bradley. Miss Camden obeyed. "Explain," said Mrs. Bradley. Miss Camden shook her head.

"You'd better ask the old man if you really want to know," she said. "But it's got nothing at all to do with this murder, I assure you."

There was no pretext upon which Mrs. Bradley felt she could detain her further, so she let her get to the door and outside it this time. Then she drew her chair to the nearest trestle table, sought for her notebook and pencil, and for the next ten minutes she was writing as fast as she could. There was nothing more to be done until afternoon school began, so, putting away notebook and pencil, she went up to the women's common room for her coat and gloves, and then sallied out to watch the hockey-practice. In a far corner of the school field half a dozen biggish boys were kicking a football about, but Hurstwood was not among them.

She watched the hockey practice for about a quarter of an hour. One side were wearing red girdles, the other green. Mrs. Bradley noticed, among the red-girdled players, Moira Malley. She was a dashing player, displaying more energy than science, and for the time being she seemed to have forgotten cares and fears both, Mrs. Bradley was pleased to notice, in vigorous enjoyment of the game. Miss Camden, too, was a different being once more. She was combining the arduous and exacting duties of referee and center half (on the side of the greens), and careered down the field in the teeth of the advancing forwards, swept the ball out with magnificent long strokes to her outside left and outside right alternately, controlled the game with her screeching whistle, which, most dangerously to herself, she held gripped between her teeth the whole time, and inspired her team with her magnificent play into scoring three goals in swift succession.

CHAPTER VII
ELIMINATIONS

"The plot," said Mrs. Bradley, "indubitably thickens."

The headmaster, seated behind his massive desk, nodded and looked interested.

"You think you are narrowing the thing down?" he asked. Mrs. Bradley cackled.

"Up to the present," she said, "I have discovered at least four persons who are temperamentally capable of the murder, and all but one had both motive and opportunity for committing it. That one had the motive, but, so far as I can discover, not the opportunity. However . . ." she chuckled ghoulishly, "many a good *alibi* has ended in smoke, so we must wait and see. Besides, I haven't quite finished. I have to interview . . ." She brought out her copy of the program of the opera once more, "Miss Freely, Mr. Poole, Mr. Kemball, Mr. Browning, the person who made up the players, the electrician, and the school caretaker."

"You'd better leave the last-named to his well-earned afternoon rest," the headmaster remarked drily. "He's a good chap, but his afternoon rest is sacred. Do you want to interview the others in here with me?"

"Without you, if you have no objection," said Mrs. Bradley. "I felt that you were an obstacle to the search for truth this morning."

The headmaster shrugged, and smiled. "One of the penalties of a job like mine is that nobody on the staff feels really at ease in one's presence. It can't be helped. I appreciate that you'll get on better without me. How's Hurstwood?"

"Better," said Mrs. Bradley.

"Good. Push that button for my secretary. She'll get anybody you want. If you should want me, I shall be"—he consulted the timetable—"in Room B. Good-bye for the present, then."

Mrs. Bradley pressed the buzzer and sent for Mr. Poole. That cheerful man smiled at her and asked her jokingly whether she had the handcuffs ready.

"Be serious," said Mrs. Bradley, "and answer my questions. First, did you murder Calma Ferris?"

"No," said Poole, serious at once. "Has anybody said I did?"

"No. Secondly, do you know anything which might indicate the manner in which she met her death?"

"Why, she was drowned, wasn't she?" asked Poole seriously.

"Thirdly, what did you do before your first entrance on to the stage?"

"Do? Let's see. Except for Miss Ferris and Smith, I was the last of the principals to be made up, and the curtain was rung up while the little dame who did the making-up was still busy on my face. Marvelous woman! Wish she'd take a part. I'd like to see her as Volumnia. Grand!"

"Wait a moment," said Mrs. Bradley. "How long did it take her, do you think, to make up each principal?"

"Varied a bit," replied Poole. "The longest were the last two, Katisha and the Mikado, I should say, but as she had nearly the whole of the first act in which to do them—Oh, but Katisha *was* made up. Oh, *I* dunno! Sorry!"

Mrs. Bradley pressed the buzzer.

"I wonder if you have the address of the ex-actress who made up the faces of the performers on the night of the opera?" she said, winningly, to the headmaster's secretary. The secretary disappeared, and returned almost immediately with a visiting-card which bore the legend: "Madame V. Berotti, 16 Coules Road, Hillmaston."

Mrs. Bradley made a note of both name and address, and then asked the secretary for Mr. Smith.

"Does that mean you've finished with me?" asked Poole.

"Not quite. Don't be impatient," said Mrs. Bradley. "You haven't finished telling me what you did before you went on to the stage."

"Oh, nothing, really, you know. When I was ready to go on I collected the small urchin who followed behind with the axe—I was the Lord High Executioner, you know—and we stood in the wings until our cue came. I was so interested in watching the stage that I did not think about anything else."

"I see. Thank you very much. That's all, then," said Mrs. Bradley. "Oh, by the way, do you box?"

Poole looked surprised.

"Well, I do," he answered. "Middleweight, you know. Who told you?"

"I deduced it," said Mrs. Bradley with a mirthless cackle. "I wish you'd teach Hurstwood."

Poole grinned.

"The head would have a fit. 'Brutal and degrading sport,' exalting the physical or animal nature at the expense of the spiritual or god-like—and all that sort of wash, you know. But I *will* teach him if he likes. Do the chap good. What is he? Lightweight?"

"My dear child, how do I know?" inquired Mrs. Bradley.

"Thought you might have deduced it," retorted the irrepressible mathematics master, nearly cannoning into Mr. Smith in the doorway. Smith shut the door behind his colleague and then stood in the center of the study. He looked round nervously, as though to make sure that Mr. Poole really had gone out.

"Don't be peevish, child," said Mrs. Bradley briskly, "but when you cannoned into Miss Ferris and broke her glasses, were you made up ready to go on the stage?"

"Of course not," said Smith. "The woman wanted to do me, but I said I wasn't going to put up with that mess on my face longer than I could help, to please anybody! Have you ever been made up as the Mikado?"

"Never," replied Mrs. Bradley, with perfect truth.

"Tons of muck!" said Smith violently. "Tons and tons of beastly sticky muck! I wasn't going to have any. Told her I'd come back half-way through the act. Why, even my nose had to be enlarged with modeling clay! Horrible!"

"Why were you in such a hurry that you collided with Miss Ferris without seeing her?"

"I couldn't see her because it was dark. Didn't you hear about one of the lights going west? That's why, on thinking things over, I think it's silly to attach so much importance to the fact that that light in the water lobby had given up the ghost. Still, it's no business of mine."

"So you didn't even know that Miss Ferris had cut herself?" asked Mrs. Bradley.

"No. How could I? I had no matches—nothing. And it was as black as Erebus along there. I apologized, and went on the way I was going, and she accepted the apology, laughed and said it was all right. She said she had another pair of glasses at school, and that she wasn't hurt, and went on the way she was going. That's all I know."

"I see. Thank you. Yes, that's all," said Mrs. Bradley. "If you're going back to your class, I wish you'd send somebody for Hurstwood. It will save the secretary a journey."

"Right," said Smith; and in due course Hurstwood appeared.

"Child," said Mrs. Bradley, "on which side of the stage were you when you encountered Miss Ferris and lent her your handkerchief to bandage her eye?"

"On the same side as the men's and boys' dressing rooms," Hurstwood answered. "You asked me that before," he reminded her.

"Not exactly that," said Mrs. Bradley. "Tell me, what would Mr. Smith want on the *other* side of the stage, then?"

Hurstwood grinned.

"I expect he went to potter about in his beloved art room. That's round the other side, you know."

Suddenly the full significance of what he was saying seemed to dawn on the boy. His face went white.

"I say! That clay in the waste pipe!" he said.

"Exactly," said Mrs. Bradley. "And now tell me what on earth possessed you to tamper with the electric light in that water lobby when you came off the stage that time?"

"Which time?" said Hurstwood, suddenly sullen and obstinate. Mrs. Bradley, who had met this boyish trick before, said gently:

"You know which time I mean. Don't be foolish."

"Well, I wanted my handkerchief back—I thought I could dry it on the hot-water pipes—so I went to the water lobby, to which I thought Miss Ferris would have gone, to see whether I could find her and get it back. When I got to the water lobby—well, I've told you all this before!" cried the boy. "I'm not going to say anything different, so what's the use of going over it again?"

"I suggest," said Mrs. Bradley calmly, "that you switched on the electric light, although you thought nobody could be in the lobby in the dark, and that, finding Miss Ferris' body there, you deliberately tampered with the light so that nobody else should see what you had seen. Isn't that right? It proves to me, also, that you believed you had discovered the identity of the murderer. What do you say, child?"

"How could I tamper with the beastly thing? I had no tools!" The boy was flushed and thoroughly belligerent now. Mrs. Bradley sighed.

"True," said she, as though crestfallen. "True, child. Very well. That's all, then. Ask Mr. Kemball whether he can spare me five minutes, will you?"

Mr. Kemball was annoyed. Hurstwood's entrance was the third interruption he had suffered during a lesson which, in any case, only lasted thirty-five instead of the customary forty-five minutes, so that he arrived on the headmaster's mat in a frame of mind that can best be described as thoroughly ill-tempered.

"You sent for me, Headmaster?" he began in a tone which was calculated to render Mr. Cliffordson red with the conscious guilt of having lured a painstaking teacher from the path of duty.

"Come in, Mr. Kemball," said Mrs. Bradley, in her deepest, richest tones. Kemball, deflated, entered and stood awkwardly. He was a thin, anxious-looking individual, gawky and spasmodic in his movements, and had the scraggy look common to Methodist local preachers. He was not as well-dressed as the other masters Mrs. Bradley had already interviewed, and had the harassed appearance of all middle-aged men whose family responsibilities are still widening but whose salaries have already reached the maximum.

"Sit down, if you can spare the time," said Mrs. Bradley, winningly. She eyed him with the glance of a predatory beast for its prey, and Kemball, who would ordinarily have replied to such a suggestion with a trenchant reference to his teacherless class, sat down on the edge of the nearest chair and waited to hear what she had to say.

"You took the part of Pish-Tush, a Japanese nobleman, in the recent production of the opera, I think?" said Mrs. Bradley formally. She consulted the program she held as though to indicate that if he had thought of denying the fact she had proof incontrovertible of it. Kemball meekly agreed that he had taken the part as stated.

"A small part, but an important one, I believe?" said Mrs. Bradley. "You had a solo, for instance, and some interesting business with one or two of the chief characters?"

Again Kemball assented. He was beginning to thaw, she observed.

"You had some time to spend, however, when you were not actually on the stage," pursued Mrs. Bradley.

"Yes. Several long waits," replied the history master.

"Do you know who murdered Miss Ferris?" said Mrs. Bradley suddenly. Kemball said blankly:

"Who *murdered* Miss Ferris?"

"Yes."

"But I understood that all the available evidence pointed to suicide. I have not studied the facts, but—"

"All the available evidence pointed to murder," said Mrs. Bradley, "if people had been able to use it sensibly."

"Well, I'm glad to hear that," said Kemball surprisingly. "I couldn't imagine that woman committing suicide, somehow."

"What is your reason for saying so?" inquired Mrs. Bradley. She had neat little lists at the back of her notebook consisting of the names of those who agreed with the suicide theory and of those who rejected it.

"Well, consider her case: no ties, no worries, enough money, no encumbrances, no debts, free to please herself in everything—what more could any human being ask for? A person in that position doesn't commit suicide. It's poor devils like—" Mrs. Bradley could have added the word "me" for him with perfect correctness, and, mentally, did so, but Kemball broke off to say: "But you were asking me about her death."

"Yes. When did you last see her alive? Do you remember?"

"I don't. You see, I was one of the first people to be made up by Mrs. Berotti, and almost immediately I was called to the phone."

"Ah, yes. I see. How long were you at the telephone, do you think?"

"Rather a long time. I used the school phone, of course, and first of all I talked to my wife, who had rung me up, and discussed some purely domestic business with her. She's—er—well, she's—we're expecting another child, you know—and I inquired after her and gave her some impression of the audience—all that sort of thing—and scarcely had I rung off when somebody else rang up. I answered the call, as I happened to be there, and found that it was important. The electrician could not come, but was sending along a man and asked whether he could be met at the school gate, as it was dark and the back entrance is difficult to find. I replied, and went myself to the gate, as the telephone message advised me that the man was already on his way. At about five minutes before the opera was due to commence, the man arrived, and I conducted him round to the back and left him, as I had to be prepared to make my first entrance almost immediately. During my offstage waits I sat next to Mr. Browning, who was acting as prompter, and read the proofs of my monograph on the Renaissance popes."

"What about the interval?"

"I read my proofs during the interval."

"You did not see Miss Ferris at all, then, during the whole of the performance?"

"Not consciously. In fact, I don't think I could possibly have seen her, consciously or unconsciously."

"Could you identify the electrician if you saw him again?"

"Decidedly I could. He was less like a mechanic than anyone I ever saw. I should have taken him for a commercial traveler of a particularly brazen type. He insisted upon addressing me as 'old boy,' in a manner that was quite repulsive. The funny thing is that the electrical people sent him without being asked. The headmaster is under the impression that Pritchard asked for someone to come and see to the footlights, but that is quite a mistake. He came of his own accord."

"Thank you," said Mrs. Bradley cordially. "I rather fancied that the electrician came into the story somehow. You must please put my name down for a dozen copies of your monograph. The Renaissance popes," she concluded, with magnificent mendacity, "form for me one of the most fascinating themes in history."

"To a psychologist," replied Mr. Kemball, now completely restored to good humor, "they must certainly appear interesting. A dozen copies? That is extremely kind of you."

"Make it fifty, dear child," said Mrs. Bradley, waving a skinny claw as though she were scattering largesse—as, indeed, thought poor Kemball, reflecting that if he sold a hundred copies of his work he would be doing very well indeed, she was!

The next person to throw light on the dark question of the electrician, thought Mrs. Bradley, would probably be the school caretaker, so she allowed Mr. Kemball five minutes to get back to his form, and then she descended the stairs, crossed the hall, left the school building and knocked at the door of the school keeper's house. The house was separated from the school building by a small gravel courtyard and the school bicycle shed. Mrs. Bradley was admitted to the house by a small woman who was suffering from a severe cold in the head. She informed Mrs. Bradley flatly that the school keeper was having his afternoon rest, and could see no one, but the next moment, having crossed glances with the visitor, she found herself asking Mrs. Bradley to sit down. In another moment the school keeper appeared.

"I'm sorry to disturb you," said Mrs. Bradley, "but who was the electrician who came to the school on the evening of the opera?"

"Ah, ma'am," said the caretaker, "don't I wish I knowed! I'd electrician him! Been up to the firm twice, I have, and he don't belong there. That's all I know. And they never phoned the school he was coming or nothing! No wonder murders 'appen!"

"What reason had you for visiting the firm?" asked Mrs. Bradley.

"What reason? Lorst me watch, lorst me wallet with two pounds in it, lorst me new waterproof, lorst a spanner, a wrench, a pair o' pliers and a screwdriver what I lent him, and everything. And no redress! No compensation! And daren't tell the 'eadmaster, because I was where I'd no business to be when it all 'appened."

"And where was that?" inquired Mrs. Bradley.

"Round at the Pig and Whistle, all along of that same chap, too, and all. ''Ere, mate, you pop round and 'ave a drink,' 'e says, same as I might say to anybody. 'I'll keep an eye on that there curtain,' 'e says. 'You won't need to do that,' I says, 'because they don't finish for near enough another hour and a quarter,' I says. And off I went, getting back in half an hour from then, with the opera still going strong, you might say, but no sign of the bloke, no watch, no wallet, no waterproof, no spanner, no wrench, no pair o' pliers or no screwdriver."

"An interesting, but not unusual sequence of events," said Mrs. Bradley briskly. "Describe the electrician as best you can."

"Tallish, plumpish, fatty kind of self-satisfied face, little mouth, no mustache, reddish bristly 'air, fat 'ands with 'airs on the backs, short fingers, aged about forty-three or four, gray suit, black boots, no overcoat, suede gloves, no tools with 'im when he come; London voice—not cockney but not a gentleman's voice neither—big ears with no lobes to 'em. That's all I can recollect of 'im."

"You are a remarkably observant man," said Mrs. Bradley.

"Well," said the school keeper, pleased at the compliment, "my boy's a Scout, and he learned me to play the Scouts' games. Consequently I find meself taking notice whether I want to or not. He's a King's Scout, my boy is."

"Splendid," said Mrs. Bradley heartily. "You remember the switch in the water lobby, don't you? The one which was out of order on the night of Miss Ferris' death?"

"The one them boys tampered with, ma'am?"

"The same. I suppose it wasn't the electrician who tampered with it?"

"I could believe anything of that bloke," said the school keeper, "except that 'e knowed enough about electricity even to put a switch out of order. You recollect one of the lights fused? 'E couldn't do nothing whatever with it. I 'ad to get Mr. Pritchard 'isself to 'elp me, me being tied up with that there blessed curtain."

"When did Mr. Pritchard see to it?"

"See to it, ma'am? About 'arf-way through the first act, I think."

"One more question before you return to your well-earned rest," said Mrs. Bradley. "Apart from the electrician, was any other stranger behind the scenes on the evening of the opera?"

"Barring the Eye-talian lady what puts the greasepaint on for 'em, nobody, ma'am."

"Thank you very much," said Mrs. Bradley. "I presume that the stolen articles were taken from this house?"

"That's right, ma'am. I 'adn't locked up, you see, the 'ouse being right inside the school grounds, and my wife at the back of the 'all to see the show, and my boy with 'er. But the watch and the wallet, 'e must 'ave picked me pocket for 'em, as 'e stood talking to me, ma'am, and that's a fact."

"I see. It was only the waterproof coat that he took from the house?"

"That's right. Saved up me coupons for months to get it, and that's what happens. Thanking you very kindly, ma'am. Much obliged, I'm sure, though I wasn't meaning to make an 'ard-luck tale of it."

It occurred to Mrs. Bradley that if she could get Mr. Browning to corroborate Mr. Kemball's story and Mr. Kemball to assert, independently, that Mr. Browning had not moved from the prompter's stool at all during the first act of the opera, during which the murder had been committed, she would be in a position to eliminate both of them from the list of persons who had had opportunity for the murder. A further point at issue was the alibi of Miss Camden, who, by reason of having been a member of the audience, was in the same solid position as Browning and Kemball if it could be proved that she had not left her seat in the auditorium until the interval. If, on the other hand, it could be shown that she had left the auditorium at any point during the first act, she would immediately be in the same position as the other persons who had had both motive and opportunity.

She waited until afternoon recess to tackle Browning and Kemball. Appealed to separately, each was prepared to swear that the other had been in the wings on the prompt side during the whole of the first act, except for the times that Kemball was on the stage. Alceste Boyle, appealed to next, was prepared to state that Mr. Browning had not risen from his stool during the whole of the first act, and Mrs. Bradley, with a sigh of relief, felt that she could safely disregard Browning and Kemball during the rest of the investigation.

CHAPTER VIII
THEORIES

Coules Street, Hillmaston, whither she journeyed at three-fifteen to interview Mrs. Berotti, the ex-actress who had put on the makeup for the principal players, proved to be a short, neat, select cul-de-sac in the best residential quarter of the small town. A maid opened the door, and, in response to Mrs. Bradley's inquiry, said that her mistress was resting, but took Mrs. Bradley's card and asked her in.

In a few moments she returned and asked Mrs. Bradley to follow her. In a small, comfortable, warm room at the back of the house, Mrs. Berotti was lying on a chesterfield drawn up near the fire. She greeted Mrs. Bradley charmingly and told the maid to bring tea. She was a very old lady, nearer eighty than seventy, Mrs. Bradley imagined, but her dark eyes were alive with zest and amusement, and she made gestures as she talked.

"I've come about the murder of Calma Ferris," said Mrs. Bradley abruptly, after casual remarks had been exchanged.

"Do I know her?" asked Mrs. Berotti, with a little frown of concentration. "Ah, yes, I know her. The little plump one, plain, and very anxious to do well, who dies instead of playing the part. Unprofessional."

Mrs. Bradley hooted with laughter, and the ex-actress wrinkled her old face into a smile which beautifully blended malice and childlike fun.

"She could not help dying. She was murdered, I tell you," said Mrs. Bradley firmly.

Mrs. Berotti nodded and her expression changed to one of thoughtfulness.

"Yes. I thought so myself," she said. "But one could not say so. There was no evidence. Nothing."

"Were you present at the inquest?" Mrs. Bradley inquired.

"I was present, yes. I was asked whether I had made her up. I replied that yes, I had made her up. Was she drunk? Imagine asking *me* such a question! I replied, in a manner which abashed them, I hope, that never

100

had I been in the company of a drunken person, man or woman, all my life. Had she troubles? I was firm over this, my friend. I replied that if she had no troubles, we who understand good acting, would have had troubles had she been permitted by Providence to come before an audience and play that nice part so badly!—*so badly!* That dress rehearsal! Never shall I forget it! It was terrible!"

She shook her head, smiled wistfully and added, "I informed them that I, too, should have committed suicide if ever in my life I had played the part of a strong, hard, middle-aged, grasping, tormented woman so slowly, so carefully, so—so"—she spread her hands wide apart as though to embrace the right word when it came—"so *inoffensively*, my friend!"

Mrs. Bradley cackled. She had formed a very complete mental picture of Calma Ferris since the beginning of her investigation.

"But the other—the magnificent, large, personable goddess of a woman who played it on the night!" went on Mrs. Berotti ecstatically. "Never have I seen a performance like it! She had lost her temper when she came to me in the interval to be made up. She had made herself up, well but hastily, for the end of the first act, but she came to me in the interval.

" 'For God's sake keep the woman out of the way, Madame, if she *does* turn up,' she said. 'I've got to finish now, whatever happens.'

"My work was over when the interval ended. There are but two acts in *The Mikado*. So I went in front, to a little charming seat right in the middle of the third row kept for me by my good friends, and I saw and heard everything. Imagine it, my dear friend! The poor young plump one, with her unproduced voice, too high, too thin, her careful gestures, her insignificant height—all this by Providence and the grace of God withheld from us; and instead—Alceste Boyle! You did not see it? My good friend, you will go to heaven! God will compensate you because you did not see it."

Mrs. Bradley would like to have stayed much longer than she did, but she was anxious to get back before school ended for the afternoon. One or two questions bearing on the case she managed to get answered, however, before, at five minutes to four, she took her leave.

"Did you know that Miss Ferris had met with a slight accident near the beginning of the first act?" was the first of these.

"One of the schoolgirls told me, but I was very busy," replied Mrs. Berotti, "and I understood that somebody was helping her, and so I did not go to see. That the makeup should be put on correctly was my first concern."

"You had already done Miss Ferris when she cut herself?"

"I had. I had made her up beautifully. I am an artist, me! She told me she had to go on in Act One. 'But not until almost the end,' I said. But she persisted, so I did her. 'You'll be hot and uncomfortable,' I said. She did not mind that, she assured me. I think she was afraid that she and Mr. Smith, the Mikado—he was fine, that one!—would be left alone together in the makeup room. They had quarreled, I understand. So I did her. The poor little one! So inoffensive! Such an offense herself against my beloved art!"

There seemed to be nothing else that Mrs. Berotti could tell. She again eulogized the performance given by Alceste Boyle, informed Mrs. Bradley that the professional stage had lost a treasure when Alceste left it, and, when Mrs. Bradley very reluctantly announced that she must go, rose and escorted her to the door. She expressed delight that Mrs. Bradley had visited her, and begged her to come again.

Mrs. Bradley walked back to the school as quickly as she could, and arrived inside the building at six minutes past four. The school closed at half-past, but the staff had been requested by Mr. Cliffordson to remain in the building until five o'clock, in case any of them were wanted. Mrs. Bradley had opposed this move, but Mr. Cliffordson insisted that since the whole staff knew the reason for her presence, they could scarcely, in fairness to themselves, refuse to submit to questioning.

During what was left of the afternoon, therefore, Mrs. Bradley sat in the staff room talking to Alceste Boyle.

"First," she said, "I want to know at what point in the proceedings you missed Calma Ferris."

Alceste, blue marking-pencil in hand, thought for a moment, and then said:

"A quarter of an hour before her first entrance. Do you know the script of *The Mikado*?"

"Intimately," replied Mrs. Bradley. "It has been my bed-book ever since I came down here."

"Then you remember that the first entrance of Katisha comes almost at the end of the first act," Alceste continued. "Well, it is my rule that people are to be ready a quarter of an hour before the time their cue comes. It means a certain amount of hanging about offstage, but it's worth it. I had a fourth-former acting as callboy, and she had orders to report to me immediately if people did not respond to their call. She found me, therefore, as soon as Miss Ferris did not appear, and I sent her to the women principals' dressing room and round and about, but no Miss Ferris was to be found. It was approximately half-past eight. I then went to the women principals' dressing room myself, sat down and waited for the girl to find Miss Ferris. She couldn't find her, so I went along to the W. C. in case she had been taken ill in there, or had locked herself in and could not get out. But there was no sign of her anywhere. Time was getting short, so I went into the hall and found Miss Camden—all the staff sat together at the right-hand side of the hall as you look at the stage, so it was easy enough to spot her—got her out into the passage and tried to persuade her to take the part. She refused. I got her into the women principals' dressing room to argue the point with her, but she stood firm. She said she could not undertake the part at a moment's notice, and I didn't blame her. She had been turned down in favor of Miss Ferris, you see, and I suppose she didn't see why we should come moaning to her to get us out of a hole. In the end I took the part myself. It was the only solution. In case you suspect Miss Camden, I ought to say that she went back into the auditorium. I watched her enter the hall."

"Thank you," said Mrs. Bradley, and for the next two minutes both were busily engaged—Alceste in correcting a set of exercises and Mrs. Bradley in writing notes. At the end of the ten minutes Mrs. Bradley, having waited while Alceste finished marking a book, asked pointedly:

"Who sat on either side of Miss Camden during the first act?"

"There was nobody on her right. She occupied the end seat in the row. She had been stewarding, you see. On the other side of her sat Mr. Pritchard, the senior science master."

"Ah!" said Mrs. Bradley, making a note of it. "And next to him?"

But this Alceste did not know, so Mrs. Bradley decided to waylay Mr. Pritchard after school was over and ask him. She decided, too, to inquire about the electric light that had gone wrong. There were still several things in connection with Miss Ferris' death which she did not understand. It must, she decided, have been entirely fortuitous that, owing to the failure of the light, a collision had occurred which resulted in Miss Ferris' glasses being smashed and her face cut. Mrs. Bradley was fairly certain that Miss Ferris must have gone, not once, but at least twice to the water lobby to bathe the cut, for it was inconceivable that the murder should have been premeditated; or rather, not so much that it could not have been premeditated, but that the murderer could have known beforehand that Miss Ferris would injure her face so that she was compelled to enter the water lobby and so render herself liable to be done to death in the particular manner in which death had come to her. The clay in the waste pipe was the result of a deliberate act, and to that extent the murder was premeditated, but the murderer must have prepared for the crime between Miss Ferris' first and second visit to the lobby. That meant, Mrs. Bradley decided, that the murderer was a person quick-witted enough to take advantage of the entirely fortuitous set of circumstances—i. e., the cut under Miss Ferris' eye and the fact that she bathed it over a school washing-bowl—which Fate had provided, courageous enough to take the risk of being discovered in the act of murder, sufficiently determined to use the method which presented itself, cruel and barbarous though it proved to be, and—Mrs. Bradley was compelled to admit—self-possessed enough not to have been guilty of self-betrayal.

"Unless," thought the little old woman, "I haven't met the murderer yet!"

Her thoughts returned to the electrician, whom already she was calling "Mr. Helm."

To fill in the time at her disposal she sent for Miss Freely, who arrived looking scared.

"I don't know anything about it, and I don't want to," was the burden of her song when Mrs. Bradley questioned her. Mrs. Bradley decided that she really did know nothing, for she was able to account satisfactorily for all the time she had spent off the stage by announcing that she had sneaked into the auditorium and sat on a stool next to the pianist. As this was corroborated by the pianist, who was one of the girl pupils, Mrs. Bradley dismissed Miss Freely from her mind and sent for Mr. Pritchard.

"You repaired an electric switch during the first act of *The Mikado*, didn't you, Mr. Pritchard?" she asked without preamble, when he entered.

"Repaired nothing," said Mr. Pritchard in a loud, cheerful voice. "I had one go at the damn' thing before the opera started, and I was sent for again halfway through the act. Couldn't do anything by myself, so I fetched along the electrician fellow who was gassing with Smith, but the silly ass had no outfit with him. Sent him to borrow stuff from the caretaker, and never saw him again. Oh, Lord! that reminds me! I've still got the caretaker's kit! What the thing wanted, I discovered in the end, was a new lamp, so I pinched a bulb out of one of the classrooms on the top floor."

"Who sat next to you in the auditorium?" asked Mrs. Bradley.

"Miss Camden sat on my right, and there was an empty seat next to me, and then came some of the audience. We were really stewarding, you see, so we just took the end seats, where there were any, on that side."

"Thank you," said Mrs. Bradley. "You are an expert, I believe, at everything connected with electricity?"

Pritchard, a large, cheerful young man, laughed.

"Sounds like it if I deduce a fuse and it turns out to be a worn-out bulb, doesn't it?" he said. "I've received a lot of undeserved applause for constructing a school wireless set, but it's one or two of the boys who are the real star turns."

"Hurstwood?" inquired Mrs. Bradley.

"Well, I don't get him now. He's gone over to arts, you see. But in the Fifth he was rather good."

"Did he know enough to disconnect a switch so that no light could come on?"

"Oh, Lord, yes. Anybody could do that!"

"Thank you."

"Not at all. May one inquire—?"

"Yes," replied Mrs. Bradley. "I am trying to find out who murdered Calma Ferris."

"*Murdered* her?"

"Yes."

"Were you the first person to decide that she had been murdered?"

"No, young man."

"H'm!" said Mr. Pritchard, walking to the door. Mrs. Bradley sat staring at it after he had closed it behind him. She stared at it for several minutes. When it opened to admit the headmaster, she looked quite surprised. There was, however, a question she wanted to put to him.

"Is there any reason why you should refuse to write a testimonial for Miss Camden if she wanted to apply for another post?" she asked. Mr. Cliffordson sat down at his desk, moved his pen tray and blotting pad, and fidgeted with a jotter and a small metal ruler, and then inquired:

"Did she tell you I wouldn't?"

"Yes, dear child."

"Oh? I would, of course, if she asked for one. I couldn't very well refuse. But I know what she means." He put down the ruler and drummed on the desk with his fingers.

"There was a funny business about some money," he said, obviously unwilling to embark on the explanation. "Mind, I accuse nobody—except myself, for leaving my checkbook about. I had made out a check for nine pounds to self, and left the leaf in the book—signed, of course,—while I went down to take a class. The check disappeared, and was later cashed for *ninety* pounds, and—well, it rather appeared that nobody could have had access to it except Miss Camden, who was helping me that day with my correspondence in place of my secretary, who was down with influenza. I did not accuse her then, nor do I accuse her now, and, of course, the thing went no further than the four walls of this room. I should never have mentioned the subject again had not your question prompted me to do so. I *do* know that the poor girl is very extravagant. I heard from one of the men that she had told the staff she even had to wire home for the money for a return journey from Monte Carlo this last summer. But I don't believe she is dishonest. Please forget all this. The subject is very distasteful to me. I shall never be sufficiently sorry that my own carelessness tempted someone into dishonesty. But I certainly *could not* refuse to give Miss Camden a testimonial."

"Thank you," said Mrs. Bradley. "And now I want to leave the school for a few days. I am going to visit Miss Ferris' aunt at Bognor Regis. There is a missing diary which ought to be found and read. I am hoping that the aunt collected it up with the other personal belongings of Miss Ferris when she came here to attend the inquest."

"And you think the diary may throw some light on the identity of the murderer?"

"I doubt it," replied Mrs. Bradley. "But in any case I think I know the identity of the murderer. No. I want the diary for purposes—nefarious ones"—she screeched joyously—"of my own!"

"Extraordinary woman," thought the headmaster. He was not at all certain whether he was pleased or sorry that he had called her in to investigate the murder of Calma Ferris. As though she guessed his thoughts, Mrs. Bradley turned round when she reached the door.

"Who sups with the devil must have a long spoon," she said. "Do you know, I have a shrewd suspicion that if anyone is hanged for the murder of Calma Ferris, it will be that elusive electrician of yours—or possibly your Mr. Pritchard," she added, chuckling.

"Pritchard!" said Mr. Cliffordson, startled. Mrs. Bradley nodded.

"Pritchard. He pretended to me just now that he didn't know a fused wire from a worn-out lamp. What do you think of that?"

The headmaster did not have the chance of telling her what he thought of it, for by the time he was ready she had gone.

CHAPTER IX
EVIDENCE

It was surprising that Mrs. Bradley noticed the small paragraph in the morning paper. She was less a reader than a skimmer of the daily news. She would glance at the headlines, then read the column below, if she were interested in the topic. Then she would glance at the leading article, and, on the same principle, read it or not, as the spirit moved her. The small paragraph, which was tucked away almost at the bottom of one of the inside pages of the newspaper, would not have attracted her attention but for the sight of her own name, which happened to occur toward the end of it. Not imagining that she herself was being referred to, she read the paragraph nevertheless, and discovered in it a fact of peculiar interest. This was nothing less than a notice of the sudden death of Mrs. Frederick Hampstead at a private asylum. The cause of death was drowning, and it was stated that the unfortunate woman had fallen by accident into a small ornamental lake in the grounds of the institution. At one time, the column asserted, the deceased had been under the care of Mrs. Beatrice Lestrange Bradley, the eminent psychoanalyst and specialist in nervous and mental disorders.

"Curious," said Mrs. Bradley, referring to the sudden decease of Mr. Hampstead's unwanted wife, and made a note in her small book while she was waiting for the train which was to take her to the home of Calma Ferris' aunt.

It was a long and tiresome journey from Hillmaston to Bognor Regis, and Mrs. Bradley employed her time during the actual time the train was in motion, and also during the long periods of waiting for a connection, by thinking out the facts bearing on the death of Calma Ferris, to see whether any new angle could be obtained from which to view the case. She had made up her mind that it was going to be difficult, if not impossible, to obtain clear proof of the murderer's identity, although, in her opinion, the psychological proof was already overwhelming. But, partly for amusement and partly to test her theories by thinking them out from the beginning, she took each person who had had both opportunity and motive for the murder, then those who had had motive, but seemingly no opportunity, then those who had had opportunity but no apparent motive, and she reserved to herself the right to think over any unexpected developments which might have arisen during the time she had spent at the school in working on the case.

First, there was the boy Hurstwood. Temperamentally, Mrs. Bradley decided, he was capable of murder. He had had sufficient opportunity and a reasonably strong motive—Mrs. Bradley decided that to a schoolboy of seventeen the consequences of his having been discovered passionately kissing a member of the staff might appear far more disastrous and overwhelming than they would to an adult, especially if that adult were a man of the world, as Mr. Cliffordson appeared to be. The boy had known that Miss Ferris had injured her eye. He had known that she had gone into the water lobby to bathe it. He had even lent her his handkerchief, and the handkerchief had certainly reappeared in what had to be considered suspicious circumstances. Miss Cliffordson had had possession of the handkerchief. If Hurstwood were not to be regarded with suspicion that handkerchief ought to have been found on or near the body.

Other questions had to be interpolated here, Mrs. Bradley decided. The first one was: Were Miss Cliffordson and Hurstwood in collusion? Miss Ferris' unfortunate discovery of the love affair affected them equally up to a certain point. The second question was: Had Miss Cliffordson found the handkerchief and recognized it, and then kept it in order to shield Hurstwood? If so, why had she weakened sufficiently to show it to Mrs. Bradley, and confess it was Hurstwood's? This question was doubly difficult to answer in that the handkerchief was unidentifiable since initial and marking-cotton had both been picked out. The third point was this: Did Miss Cliffordson believe that Hurstwood had committed the murder? Did she accept the finding of the handkerchief (if it *was* found, and not handed to her for safety by Hurstwood himself) as proof of his guilt? And did she fear for her own safety? She had reason to know that Hurstwood could be uncontrolled and unmanageable, and that physically he was much stronger than she was. It was possible, thought Mrs. Bradley, that fear had caused her to produce the handkerchief.

Against all this were several points which told in the boy's favor. He had admitted that he knew of Miss Ferris' injured face and that she was going to bathe it. Would an obviously intelligent boy have made such a damaging admission if he had had anything to fear? He was nervous, imaginative and sensitive. If he had committed a horrible crime against an absolutely inoffensive person, would he have been able to brazen it out? Mrs. Bradley thought it very doubtful, unless he felt that by killing Miss Ferris he had saved Miss Cliffordson from the consequences of his own tempestuous behavior on the night of the rehearsal. A boy of Hurstwood's temperament might easily imagine that he owed it to Miss Cliffordson to get her out of the trouble into which his own madness and lack of self-control had placed her.

A different type of evidence was offered by the failing of the electric light in the water lobby. There seemed no reasonable doubt that the light had been deliberately disconnected. If Hurstwood were responsible for tampering with the switch, it was for one of two reasons: either to cover up the murder he himself had committed, or the murder he believed one of his friends had committed. Putting it another way, said Mrs. Bradley to herself, if Hurstwood had any reason whatsoever for believing that Miss Cliffordson had killed Miss Ferris, he might have performed the two rash acts of giving his own handkerchief up for her to produce as evidence of his guilt instead of her own, and of disconnecting the electric light so as to put off the evil hour of the discovery of the body as long as possible. Taking into consideration his temperament, his reactions and his state of mind, the evidence was as much in his favor as against him, Mrs. Bradley decided. She reconsidered his fainting fit in the headmaster's room. It was the direct result of learning that Mr. Cliffordson knew all about his love for Miss Cliffordson, and that the headmaster, in a semi-facetious manner, sympathized with instead of condemning him. In such circumstances, the fainting, followed by the boy's hysterical tears, had been entirely understandable, and need have had no connection with the murder at all.

She dismissed that train of thought and returned to the question of the electric light. Could there be any connection between two lights that failed on the same evening? It was a coincidence, certainly, but a possible one. Suppose, for instance, that the caretaker was wrong about

the switch in the water lobby? Suppose nobody, either in jest or earnest, had tampered with it. Suppose, also, that Hurstwood had been
telling the truth when he had told the headmaster that after his first exit
he had gone to the water lobby to find Miss Ferris and ask for the
return of his handkerchief—boys usually went provided with one only,
Mrs. Bradley suspected, so that it was all quite plausible so far. Suppose the boy had discovered the place in darkness, discovered furthermore that he could not switch the light on, went back to the men's
dressing room and talked with Mr. Smith before going on the stage
again.

There were a lot of gaps in Hurstwood's story, she was compelled to
admit. On the other hand, it might easily be the truth. She wondered
whether it might be necessary later to reinvestigate it. Not even
Hurstwood's youth was on his side in a case like this. So many unstable boys in their teens had murdered women. There were numerous
newspaper accounts of such crimes, besides the psychologically classic instances. She shook her head, and began to consider the case of
Gretta Cliffordson.

Vindictively or not, Miss Cliffordson had certainly tried to incriminate Hurstwood, and that, on the face of it, looked bad from one who
had at least as strong a motive as the boy for wishing to shut Miss
Ferris' mouth. Some of Mrs. Bradley's patients had been schoolmas-
ters and schoolmistresses, and she knew that one of the most dangerous effects of the most unnatural life in the world was the importance
which trivialities were apt to assume in the minds of those who spent
their lives among undeveloped intelligences and small events. It might
easily be that Miss Cliffordson, for all her seeming pertness and inde-
pendence, dreaded her uncle's anger and contempt above all things,
and thought that by allowing matters between herself and Hurstwood
to get to the point at which Miss Ferris had discovered them was to
court disaster indeed if word ever came to Mr. Cliffordson's ears of
what had occurred. On the other hand, there was Miss Cliffordson's
entirely voluntary confession to Mrs. Bradley that Hurstwood was "being rather difficult." The point at issue here, Mrs. Bradley decided,
was this: Did Miss Cliffordson believe that Hurstwood was the murderer? If she did, it was a heavy indictment of the boy, for Miss Cliffordson might reasonably be expected to know a great deal about him
and about the impulses which might have prompted him to such a terrible deed.

Mrs. Bradley, loath to believe evil of the boy, to whom she had taken a liking, tapped her notebook with the end of her silver pencil, and looked unhappy. On considering the rest of Miss Cliffordson's evidence, however, her face cleared, and her black eyes lit up with fresh interest. Miss Cliffordson's realistic description of the murder returned to her memory as she reread her notes.

"It was such an easy way to kill anybody," Miss Cliffordson had said—she could hear the carefully modulated, overrefined tones all over again—"especially anybody who was sitting down. You offer to help—you lend a handkerchief—you stuff the waste pipe up with clay . . ." (Ah, but there, thought Mrs. Bradley, is the rub. At what point in the proceedings, precisely, do you stuff the waste pipe up with clay? Have you, so to speak, a lump of clay in your left hand while you proffer a handkerchief with your right, or *vice versa?* Or have you prepared a bowl beforehand so that the water won't run away, and do you then guide the predestined victim to that particular bowl when she wants to bathe the cut on her face?)

Mrs. Bradley shelved the point for the moment and went on reading.

". . . and press the tap," Miss Cliffordson had said—"school taps are never of the type that have to be turned on and off, for obvious reasons," Mrs. Bradley reflected—"and talk—any kind of nervous, silly talk, so that no suspicion is excited. . . ."

Yes, but it was just that flow of talk, so essential for the relaxation of the victim's mind, so impossible to the male adolescent under such circumstances, that Mrs. Bradley found it impossible to associate with Hurstwood. Obviously, if the element of surprise which was so necessary in this particular kind of crime was to be maintained, conversation of an interesting, or, at any rate, a non-interruptible kind, had to be provided by the murderer. No boy, surely, could have watched that basin filling and filling—school taps are usually of small bore and do their work slowly and splashily—and riveted his victim's attention upon something so interesting that at the crucial moment he could have thrust her head under water without her having experienced the slightest premonition of danger? On the other hand, though, what if Miss Ferris had herself provided the conversation? By all accounts she was the kind of woman whose conscience might have troubled her sorely over the Hurstwood-Cliffordson—or even the Boyle-Hampstead—affair, and she might have regarded the advent of Hurstwood as a God-given opportunity for easing her conscience by speaking her mind. That this argument would apply equally if Alceste Boyle had committed the crime Mrs. Bradley pigeonholed in her mind (and at the back of her notebook) for future reference.

"Then," concluded the portion of Miss Cliffordson's evidence in which Mrs. Bradley was most interested, "as the basin fills, you begin to press the woman's head down."

"But you don't, of course," Mrs. Bradley decided. "You don't dare to risk touching the woman's head until the basin is full. You daren't risk a scuffle and a struggle and a half-drowned victim who will proceed immediately to the nearest police station."

She shook her head. Miss Cliffordson, she decided, had visualized the murder, but had visualized it imperfectly. It was almost certain that she was not the criminal.

As the similarity, in one sense, of the motives which might have governed the conduct of Alceste Boyle and Frederick Hampstead struck Mrs. Bradley, she considered their case next. Frederick Hampstead she immediately dismissed from her mind. On religious, moral and temperamental grounds she considered him an unlikely person to commit any murder, let alone a murder whose motive, in his case, would have been sordid in the extreme. Besides, it seemed impossible that he could have had any opportunity for the crime. It had most certainly occurred during the first act of the opera, and during the whole of that time he had been in position as conductor of the orchestra. Guarded inquiries among the players, who were all schoolboys and schoolgirls, had revealed the fact that not for a single instant after the first note of the overture had Frederick Hampstead left his place until the interval. And it was inconceivable, Mrs. Bradley decided, that he should have found Calma Ferris in the water lobby during the interval, murdered her, disconnected the electric-switch, gone away, and left Moira Malley immediately to discover the body. Besides, in that case, Calma Ferris would have been alive to take her cue in the first act. Mrs. Bradley felt that nothing was to be gained by thinking that Frederick Hampstead could have had any connection with the affair, but the recurring idea of the switch brought her again to the question of Miss Cliffordson's guilt. Suppose Hurstwood imagined that Miss Cliffordson was guilty, would he not perhaps have tampered with the switch? The desire to hide dreadful deeds from the light is characteristic of the young.

She sighed, and then turned over a couple of pages in order to consider the case of Alceste Boyle. Mrs. Bradley was not one of those psychologists who divide humanity into two groups—those capable of committing murder and those incapable of it. Her view was that, given time, place, opportunity and circumstances, it was impossible to say that any human being was incapable of such an act. Nevertheless, on temperament, she was forced to admit that Alceste Boyle was not the person she would have picked out as the murderer of an inoffensive person like Calma Ferris. The only reason which could be found to explain why Alceste Boyle should murder anybody would be that great danger threatened someone whom she loved. Could this reason be found to operate in the particular case Mrs. Bradley was studying? Frederick Hampstead, it appeared, was the person Alceste loved. The only danger which could have threatened him was the danger of being dismissed from his post at the school. Surely a levelheaded, sane, well-balanced, admirably sensible woman like Alceste Boyle would not have committed a horrid crime to prevent the dismissal of Hampstead? Besides, thought Mrs. Bradley, it was most unlikely that Calma Ferris would have betrayed the lovers to Mr. Cliffordson, and it was almost impossible to believe that Mr. Cliffordson would have taken a very grave view of the matter if she had. Even supposing he had gone so far as to dismiss them, surely the dismissal of one or both from the staff of the school would have been private, not public; friendly, regretful, apologetic on the one side; ruefully but comprehendingly accepted on the other. The senior English mistress, familiar with the classic situations in Greek and Shakespearean tragedy, would never have been sufficiently misguided to confuse the greater with the less to the extent of preferring Calma Ferris murdered to Frederick Hampstead dismissed. It was unthinkable. There was, of course, the question of opportunity. Alceste, free to rove about behind the scenes during the whole of the first act, her comings and goings, appearances and disappearances unquestioned, had had as much opportunity as anyone of drowning poor Miss Ferris if she had made up her mind to drown her. On the other hand, her general behavior, described by herself and corroborated wherever a corroboration was possible by members of the company, was not that of a murderer coming fresh from the scene of the crime. She had searched, and had set others to search for Miss Ferris. She had appealed to Miss Camden to play the part, had been refused, and had gone on herself to play it. Would she have risked sending out a search party if she thought there was any chance of their discovering the body of the victim? It seemed unlikely. On the other hand, again, a very

clear, farseeing and courageous person might have risked it, and Alceste could certainly be described by those three adjectives, Mrs. Bradley reflected. But the electric light! Could Alceste have tampered with
the switch? If she had, it would go to prove that she had taken the
minimum of risk when sending out the search party, for nobody would
be likely to explore a place that was in pitch-darkness. But very few
women would have thought of disconnecting the switch. Most would
have turned off the light and trusted to luck. Then, again, Alceste had
immediately disposed of her own supposed motive for the murder by
confessing to the headmaster the love she had for Hampstead. True,
she had refused to give the name of the man, but it was easy enough for
Mr. Cliffordson to put two and two together. It had to be Hampstead or
Smith, and with Smith there would have been no obstacle to the marriage, since he was a bachelor. Under the heading of opportunity, Alceste remained on Mrs. Bradley's list of suspected persons, but on every other count she was ruthlessly crossed off.

The next suspect on Mrs. Bradley's list was Mr. Smith. Her feelings
about this man were mixed. That he was capable of murder she felt
certain. That he had committed this particular murder she was slow to
believe. Any motive which she could assign to him was weak. Admitted that he might have nursed a desire to retaliate on Miss Ferris for the
loss of his Psyche, it was difficult to believe that he would have killed
her as an act of revenge. The only other motive which he may have
had, Mrs. Bradley decided, was that of saving Alceste Boyle, whom he
loved in the way that some small boys love their mothers, from the
consequences of Calma Ferris having discovered her relationship with
Frederick Hampstead. The point at issue here, Mrs. Bradley told herself, was whether Smith knew of Miss Ferris' discovery of Alceste's
secret. Alceste, she felt certain, would not have discussed the point
with Smith, and Hampstead would scarcely have deemed it delicate to
do so. Apart from the question of motive, Smith would have to remain
fairly high on the list of suspects, she thought, since he was one of
the people who had had the whole of the first act in which to commit the crime.

The other person with almost unlimited opportunity was the ex-actress, Mrs. Berotti. Here, although temperamentally she would make
an ideal murderer, possessing the artistic instinct, courage, a sort of
divine exasperation with fools, resourcefulness and an actress' self-
command, it was difficult to assign to her any motive for the crime. A

murder without motive is the act of a maniac, and Mrs. Berotti, whatever her shortcomings of temper and impatience, was certainly not mad.

The bogus electrician, Helm—if Helm it had been: a theory that needed proving—must have had opportunity, but where, again, was his motive? Calma Ferris had left a will bequeathing her property—two or three hundred pounds—to the school. She would have inherited something from her aunt, it was true, but only if she had survived her. Helm had offered her marriage, by which ultimately he might have gained something, but, as matters stood at the time of Miss Ferris' death, he could gain nothing whatever by that death.

Miss Camden was the most likely person to have committed murder, it seemed. She was extravagant enough, perhaps, to waste life as well as money; she was perverse, ill-dispositioned and thwarted; she had hated the dead woman and had intended to be revenged on her. . . .

At this point Mrs. Bradley discovered that she had to change at the next station, so she stowed away notebook and pencil and sat staring out of the window on to the flying landscape. Grays and browns predominated in the coloring of vegetation and sky. It ought to have been a dispiriting reflection that winter was only just beginning, but Mrs. Bradley, who was insensible to changes in the weather, and was equally undisturbed by the climates of Greenland and Southern India—she had experienced both—did not find it so. Instead, when the train drew up at the next station, she hopped blithely on to the platform and was greatly surprised to find a young friend of hers, the Reverend Noel Wells, seated upon the nearest bench, his long black-trousered legs uncanonically sprawling, his soft black hat tilted over his eyes, his mouth wide open and an expression of imbecile contentment on his vacuous, sleeping face. Mrs. Bradley set down her small suitcase and prodded him gently with the ferrule of her neat umbrella.

"Well, child," she said. Wells sat up and stared.

"Well, I'm blowed," he said. "What are *you* doing here?"

"I am chasing a murderer," said Mrs. Bradley, concisely. "And you?"

"Doing a locum job at Bognor. At least, it's a little village outside. I've got to go to Bognor and then walk or bus or something. Wouldn't be bad if it were August, of course."

"And Daphne?" inquired Mrs. Bradley.

"South of France. You knew we were married? I suppose you're not going to Bognor by any chance?"

"But I am," said Mrs. Bradley. "This is splendid. Listen. If the circumstances warranted it, would you be prepared to practice a little innocent deception?"

"Certainly. What is it?" inquired the young curate immediately.

"Pretend to be my son," said Mrs. Bradley.

"Rather. I get you, although you might not think I could rise to it," said Wells. "You want to persuade someone that you're a bit of a goop, and you think that the party will take one good look at me, shake his or her head sadly, observe pensively, 'Like mother, like son,' and that'll be that."

"You know," said Mrs. Bradley, in all sincerity, as she stepped back a pace to get a better look at him, "there are moments when your intelligence staggers me."

"It's being married to Daphne," the young curate explained modestly. "Bucks up the intellect no end. I'm supposed to be having a chance at a bishopric, you know."

He laughed, and they talked about matters of interest common to them both until the train came in.

"And now," said Mrs. Bradley, when they were settled in opposite corners of the compartment, "for a little further investigation into the case of Mr. Donald Smith." And, without taking any further notice of the Reverend Noel Wells, who proceeded to smoke his pipe and gaze peacefully out of the window, she took out her notebook and pencil, turned up the pages she had devoted to the evidence supplied by and on behalf of the senior art master, and reconsidered it. Smith worried her. He was almost as obvious a choice for the murderer as Miss Camden. Motive and opportunity here were strong, she decided, again. The whole of the first act had been Mr. Smith's opportunity, the damaged clay figure of the Psyche his chief motive. But there were snags. Mr. Smith was not the type to brood for two or three days over a wrong. If he had been going to kill Calma Ferris for damaging his work he would have snatched up the nearest heavy object and brought it down on the top of her head there and then, Mrs. Bradley decided. Besides, the motive, in his case, was not so strong at a second glance as it had seemed at first sight. He was not interested in that particular figure, it appeared, except as a money-making proposition. It had been commissioned, and he was in debt, and with the money he obtained from the sale of the commissioned work he was going to pay his debts. Well, the clay figure had been damaged past repair by Calma Ferris, but Alceste

Boyle had come to the rescue, lent the money and comforted the artist. True, Smith had been the person to cause Calma Ferris' injury, but it was permissible to believe that the collision in the darkened corridor was accidental. It was not to be supposed that Smith imagined he could seriously injure the unfortunate woman by charging down the corridor, since he would not even have known she was there until they collided; for there was nothing to show that he had asked Calma Ferris to come that way or that he could have seized upon the exact moment of her coming. He might possibly have foreseen that she would be wearing eyeglasses with her makeup, but not that she would cut her face; nor that she would have gone to that particular water lobby to bathe the cut, since it was not the only place on the ground floor behind the scenes where running water was available. Smith might have tampered with one or both of the electric lights that failed, since he had plenty of time on his hands, but it was fantastic to suppose he had done so before the murder, unless he had experimented on the corridor light that went wrong in order to make certain that he could cut out the one in the lobby when the time came. His plea of a bad memory was suspicious, if he were the murderer, but, on the other hand, people of his peculiarly erratic, nervous type often did have bad memories. The business of the modeling clay from the art room which had been used to stop up the waste pipe reacted for and against Smith, Mrs. Bradley decided. On the one hand, it was the kind of nonporous agent which would have occurred to a man who had been using it for modelling purposes a short time previously, but, on the other hand, would any murderer have been so foolish as to use something which so obviously suggested his guilt? Mrs. Bradley, shaking her head over all the classic instances of murderers' foolhardiness, reluctantly confessed to herself that Smith might easily have used the modeling clay to stop up the waste pipe. One more thought presented itself in connection with the clay. Had someone else used the clay, foreseeing that its discovery in the waste pipe might incriminate Smith? It was an interesting question which, up to the moment, was impossible to answer. The very proximity of the art room to the water lobby might in itself have suggested the clay, and the murderer might never have considered for an instant that the discovery of the clay might implicate Smith.

At this point a new idea came to her, and an unwelcome one. She looked across at Wells and said:

"If you were going to make a statue called Psyche, how old do you think your model would have to be?"

Wells rubbed his nose and, having given the question a good deal of earnest thought, replied vaguely:

"Oh, I don't know. Somewhere between fifteen and eighteen, I suppose."

"Exactly," said Mrs. Bradley. "Child, I'm alarmed."

"Bottom fallen out of your conclusions?" inquired Wells, sympathetically. Mrs. Bradley shuddered.

"I hope not. But I am conscious of dark and hideous doubts."

She had wondered once or twice what Smith's reason could have been for doing his modeling at school instead of in his studio at home. It struck her now that the reason must be that he was using someone at the school for a model—someone who could stay at school after hours, perhaps, but who could not have gone alone to Smith's studio.

"At the next stop I must telephone," she said. She put through the call to Alceste Boyle.

"Please find out for certain whom Mr. Smith was using as a model for his Psyche, will you?" she said, when communication between herself and Mrs. Boyle had been established. The reply was a foregone conclusion.

"Moira Malley. He was using her figure, but not her head," said Alceste.

"No wonder," said Mrs. Bradley, when they had again made their connection and were en route for Bognor Regis, this time on a main line and in a much faster train, "that Mr. Smith was sufficiently in touch with Moira Malley to get her to promise not to tell anyone that he was responsible for the accident to Miss Ferris' glasses."

But the outcome of this new discovery was likely to be perturbing in the extreme. Mrs. Bradley had never seriously considered the sixth-form Irish girl as a probable murderer, but it was possible to suppose that she had given the sittings secretly to Smith, and it was possible that Miss Ferris had discovered that she was sitting to him. Mrs. Bradley decided that if the spectacle of Hurstwood kissing Miss Cliffordson had shocked Miss Ferris, the spectacle of a naked sixth-form girl posing after school hours for the art master would have shocked her a good deal more. Another point at issue was that although Smith himself had probably regarded the girl's action as natural, justifiable, convenient and right (and probably, too, in view of the girl's chronically impecunious state, as a business proposition entirely), Mrs. Bradley thought it more than possible that to the girl herself, fanatically chaste and unreasoningly modest as only an Irish person can be, the sittings were a source of constant war between her conscience and her desire to please Smith, with whom, thought Mrs. Bradley, groaning with humorous despair, she was probably in love.

There was nothing humorous about the conclusion toward which this latest discovery tended. If Moira Malley thought that Miss Ferris would report to the headmaster that she had discovered her standing naked in the art room, no matter for what purpose or reason, the motive for Moira Malley's having killed Miss Ferris was overwhelmingly strong. Mrs. Bradley felt old and tired. Her previous conclusions as to the identity of the murderer began to rock on their foundations. Fortunately, she decided, it would be impossible now to prove whether Miss Ferris had known of the sittings or not, and, without such proof, the case against Moira Malley fell to the ground. All the same, a little demon insisted upon repeating in Mrs. Bradley's mental ear a snippet of the conversation she herself had had with Moira Malley on the subject of the time the girl was expected to be home from school.

—"But what about your people?"

—"Aunt doesn't mind. Often she doesn't know whether I'm in the house or not, until suppertime. . . ."

"Oh, dear," sighed Mrs. Bradley. "I do hope you didn't do it, you poor child, because you'll never get over it if you did."

There had been the girl's outburst, too, when Mrs. Bradley had suggested that she should conduct her to the water lobby where the body had been found.

—"I can't go round there after dark! I won't face it!"

Well, it was natural enough, considering that the girl had been the first person to discover the dead body. On the other hand, that "discovery" in itself was suspicious. So many murderers, overcome by their own nervous inability to escape from the scene of the crime, have "discovered" the body with intent to begin the very inquiries they most dread having set on foot.

It looked bad—Wells, looking across at Mrs. Bradley, noted the sunken lines round her mouth and the pucker between her brows—it looked very bad for Moira Malley. But still—Mrs. Bradley turned over another page of her notebook—there were several other people to be considered. There was still Miss Camden, for example, and there was still the electrician. If the electrician *should* prove to be the man Helm, he would have to explain away a good deal of very suspicious matter in connection with his obviously clandestine visit to the school, Mrs. Bradley decided. She resolved not to consider him further until she had visited Miss Ferris' aunt at Bognor Regis and had learned all she could from her about Helm and the dead woman.

Miss Camden, however, was in a different category of suspects. In her case the motive seemed fairly obvious—she had had what might be called a double motive, in fact—and temperamentally she was capable of murder. She possessed a good many, if not all, of the qualities required in the carrying out of this particular crime. Her course as a physical training and games mistress had made her alert, physically powerful, able to grasp opportunity quickly, ruthless in the sense that in her had been developed the "will to win" at the expense, so far as Mrs. Bradley could determine from a very imperfect study of the girl, of gentler qualities. The difficulty in her case, Mrs. Bradley repeated to herself, was the question of opportunity. But the more Mrs. Bradley thought it over, the more possible it seemed that Miss Camden might have had as much opportunity as any other person with a motive for committing the crime. It was easy enough to prove that she had been seated at the end of a row in the auditorium at the beginning of the performance, and it was apparent, from Alceste Boyle's evidence, that she had been in the same seat toward the end of the act. But the point at issue, so far as Mrs. Bradley was concerned, was whether she had remained there during the whole of the intervening time. If it could be shown that she had left her place at any point between, say, half-past seven and a quarter-past eight, for instance, there would be a certain amount of reason for keeping her high on the list of suspected persons. She was a person with little or no power of thinking ahead; she was inclined to yield to sudden temptation (if the story of the cashed and altered check was true); she was a disillusioned creature, and she was obviously the victim of nervous strain brought on by overwork. On the other hand, she had admitted to having had what she called "a row" with Miss Ferris, and she had sufficiently confessed the incident of the headmaster's check for Mrs. Bradley to find out the complete story. It was difficult, too, to determine exactly how she had discovered that Miss Ferris had been using the water lobby. Mrs. Bradley wrinkled her brows over this. Suddenly light came.

When she and Wells left the train at Bognor she ordered the taxi to stop at the first post-office. From there she sent Alceste Boyle a telegram.

"ASK GIRLS WHO ATTENDED FERRIS NIGHT OF OPERA."

To shorten the message further was to make it unintelligible, she thought. The reply came next morning in the form of a letter.

"I could not explain satisfactorily on a telegraph form," Alceste had written. "I asked in all the forms today, and when I had asked in the fourth form, my callboy girl stood up and said that, imagining I was too busy with the opera to be bothered about such matters, she had gone into the auditorium to find Miss Camden when she knew Miss Ferris had injured herself. Miss Camden is always called in when first aid is required, so that it was natural and sensible of the girl to go and find her. Miss Camden went immediately to Miss Ferris' assistance, the girl going too, and remaining to assist."

"I wonder whether the girl remained to assist all the time they were in the water lobby together?" thought Mrs. Bradley. "I wonder how and when that modeling clay was put into the waste pipe? I wonder whether Miss Camden went a second time to help Miss Ferris? I wonder how this man Helm comes into the affair? I wonder why, with four perfectly good suspects, all of them with motives, all of them with opportunities, all of them, within limits, capable of committing murder, I trouble myself to try to find a fifth?"

CHAPTER X
AUNT

Mrs. Bradley had wondered how best to attack the question of Calma Ferris' death with Calma Ferris' aunt, but found her path smoothed by the unforeseen fact that the aunt, whose name was Miss Lincallow, had heard of her fame and was prepared not only to welcome her as a distinguished guest, but to open, of her own accord and without any prompting from the black-eyed visitor, the whole subject of what she still regarded as her niece's suicide.

"But why should she have committed suicide?" Mrs. Bradley asked. Miss Lincallow shook her head.

"Before the inquest I should have said she had *fallen* and couldn't face the future," she observed, "but *since* the inquest—well, what can you think? It seems she was as virtuous as you or me."

Mrs. Bradley, who had never regarded herself as particularly virtuous in either a moral or a physical sense, nodded solemnly and assumed the somber expression of countenance which she imagined might
pass for the outward, visible sign of deep intelligence.

"Of course, one never knows," she said. To Miss Lincallow this
apparently meaningless phrase must have conveyed something at once
serious and profound, for she nodded in her turn, sighed loudly—almost groaned, in fact—while her greenish eyes turned slowly but surely
ceilingwards.

"Poor Calma," she said. "She had her suspicions of that man at once.
She sat opposite him at table the first day of her holiday here, Mrs.
Bradley, and at the end of the meal—lunch, I believe it was, but I'm
not quite sure—she came to me and said, 'Auntie, you must please
move me away from that sinister middle-aged man.'

" 'What sinister middle-aged man, dear?' I said, all middle-aged men
looking alike to me as far as sinister is concerned—you know what I
mean: all of them with wives they've got tired of—especially when
they come and stay in a nice town like Bognor all alone, or any other
high-class watering place, for that matter—'what sinister middle-aged
man, dear?' I said.

"When she pointed him out I quite understood. A commercial, Mrs.
Bradley, if ever I saw one, and you know what *they're* like when they're
away from home! Worse than *sailors*, I always say, because, after all,
sailors are subject to some sort of discipline on board ship if not actually while they are ashore, and also, of course, they do have a chaplain
to read the prayers at sea and teach them to be God-fearing on the
water, if nowhere else; but *commercials!* Why, their whole living depends on them telling more lies than anyone else can think of, doesn't
it, now?"

Mrs. Bradley, to whom this aspect of a commercial traveler's means
of livelihood had not previously presented itself, assented meekly, but,
without waiting for her hearer's comment, Miss Lincallow continued:

"And then, that night! Oh, dear! That night! Never shall I forget it!
Mind you, I could hardly believe it at the time, and looking back now it
all seems a dream. But, burglars or not—although, if I were on my
dying oath, nothing whatever was missing from the house or in any of
the visitors' rooms or anywhere—but, burglars or not, as I say, they
were in one another's rooms, both poor Calma and that man together.
Nefarious, I call it, don't you?"

Mrs. Bradley, who had seldom used the word, again assented.

"I didn't say a word to Calma, mind you," Calma's aunt continued. "It wouldn't have done. There she was, paying almost as much for her room as anyone, and *quite* old enough to take care of herself, and with her father's independent character, for all that she seemed somehow so mild. She had a strong nature, Calma had, and if she was set on doing a thing, do it she certainly would. Not headstrong, just determined in a quiet way. Behaved as though you weren't there, if you know what I mean. You couldn't domineer over her at all. So I said nothing, and he stayed a good while, longer than a commercial ought to, I should have thought, as I couldn't find out what he traveled in. And *then* we heard why. And *when* we heard why, I asked my lord to leave, quick, sharp!"

She sank her voice to a bloodcurdling whisper.

"Murder, Mrs. Bradley. But acquitted. You remember the George Bryan Cutler case last year?"

Mrs. Bradley recollected a murder trial, at the termination of which a man known as George Bryan Cutler had been found not guilty of drowning his wife for her insurance money. She nodded.

"Ah, I thought you would," said Miss Lincallow. "Well, this Helm is that Cutler, and when I heard that my Miss Sooley here had given that monster the school address where Calma was teaching, I thought the least I could do was to send the poor girl a warning. That Sooley's a fool. He happened to mention the school, and straight away she tells him that my niece is there."

"You are referring to the telegram you sent?" said Mrs. Bradley, returning to the warning message.

"That's right. I sent a telegram, and then I wrote a letter. Why, when you come to think of it, if the poor girl hadn't committed suicide she might easily have been murdered by that wretch!"

"Where is Mr. Cutler now?" asked Mrs. Bradley, not attempting to cope with the implications of the last of Miss Lincallow's remarks.

"If you ever heard such boldness, he is in this very town. At least, he's taken one of those railway-carriage bungalows further along the beach, just out of Bognor. I keep wondering whether the council ought to know. What do you think?"

"Do you know the name of the bungalow?" asked Mrs. Bradley.

" 'Clovelly,' " replied Miss Lincallow without hesitation. "But don't you go anywhere near it. I shouldn't, really. I believe he's dangerous."

For the only surviving relative of the unfortunate Miss Ferris, Miss

Lincallow did not appear to be unduly grief-stricken, Mrs. Bradley decided. She retired to her room after lunch, and made a note of the most enlightening points which had occurred to her as a result of the interview. She dismissed as fantastic a notion that Miss Lincallow was relieved rather than otherwise at the thought that her niece was dead, but it recurred so strongly that she sought further opportunity for enlightenment.

"Tell me," she said to Miss Sooley, who was what might be called Miss Lincallow's junior partner in the running of the boardinghouse, "what do you suppose Miss Lincallow thought when she received the news of her niece's suicide?"

It was the kind of idiotic question which might evoke answer false or true, or it might evoke no answer at all, Mrs. Bradley reflected, as, fixing her sharp black eyes on Miss Sooley's round, red countenance, she waited for some kind of response. Miss Sooley looked startled, twisted the black silk apron she wore into a crumpled mess, shook her head, and said that she was sure she did not know. This was a sufficiently promising beginning, from Mrs. Bradley's point of view, to warrant further research, so, with a basilisk grin intended to be propitiatory but having the result of causing Miss Sooley to retreat two steps and gaze wildly round at the bell-push with the indescribable feeling of one who has stepped on the crocodile in mistake for a log of wood, she continued:

"You mean you weren't there when the headmaster's telegram arrived?"

"Oh, yes, I was," returned Miss Sooley, somewhat comforted by Mrs. Bradley's dulcet tones, which issued so unexpectedly from the beaky little mouth. "It was I who held the smelling-bottle ready as she went to open the nasty thing."

"Ah," said Mrs. Bradley, managing to introduce a sympathetic inflection into the monosyllable.

"Oh, yes," went on Miss Sooley. "And all she said was to ask me to tell the boy there would be no reply."

"And then?" prompted Mrs. Bradley, after a pause.

"That's all," said Miss Sooley. "As sure as I'm standing here, that's all she said. And her having been to see the poor girl only the evening before."

"She went to see her on the evening before her death, do you mean?" said Mrs. Bradley, who found it difficult to assimilate this amazing piece of information. Miss Sooley nodded impressively.

"Didn't Miss Ferris write and ask her auntie and me to come and see her act in the school concert?" she demanded. "Here, I'll get the letter. It was sent to *me*, as a matter of fact, because Miss Ferris thought I could persuade her auntie to come, me being quite a theater-goer in my young days. Come upstairs a minute."

In the pure human joy of having something to impart, she appeared to have forgotten her nervousness, and ran upstairs, followed closely by Mrs. Bradley. For Miss Lincallow actually to have gone to see Miss Ferris act in *The Mikado* on the night of the murder, and then to have betrayed so little emotion upon the receipt of the headmaster's telegram announcing her death, was sufficiently extraordinary, but even more startling was the question which Mrs. Bradley put to herself as she ran up three flights of stairs. Had they managed to stay to see the whole of the performance and then had they made that maddening cross-country journey back to Bognor by train on the same night? The headmaster would have sent off his telegram at about half-past nine on the morning after the murder. They had been back in Bognor to receive it. There was a certain amount of mystery in those statements which Mrs. Bradley wanted to have cleared up as soon as possible. Had Miss Lincallow not asked to see her niece after the performance?

The letter, produced from some hidden store of correspondence by the now thoroughly excited Miss Sooley, was short, but there was no mistaking the genuine desire of the writer for her aunt's company at the school entertainment.

"Dear Aunt Sooley," it began ("She always called me her aunt, the same as Miss Lincallow, but of course I'm no relation, really," interpolated the recipient of the communication, peering shortsightedly over Mrs. Bradley's shoulder at the even, legible, schoolmistress-careful script).

"I hope you and Auntie are well. I am still feeling the great benefit derived from my very delightful holiday with you. Next week, on Friday evening, we are doing Gilbert and Sullivan's *Mikado*. I enclose two tickets. You will see the time of the performance on them. I know it is a very long and tiresome journey, but I do wish you and Auntie would come. I have one of the chief parts, that of Katisha, the daughter-in-law-elect of the Mikado of Japan. It is an extremely humorous part. Do please try and persuade Auntie. I could arrange with my landlady for you to stay the night at my lodgings, as it will be too late for you to get back to Bognor when the performance is over, if you would not mind a double bed just for the one night."

It ended, "With love, Calma Ferris," and there was a postscript: "Do come."

"And you went?" said Mrs. Bradley. Miss Sooley nodded, glanced at the two closed doors on the landing, put one finger to her lips and then whispered:

"Miss Lincallow is resting. She'll be in her room an hour at least. Come down to the second sitting room."

The second sitting room contained a settee and two easy chairs, all of a period sufficiently far back in history for its furniture to be obsolete, but not sufficiently removed from the present-day for it to be respectable from a collector's point of view. There was also a bookcase crammed with commentaries on the New Testament, the Victorian poets in faded bindings, some light reading, but of an improving character (Sunday-school prizes won by Miss Ferris between the ages of seven and thirteen, said Mrs. Bradley to herself); and the lives of several obscure divines. In addition there were a large deal sideboard stained mahogany-color and bearing a large, ornate, empty *épergne*, two pictures of rough seas at Hastings, and a depressing oleograph of a whiskered gentleman grasping the back of a chair ("Miss Ferris' father," thought Mrs. Bradley). A large writing desk, a small piano, three small chairs with knobby backs and shiny leather seats, an enormous dining table and a footstool, completed the furnishing, and made a curiously depressing *ensemble*.

Mrs. Bradley selected the smaller easy chair and seated herself. Miss Sooley occupied a small chair, folded her hands in her lap with great care, and prepared to unfold the tale.

"I didn't have half the job persuading her I thought I should," she began. "She said, as soon as I showed her the letter, how much she'd like to go and how Calma was coming out since she'd met Mr. Helm in the summer here. Then I said why should we not go? But she said it was too far, and too many changes on the train; and then I had a real brainwave. I said why should we not, just for once, hire Mr. Willis' car? He would oblige us cheaply, I said, owing to our getting him a lot of custom with the visitors in the summer, what with private hire to the station and trips round and about for those visitors that are afraid to go in motor-coaches and too proud to take the bus to places of interest in the neighborhood—and, of course, Mrs. Bradley, Bognor is *very* well situated for places of interest—so that if he could not oblige us, who can?"

As the question appeared to be directed at her, Mrs. Bradley said:

"Quite, quite," in conciliatory tones, and the narrative proceeded.

"Well, we knocked him down to two pounds seventeen-and-six, no tips, and the driver to be responsible for garaging the car at Mr. Willis' expense, and really, you could hardly grumble at that, especially as we understood from the letter that poor Calma quite expected to pay for our lodgings herself. So at half-past ten that Friday morning off we set."

She paused.

"Very pleased at the idea of your outing?" Mrs. Bradley suggested. The question had the desired effect. Miss Sooley's round red face clouded and her eyes looked troubled. She shook her head.

"We weren't on speaking terms. Very unfortunate it was. Miss Lincallow thought it would be nice to send Miss Ferris a telegram to say we were coming, and, as luck would have it, that made me say, just careless-like:

" 'Then she'll have all sorts of surprises.' Well, though perhaps it isn't for me to say so, Miss Lincallow is a little bit nosey and suspicious. Well, you have to be if you take in visitors at a seaside resort, even a high-class one, you know, Mrs. Bradley. So she pounced on me directly for saying that, and asked me what I meant.

" 'I mean this,' I said. 'That saucy Mr. Helm was on the promenade yesterday, and he stopped when he saw me, raised his hat, quite the gentleman, asked after you, Miss Lincallow—very correct he was— and then he turned the talk on to Miss Ferris, and really, before I realized what he was getting out of me, he was scribbling her school address on the back of an envelope he took out of his pocket, and was raising his hat and wishing me good-day as cool as you please, and before I could find my breath sufficient to run after him and ask him what he wanted it for—because I could just *imagine*, Miss Lincallow, what you would say—he had stepped into the Chichester bus as it was starting, and off he had gone. Of course I didn't *give* it him. He happened to mention the school, and I said she was there.'

"My word, she *was* cross with me. You would scarcely credit, Mrs. Bradley, what a temper she has got when she likes! Anyhow, it all ended up with her sending the telegram to warn poor Calma against him, and when I said ought we not to let her know we were coming, she

said she could not afford two telegrams, and that what could not be
said for a shilling had better go unsaid, and that *she* wasn't made of
money, even if *I* was, but that she hoped she knew her duty to her
niece, even if *I* didn't, and then at last, out it came. It seems she had
been talking to Mr. Willis about the car, and somehow, talking of poor
Calma, the conversation had got round to Mr. Helm, and Mr. Willis
said surely she knew about Mr. Helm? And she said, 'No. What?' And
he whispered it. That he was really that monster Cutler, who had
drowned his wife in the bath for her insurance, and had been acquitted
because there wasn't enough evidence to hang a dog. The thing that
spoilt her temper the most, though, was when she found that no way at
all could she get the warning to Calma into a shilling telegram. Not
that she is really mean with money, but she has her little foibles, and
twopence or threepence extra on a telegram is one of them. Of course,
she was a bit cross about poor Calma coming to us for her summer
holiday, really. She never let on to me about it, but I guessed.

" 'Comes here to have a holiday on the cheap! Wants the best room
for the least money just because she's my niece,' she said to me one
day. I think she thought Miss Ferris might have helped with the visitors
a bit, too, but poor Calma never offered to. Still, her auntie was very
nice to her face, I will say that."

"So the fact that you went by car accounts for your having been able
to return to Bognor immediately after the entertainment," said Mrs.
Bradley, who was getting far more information from Miss Sooley's
rambling discourse than she could possibly have expected.

"Well, thereby hangs a tale," said Miss Sooley portentously. She
was obviously enjoying herself to the full. "It was like this. Mr. Willis
himself drove us, as Miss Lincallow wouldn't trust herself with young
Tom, and, Calma not expecting us, we had tea in the town and got Mr.
Willis to drive us on to the school in nice time for the opening of the
doors at seven o'clock. But the disappointment was that he lost the
way, although we had been directed, and what with it being dark, and
the school set in the middle of rather good-class roads, very quiet, you
know, and for more than a mile and a half nobody to ask the way of,
and Mr. Willis surly and Miss Lincallow what you might call annoyed
to think we were paying all that for the car and not seeing the show,
after all, that when we did arrive at the school gates she said she wouldn't
go in. She gave Mr. Willis her ticket, as I wouldn't go in alone, and him
and I went in nearly at the end of the first part. We hadn't sat down

hardly five minutes when down came the curtain and up went the lights, and everybody round us laughing and talking and eating sweets, and Miss Lincallow nursing her crossness out in the car, and no sign of Calma, either on the stage or off it. Well, I was ever so disappointed, but right in the very middle, just as I was having a really good laugh at that Ko-Ko, up comes a nice little chap with a message. 'The door-keeper says there's a lady outside wants you to go home now.'

"It was my lady Lincallow, of course, sick of waiting and having caught her death sitting out there at that time of the night, in December, too, and small wonder at it! Anyway, out we had to go, Mr. Willis and me, and off we drove, straight back here without seeing Calma or the opera or anything, except if it ever comes to Bognor I shall go and see it, Lincallow or no Lincallow, temper or no temper," concluded Miss Sooley with unlooked-for spirit.

After being compelled to listen to some unimportant details relative to the drive home, Mrs. Bradley escaped to her room and spent the time that remained before the ringing of the bell for tea in making notes. The most important points, she decided, were that Miss Lincallow had betrayed neither surprise nor agitation at the news of her niece's death and that she had arrived at the school and had contrived to separate herself from her two companions before the interval; that was to say, before the finding of the body.

The first thing to be done was to seek out Mr. Willis and compare his version of the affair with Miss Sooley's account. She did not want either of the boardinghouse proprietors to know that she was going to question Willis, so she did not ask for his address, but went out after tea to find him. His house adjoined his garage, and his garage was, as she had suspected, at the end of the road in which Miss Lincallow resided. Willis, a homely, pleasant man of about fifty, scratched his head with an oily hand, smiled at the recollection of Miss Lincallow's annoyance, informed Mrs. Bradley that she had refused to pay a penny for the hire of the car, and finally (without realizing in the slightest that Mrs. Bradley's manipulation of the conversation had brought out the information), that he should say that he and Miss Sooley had been seated in the auditorium for a quarter of an hour at least, and probably longer, before the curtain came down upon the first act. Mrs. Bradley then led the conversation to channels which resulted in her hiring the car for a short drive on the following morning, and she and Mr. Willis parted on terms of mutual goodwill. It was extraordinary, she reflected, how people's ideas about the passing of time varied.

She sought out Miss Sooley again, and was able to elicit the fact that she and Willis had seated themselves in the auditorium some moments before the first entrance of Katisha. That settled it. Although Mrs. Bradley was perfectly certain in her own mind that Miss Lincallow had done nothing whatever that night except sit in the car outside the school door, nursing a grievance against Willis, it was obvious that she could have had the opportunity to murder her niece. On the face value of the evidence offered by Willis and Miss Sooley, she had no alibi for the time the murder might have taken place, and her determination to return that night to Bognor instead of staying at Calma Ferris' lodgings might turn out very awkwardly for her if it could be proved that she had had any motive for wishing her niece out of the way. Had she had such a motive?

Mrs. Bradley sighed. She felt convinced, in spite of herself, that Miss Lincallow *had* had such a motive. Everybody who was mixed up in this queer case seemed to have had a reason for disliking poor Miss Ferris. It was ridiculous!

It was also interesting. Mrs. Bradley went to bed early that night, and by the morning her brain had produced the motive, mocked itself for producing any suggestion so farfetched, rebuked itself for its own mockery, and, finally, compromised with itself by deciding to wait and see.

There was another task awaiting her that day. She decided that it was time to go and interview Mr. Helm. She confidently expected that he would deny ever having been at the school, and she realized that, so far, there was nothing whatever to connect him in any way with the crime. She wondered how she could introduce herself to him, and decided that audacity and mendacity would have to be the weapons of attack. After breakfast, therefore, she went for her drive in Mr. Willis' car and arranged with young Tom, who drove, that he should wait outside the railway-carriage bungalow for half an hour.

"At the end of half an hour," she observed to young Tom, "you will knock loudly upon the front door and demand admittance."

"Seems to me, ma'am," said young Tom, pushing his peaked cap farther back on his fair head, "you'd be better not calling on him. I haven't heard much about him to his credit."

"Charity begins at home," said Mrs. Bradley, obliquely. She walked up a path of pebbles and banged on the front door. Tom, who was a chivalrous lad, opened the bonnet of the car and, under pretense of looking at the engine, covertly watched proceedings. When the front door closed behind Mrs. Bradley, he sat on the step, looked at his wrist-watch, and prepared to rush into the bungalow at the first suspicious noise that issued from it.

Mrs. Bradley's tactics in order to gain admission to the bungalow had been simple. The door was opened by Helm himself, whom she recognized, even from a newspaper photograph, as Cutler. This was promising. She remembered the trial in which he had figured, chiefly because it had been the particularly brilliant defense conducted by her son, Ferdinand Lestrange, which had led to Cutler's acquittal. Ferdinand had torn to shreds the case for the prosecution, and had exposed the fact that it was based on insufficient evidence. Mrs. Bradley had believed the man guilty, but the evidence against him was purely circumstantial and its strongest link was the fact that he drew his wife's insurance money, and had himself been the person responsible for insuring her life.

The man looked inquiringly at Mrs. Bradley. She grinned in what she imagined was an ingratiating manner, and he retreated a step.

"Good-afternoon, Mr. Helm," said she. "You *are* Mr. Helm, of Hillmaston School?"

"Well, no, madam, I regret to say that I am not."

"Oh, but *surely*," said Mrs. Bradley, in fatuous tones. "I mean to say, they told me you were he. I want to know all about the school on behalf of my daughter-in-law, who is thinking . . ." She was comparing him with the description of the electrician. *Was* he . . .?

"Who told you to come to me about it?" asked Helm. "Look here; come in. We can't talk here."

Mrs. Bradley had gained her point. She was admitted. The railway-carriage bungalow consisted of two rooms, all the partitions except one having been knocked down. The room into which the front door opened was simply furnished with a small, narrow table, two chairs, two of the original railway compartment seats, a strip of matting in dull shades of crimson and purple, and a large portable bath made of galvanized iron. A gleam of interest in Mrs. Bradley's bright black eyes when they discerned this last sinister object caused Helm to explain modestly that he was not fond of bathing in the open sea at that time of year, but that he considered sea water so beneficial that it was his habit to walk down to the water's edge at high tide with a large pail, and, by taking several journeys, to transport sufficient water from the sea to fill his copper, which he pointed out with great pride. It was a small affair, placed in the "corridor" of the carriage. When the water was warm he emptied it into the bath by means of a large enamel jug, and so had a warm sea water bath twice a day.

"And you wouldn't believe," he said, smiling enthusiastically and waving his arms, "how much good it does me. But this school of yours, dear lady,—I know nothing about it whatever."

"Lie number one, if Miss Sooley is telling the truth," thought Mrs. Bradley, delighted at this discovery.

She drove back to Bognor thinking hard. He had denied ever having visited the school. His appearance did not altogether coincide with the description of the electrician which she had received from the care-taker. The ears were right, though. His manner did not coincide with the picture conjured up by Miss Ferris' aunt of a bold, bad commercial traveler. In short, the man seemed a mental and physical chameleon, and Mrs. Bradley was suitably intrigued. She ate sparingly, as usual, but was so slow over the meal that Miss Lincallow inquired whether she were tired. Mrs. Bradley replied that she was not tired, but that the sea air had made her sleepy, so she retired to bed at about half-past ten, and was asleep before the clock struck eleven. She had managed to indicate to Helm during the course of conversation that she was a wealthy widow with no particular encumbrances—which was perfectly true as far as it went—and she had made up her mind that if he were the unscrupulous adventurer which history seemed to have painted, he would not be content to allow his acquaintance with her to drop. She was not deceived. Helm allowed the next two days to pass, and then Mrs. Bradley received a letter saying that Helm had been in touch with the principal of the school, and had secured a copy of the prospectus, which he would be pleased to talk over with her if she would be kind enough to take tea with him any afternoon that suited her. Mrs. Brad-ley went that very afternoon, and found him, very spruce, awaiting her.

"I had a feeling that you might come today, dear lady," he said. The sparse sandy hair was parted in the middle and carefully brushed. The gray suit was neat and smartly cut. Knife-edged creases down the trou-sers and a tiepin of extraordinary brilliance completed his outward appearance, and the whole effect compelled Mrs. Bradley to smile like an alligator which sees its evening meal within measurable distance of its jaws.

CHAPTER XI
ADMIRER

I

By some means or other, Helm had certainly contrived to obtain a vast amount of information about the school. He knew the names and qualifications of the whole staff, the acreage of the school playing fields; he was able to sketch for Mrs. Bradley an accurate plan of the ground-floor; he described the science laboratory, the art and music rooms, the garden, the swimming bath, and was able to indicate the many other amenities of one of the most modern school buildings in existence. Mrs. Bradley supposed that he had obtained his information from the printed prospectus. He had certainly taken great pains to learn it off by heart if that were the case. On the other hand, if he had actually explored the school with the intention of finding out the best method of murdering Miss Ferris . . .

But why, Mrs. Bradley asked herself, should he have gone to the school rather than found out the address of her lodgings, if he really intended to seek her out and kill her? She fancied that the most likely explanation was that he had considered it improbable that even Miss Sooley would supply him with Miss Ferris' private address, whereas the school address could not be so readily and plausibly withheld. But then, if Miss Sooley's evidence could be trusted, he had known the address of the school without having asked her for it. That was a most puzzling point. She began to talk about the dead woman.

"Of course, I never knew her," she said.

"I did," responded Helm. It was a piece of information he could not very well refuse to give, owing to the fact that he knew Mrs. Bradley was living with Miss Ferris' aunt, who would certainly have explained that he, too, had been a boarder there, and had met the niece.

"Oh, yes, of course! The burglars!" said Mrs. Bradley, shuddering realistically in her assumed character of silly old lady.

"Burglars my boot!" said Helm, succinctly. Mrs. Bradley conquered a genuine start of surprise, and said anxiously:

"Was it her imagination, then, poor girl?"

"It wasn't burglars, anyhow," said Helm. "Not a thing was taken."

"Oh, but I understood from Miss Ferris' aunt that the men became alarmed and fled before they actually entered the house," Mrs. Bradley said. Mr. Helm made a noise expressive of deep contempt, and suggested that perhaps she would like some tea. Mrs. Bradley, rightly suspicious of the victuals offered by (in her opinion) an unconvicted murderer, refused charmingly and said that she would not take up any more of Mr. Helm's valuable time. She thanked him for his kindness in procuring details of the school, apologized for having mistaken the meaning of the friend who (she thought) had told her he was the German master there, and took her leave. Mr. Helm watched her from the window as she walked down the pebbled path to the gate. There was an unpleasant smirk upon his face. The fact had emerged during conversation that Mrs. Bradley's life was insured for ten thousand pounds. It was insured in her son's interest. Mr. Helm's smirk widened into a cheerful grin. He walked up to the galvanized iron bath and played the devil's tattoo upon it with his knuckles.

Mrs. Bradley also wore a cheerful grin. Sheltering behind a breakwater, and with the collar of his dark gray waterproof turned up against the bitter December wind, was Noel Wells.

"Here I am," said Mrs. Bradley. She cackled harshly and pinched his elbow. Wells looked gloomy.

"I don't like it," he said. "It's playing with fire. And I'm not sure it's honest. In any case, what good am I to you, stuck out here on the beach? He could murder you and bury the body on the other side of the bungalow, and I should be none the wiser."

Mrs. Bradley took an orange out of her capacious skirt pocket.

"When you see an orange come hurtling through the bungalow window on this side," she said, "come at once to my assistance."

"But you may not always have an orange to throw," objected Wells. "And what if it's dark?"

"You'll hear the crash of glass."

"Oh, yes. Of course. But suppose you haven't an orange?"

"I shall throw the soap out."

"The soap?"

"The soap."

"But what I mean is—"

Mrs. Bradley took his arm and they walked along the deserted beach toward the town. Wells waited a little while, and then concluded his sentence.

"—won't that blighter be looking at us *now* out of the window?"

"It doesn't matter if he is," Mrs. Bradley replied. "For one thing, you are my son, in whose favor my life is at the present moment insured for ten thousand pounds; and, for another, he is at this moment in rapt contemplation of the bath I told you of. It hangs upon the wall and is to him the means of wish fulfillment. Sand!" she suddenly exclaimed. "Sand!" She waved a skinny, black-gloved claw. "Sand, dear child. How easy to dig the grave. How impossible to locate the grave! Sand!"

Wells quickened his stride.

"I heard in the town that he tried to rent one of the bungalows in that colony on the other side of Bognor," he said, "but that they would not have him because of the trial. Rather a shame, really, as he was acquitted."

Mrs. Bradley's only reply was to the effect that she was going home for Christmas.

"I shall write to Mr. Helm," she added, "and when the Christmas vacation is over I shall return to the school for a bit. There are still one or two things that need clearing up from that end. As to Mr. Helm, I cannot foretell with any certainty what his reaction to my absence will be." She chuckled and then demanded, "How long had you intended staying in the neighborhood?"

Wells was not quite sure. He would let her know, he said, and they parted at the gate of Miss Lincallow's neat front garden. Miss Lincallow, who avowed, possibly with truth, that, knowing Mrs. Bradley's life was in danger from "that awful man," whom, it was plain, she was now prepared to hold responsible for her niece's death, had remained at the first-floor sitting-room window during the whole of Mrs. Bradley's absence from the house said that she was thankful, "oh, thankful *indeed*," to see her safe home again.

Mrs. Bradley, who had not announced her intention of breaking her drive in order to call upon Helm, made no remark except to demand tea. After tea, the loquacious Miss Sooley sought her out.

"And did you really go *inside?*" she asked, with a shiver of delicious horror. "Do you know, when I think that we had that man here, in this house, all those weeks in the summer, and *never knew*, I could scream!"

"Never knew what?" asked Mrs. Bradley, wilfully dense.

"Never knew that he was a murderer," said the obliging Miss Sooley in low tones. Her eyes grew round and hard and bright, and her mouth became a little pink rosette. Her nose twitched with excitement. "And you went inside his house with him! Just fancy you being so daring, little as you are, too!"

"And old. And frail," said Mrs. Bradley. She gave vent to a deep chuckle, and smoothed the sleeve of a jumper which covered muscles of iron. Miss Sooley clicked her tongue and then said archly, and with the simpering smile of a sentimental old maid:

"But there! I suppose he must have his attractions, although *I* could never see them."

"How do you mean?" asked Mrs. Bradley.

"Well," said Miss Sooley, settling down with gusto to a scandalous story, "Miss Lincallow may say whatever she chooses about poor Miss Ferris, but it wasn't only Miss Ferris that couldn't behave herself as a lady should in a house that contains gentlemen."

"Really?" said Mrs. Bradley, afraid of saying anything which might cause the conversation to veer into a less promising channel. Miss Sooley, however, was fairly in midstream, and under full sail at that. She folded her hands—they ought to have been mittened, Mrs. Bradley decided—nodded her head, swallowed, drew in a deep breath and continued:

"Yes, indeed. Do you know, I really believe the only reason she warned Miss Ferris against him was because she wanted him herself. And her sixty, if she's a day! Did you ever! When we knew him and Miss Ferris had been in the same room on the night the burglars came, Miss Lincallow was that furious! And then her spreading that tale about Miss Ferris falling! 'She wasn't the kind to fall,' I said. 'Not without she was properly married. Too much good sense and nice feeling,' I said. But would she listen to me? Not a word!

" 'Be that as it may, Ellen,' she said to me, 'and I'm not contradicting you, the fact remains that young women *do* fall, and there's nobody can prevent it,' she said. Of course, I'm not one to discuss such things, Mrs. Bradley. I don't see the necessity, for one thing, although there are quite respectable people—yes, even in a town like this—who talk of nothing else. How they get to hear as much as they do passes my comprehension. But this I do say: I know a good girl when I see one, and I'm *sure* Miss Ferris wouldn't think of placing herself in an unfortunate position, and the inquest *proved* it, and very pleased I was, I can tell you."

"Yes. So was I," Mrs. Bradley hastily interpolated. "So you think Miss Lincallow was jealous of her niece?"

It was a bold plunge, but time was passing. Miss Lincallow might come in upon them at any moment, and Mrs. Bradley was interested in seeing whether her overnight suspicions were correct. It appeared that they were.

"Jealous?" said Miss Sooley. "I should say she was. And kept it all in, mind you. That's what's so funny to me. Nobody could be nicer to Miss Ferris' face. Quite took the poor girl in, I can tell you. But behind her back, to me, it was a very different tale. Murderer or no murderer, she took a big fancy to him, there's no doubt about that. And if you want to keep the peace with her, I shouldn't visit him again if I were you. No offense, of course, Mrs. Bradley. Just a friendly warning. Here she comes."

In spite of the friendly warning, Mrs. Bradley decided to visit Helm again before she returned to her own home and, later, to the school, but before she did so another interview took place, this time between herself and Miss Lincallow. That lady took her aside after the evening meal, saying abruptly:

"Come into my little sitting room." Mrs. Bradley meekly followed her.

"What has Ellen Sooley been telling you about me?" demanded Calma Ferris' aunt when they were seated, the one upon a horsehair sofa, the other in an uncomfortable armchair. Mrs. Bradley grinned.

"She told me how you sat out in the car whilst she and the chauffeur went into the school hall to hear the opera," she said, cautiously feeling her way.

"So I did. And very cold it was. That fool of a Willis lost his way. I got so cold that I couldn't stand it, so I got out of the car and went to the door and asked the doorkeeper to find them and bring them out. Let me warn you. Take no notice of Ellen Sooley. She's a liar from her hair-slide to her boots, and the only things she can cook are the accounts. I'm sorry I ever took her into partnership, for she does nothing but get under my feet and make eyes at all the men who stay here. That *Helm!* I can't understand the attraction from either point of view, but she was all over him until Calma came along. Then somehow he got to know that Calma was my heir, and that did it, I suppose, for I can't conceive of any man being attracted to Calma for her looks, can you?"

"I never met her," said Mrs. Bradley, gently. The situation was becoming complicated. She resolved to try whether Helm could not straighten it out.

On the following day, therefore, having rung up Noel Wells and requested him to be at his post of vantage behind the breakwater, she walked along the sands until she came upon Helm's bungalow. Helm was on the seaward side of his garden, if garden it could be called, engaged in planning a rockery. Mrs. Bradley was so delighted that she stood at his elbow and watched the proceedings for six minutes by her watch before he turned and caught sight of her. An unpleasant change came over his face. His eyes glinted dangerously like those of a treacherous dog, and his canines showed white, like fangs, at the corners of his mouth as his top lip drew back in a snarl which he quickly changed into a smile.

"Ah, digging a grave, I see," said Mrs. Bradley, in the bright and fatuous manner which she had adopted for his undoing. Helm looked startled.

"A grave, dear lady?" he said, gazing at the heap of large pebbles, small boulders, and pieces of quartz and granite which lay at his feet and which he was busily arranging.

"Yes," said Mrs. Bradley, who was enjoying herself to the full. "All murderers make a rockery over the grave of the victim. Didn't you know? The police know it, too. Don't you read the Sunday papers, dear child? The first task undertaken by the police in any case of suspected murder is to dig up the rockery and take up the crazy paving in the sunk-garden. After that they explore the cellars, and, if all else fails, they go through the left luggage at the nearest railway station."

Helm managed a sickly smile.

"You came to ask for more information about the Hillmaston school, of course?" he said. "Come inside, will you?"

"On no account," said Mrs. Bradley, cackling gleefully. "You terrify me! Yes, terrify me!" She rolled the middle letters of the first syllable of the word until they sounded bloodcurdling in the extreme. She gripped his arm between her powerful thumb and skinny first finger, so that he winced with pain and tried to draw away, but she held him fast, wagged the forefinger of the other hand in his shrinking face and, dropping her voice, said in sepulchral tones, "And *do* you know what they are saying about you in Bognor?"

"Yes," said Helm. Mrs. Bradley looked shocked, a histrionic effort which did her great credit, since some twenty-eight years previously she had given up being shocked at the many foibles of humanity.

"You *do?*" she said, in tones which blended horror with incredulity. Helm nodded. He was recovering. Mrs. Bradley released his arm.

"And is it *true?*" she asked, in breathless accents. Helm managed a shaking laugh. Against his will, and, as he supposed, against his instinctive *flair* for picking out a fool, the little old woman was beginning to get on his nerves.

"It's true that I was tried for my life," he admitted. "But it's a shame and a scandal that people should gossip about me."

"And you really are the notorious *Cutler?*" said Mrs. Bradley. "How absolutely *divinely* thrilling! How I should *love* to have been at the trial!"

She did it well; so well that Helm's relief showed plainly in his face. His crafty eyes resumed their expression of frank good nature and his wolf teeth disappeared. She *was* a fool, after all. He need never have been alarmed. He must be losing his nerve. She was easy. Ten thousand pounds!

"Dear lady," he said, "what an extraordinary desire in one so gently nurtured and so extremely well-endowed with all the feminine graces!"

Mrs. Bradley, who could throw a knife into the center of any given target at a range of thirty feet, and could break a man's wrist with a twist of her clawlike fingers, smiled amiably. Noel Wells, peering cautiously over the breakwater, saw her and Helm engaged in apparently amicable conversation, and dropped back out of sight again.

"I've really come to ask your advice about my son," said Mrs. Bradley, "and now I know that you are quite a man of the world, I shall follow out your suggestions with the greater confidence. He has become entangled with a female against my wishes."

"Disinherit him," said Helm immediately. He had all the blind vanity and egoism of the man to whom murder is neither an art nor a necessity. It was going to be too easy, he decided. Once get this nincompoop of a son disinherited—why, it was as easy as walking on the sands at low tide! He began to smile joyfully. Mrs. Bradley smiled too; hers was the thin, cruel smile of the serpent. Had Helm been one iota less full of self-conceit and villainy, he must have seen the small sharp teeth behind those thin, stretched, smiling lips.

"Disinherit him?" she said. "Well, I could *threaten* him with that, anyway, couldn't I?"

"I should give him a real good scare, if I were you," said Helm. "He gets your life assurance when you die, I take it?"

"Oh, you dreadful man! Don't talk like that, so casually, of dying!" said Mrs. Bradley. "I'm not going to die for *years!* A fortune-teller told me so."

"No, no! But to scare him into doing as you wish, why not pretend to make that life assurance payable to someone else?"

"Yes, but to whom?" said Mrs. Bradley, as though she were inclined to favor the absurd suggestion.

"That's not for me to say," said Helm, apprehensive of going too far, and scaring the quarry. Having brought matters to this promising point, it would be a thousand pities to be too precipitate, he thought. Besides, he wasn't in a hurry. He had other plans which were on the point of maturing. It would not hurt to let the old girl hang up for a bit, while he carried out his other schemes. Besides, the son was a bit of an obstacle. He did not want some great goop of a boy asking a lot of silly questions, and perhaps becoming violent. Mr. Helm, *né* Cutler, detested violence. Drowning an unsuspecting woman in a bath was one thing, but standing up to an angry young man was quite another.

"I should like to meet your son," he said.

"I will bring him with me if I come again," said Mrs. Bradley, feeling certain that the Reverend Noel Wells' tall, slightly stooping figure, vacuously cheerful expression and clerical collar would work wonders in restoring Mr. Helm's fast-ebbing nerve. "And I'll think over what you say. You won't introduce the subject in my son's presence, will you? He is epileptic and it would be most embarrassing for the poor boy to have a seizure in front of a perfect stranger. *Good* afternoon, then, Mr. Helm. Or do your friends call you *Cutler? Such* a good name for a murderer, isn't it? Oh, I forgot, though! You aren't really a murderer, are you? Not *yet!* Oh, isn't it all *thrilling!* Do you know, I believe I'll make out my assurance policy in *your* favor, and give my naughty boy a fright."

She was gone before the flabbergasted Helm could make any reply. His state of mind was comic. *Was* she a fool? He decided, finally, that, yes, she was. He gazed earnestly at his half-finished rockery when she had gone. Disconsolately he kicked the nearest piece of stone. It had cost pounds for the materials to be transported to the bungalow. What had that funny old girl said about it? He was not sure that he wanted to remember. He walked into the tiny bungalow and drummed on the large, galvanized-iron bath. Ten thousand pounds! The first thing the police do in a case of suspected murder is to dig up the rockery! How the devil had she guessed? . . . What was there to guess, anyway? She knew nothing of Susie. Nobody knew anything of Susie . . . yet!

But his peace of mind had been disturbed. He put on his hat and locked up the railway-carriage bungalow and went to the cinema.

II

Noel Wells escorted Mrs. Bradley to her lodgings and left her with Miss Lincallow.

"And you have been to see that man again!" Miss Lincallow exclaimed. "How *can* you bring yourself to associate with him?"

"Tell me," said Mrs. Bradley, making no attempt to answer the question, "did your niece keep a diary?"

"She did, poor girl," replied Miss Lincallow, "and you shall see it, for there's nothing in it of any consequence."

She went away to get it. Mrs. Bradley, a little surprised at having achieved her object so easily, was soon in her own sitting room, the diary in her hand. She skimmed through the entries for the first half of the year, her eyes sharp to discover any references to other members of the school staff, and especially to those who might have been implicated in the murder, but apart from memoranda with regard to playing tennis with Miss Freely, going to tea with Mrs. Boyle once, and with the headmaster twice, refereeing a match for Miss Camden and going on a school outing with some of the children and Alceste Boyle, there was no reference to any one of them. The various entries for June and up to the date of the school entertainment Mrs. Bradley read more slowly, but her trouble was wasted. From beginning to end of the diary there was not a scrap of information which served to throw any light upon any of the circumstances of the diarist's death. The references to Helm, for instance, were six in number, and referred to the burglar alarm, which appeared to have been genuine, various encounters with the man, together with a summary of the conversations which had ensued and which appeared each time to have taken a particularly formal turn, guided thereto by Calma herself, Mrs. Bradley supposed, and Miss Ferris' opinion that he was clever. On the other hand, it was possible to imagine that, like many diarists, Miss Ferris refrained from committing to paper any details which might be embarrassing if they were made public. There were references to the various *contretemps* which preceded the night of the opera—the quarrel about the netball match, for instance, and the damaging of Mr. Smith's Psyche; the discovery that Hurstwood was in love with Miss Cliffordson, and that she had allowed him to kiss her; but, of all the obvious omissions, the most noticeable, Mrs. Bradley decided, was that of the fact that Moira Malley had sat to Mr. Smith as a model for the Psyche. Calma may have decided not to include this fact of the sittings, but if she had not known that Moira had given them, the girl was automatically cleared from all suspicion of having committed the crime.

Mrs. Bradley went to the telephone and put through a trunk call. It was not yet four o'clock, so that afternoon school would not be over. It happened to be the last full day of the term. The school was due to break up on the following noon. Alceste Boyle answered the telephone.

"Find out whether Miss Ferris knew that Moira Malley sat to Mr. Smith for his Psyche, will you, my dear?" said Mrs. Bradley.

"*Did* she sit to him? That was awfully wrong of Donald," said Alceste. "Hold on a minute."

The seconds ticked away. Then Alceste's voice came through again.

"I couldn't get it any other way, so I had to ask the poor child. She doesn't think anybody knew. She hopes nobody knew. I'm sending her home to Ireland for Christmas. Hurstwood is top of the sixth, but poor little Moira is seventeenth out of a form of twenty. What do you think we can do about it? She *must* get her scholarship, or she can't possibly go to college."

"What is she worrying about?" asked Mrs. Bradley.

"Finding the body like that, I think. Horrible for her."

Mrs. Bradley had just rung off when tea was announced, and she was finishing her second cup when Miss Lincallow came in.

"I'm ever so sorry to disturb you, Mrs. Bradley," she said, "but there is a young man in holy orders on the front step. He won't come in, but he says he must speak to you immediately with your hat and coat on."

Noel Wells certainly had the appearance of excitement which Miss Lincallow's style of narrative had led Mrs. Bradley to expect.

"My dear boy, what is the matter?" she asked, as they ran down the steps and on to the pavement.

"I don't know," said Wells, "but I don't like it. He brought a woman home with him at half-past three, and since then he's been carrying pailfuls of sea water up to his beastly bungalow."

"Round this alley into the office of my friend's garage," said Mrs.

Bradley. Once inside, she raised her melodious voice and called, "Tom! Tom!"

Young Tom came running. He was bareheaded and in his mechanic's overalls.

"The car, quickly, Tom!" said Mrs. Bradley.

Tom was young. He grinned and jerked his thumb.

"Out there, ma'am. Shan't be a tick," he said.

"Come," said Mrs. Bradley to Noel Wells. She caught his hand and, running, took him round to the front entrance of the garage. Out came the car, young Tom at the wheel.

"That railway-carriage bungalow!" said Mrs. Bradley. "Never mind the police!"

"Good Lord!" said Tom, impressed. Luckily they did not meet a single policeman on the way. The car pulled up outside the gate of Helm's residence, and all three ran up the pebbled path. It was Mrs. Bradley who thundered on the door. It was Tom who gripped a spanner purposefully in his right hand.

Helm opened the door. He was wearing a dressing gown. His unstockinged feet were encased in carpet slippers.

"Go back to the car, Tom," said Mrs. Bradley over her shoulder. Tom obeyed.

"So sorry, dear lady," said Helm, with a nervous titter. "Just going to have a bath. No idea anyone would think of calling. A nice hot sea water bath for my rheumatism. So good. So comforting."

"I've brought my son," said Mrs. Bradley. "But we certainly must not disturb you now. Come, Noel, dear."

Wells lolled his tongue like an idiot and hoped he was not overdoing it. He was tall enough to see over Helm's shoulder. The bungalow appeared to be empty. The steaming bath of water was in the center of the floor. As though obeying Mrs. Bradley he turned and walked uncertainly down the garden-path.

"Dear lady, the loss is mine," Helm was saying.

"Go in, go in! You'll catch your death of cold," said Mrs. Bradley. "Have your nice bath. I'll come another day."

She gave him a little push, and pulled the door to. It slammed. Noel Wells was round on the bedroom side of the house, peering in at the window, his long nose touching the glass.

" 'Sister Ann, sister Ann, do you see anyone coming?' " said Mrs. Bradley, behind him.

"I'm sure she's here," said Wells. "Can't we warn her?"

Mrs. Bradley did not hear him. She was round at the living-room window, watching Helm. He was an interesting study. He was positively dancing with rage. His hands clawed the air. Three times he kicked the bath with his slippered foot.

"Come, child," said Mrs. Bradley to Noel Wells, as she came up behind him. Wells shook his head.

"I'm staying here until that woman comes out," he said, "and then I'm going to tell her who Helm is. He can't see us. It's nearly dark out here."

"You'll wait too long," said Mrs. Bradley gently. "While Helm was opening the door to us I saw her leave the bungalow by way of the bedroom window. She's halfway to Bognor by now."

"But she must have been undressed," protested Wells.

"She wasn't. She was wearing a knitted suit and a waterproof, and she is fairly young," said Mrs. Bradley gravely. "Get into the car as quickly as you can, and we'll follow her. Right away, Tom!"

The woman, whoever she was, had disappeared, however, for they overtook nobody answering to the given description. Mrs. Bradley clicked her tongue. The foolish girl, whoever she was, might at least have been given a friendly warning, if they could have found her.

CHAPTER XII
SWEETHEART

When Susan Cozens was found drowned at the Swinging Sign Inn, a week after Mrs. Bradley had come back to her home for Christmas, it was Looney Thomas who voiced the general opinion. He said he was not surprised. It was common belief that the inn was haunted. None of the local people would have dreamed of leasing it. They would not have expected customers, if they *had* leased it, and to have purchased outright, as these intrepid but foolhardy Londoners had done, seemed little short of lunacy on the one hand, or of trafficking with the powers of evil on the other, to the superstitious people of the village.

Nevertheless, there seemed little of the moon's madness, and still less of the cloven hoof, about Malachi Spratt and his wife. He was a decent, clean, cheerful man of forty when he bought the Swinging Sign on the London Road, not five miles out of Bognor Regis, and his wife Dora was a slow-moving, strong, big, industrious creature, quietly spoken, self-contained, civil and obliging. The people found her generous, too, and, in their ills and their troubles, sympathetic and comforting beyond the ordinary. She had married beneath her, it was said; but she and her husband were an excellent match—he so lithe and quick—it was rumored that he had held a wrestling championship somewhere, sometime; but wrestling was not a local sport, so nobody was sufficiently intrigued by the rumor to find out the time, district and kind of wrestling involved—she with her apparent languor behind whose slow grace burned fires of energy.

When they had owned the Swinging Sign for about twenty months, a son was born to them, and everyone in the village foretold disaster. Their luck had been too good. For one thing, although the village people feared the lonely inn, motorists on the London Road did not. Spratt's bar might often be empty, but his saloon lounge, his bar-parlor, his six fine bedrooms and his garage were often filled to capacity with Scotsmen and Londoners and their cars. He had twice entertained a Gretna couple, and once a man absconding with company funds. All who came were welcome, as long as they were quiet and paid their score. Many people came again and again, for the reckoning was moderate, the food and drink reasonably good, and the beds comfortable. By the time young John was rising twenty, his father was sufficiently rich to be thinking about rebuilding the Swinging Sign and laying the ghost.

Upon mentioning this to one of his clients, however, he was persuaded by the young fellow to give up the idea. The ghost was advertised in an important and distinguished Sunday paper as an extra inducement to stay a weekend at the Swinging Sign and business became more brisk than ever. Unfortunately, the luck did not last, for, almost coincident with young John's twenty-first anniversary, a new bypass road was opened which diverted traffic from that part of the London Road which led past the inn, and the Swinging Sign was left like an eyot in a looped backwater—not high-and-dry exactly, but subject to the fluctuations of weekend and holiday tides of traffic. Some motorists preferred the narrow highway to the broad new arterial road, and for these the Swinging Sign catered adequately as of old; but the high tide of prosperity had passed, and the villagers revived the old tales of ghosts, ill-luck and sudden death, to the annoyance of young John and the amusement of his father. Neither husband nor son could tell what effect the change in fortune was going to have upon Dora. Slow-moving, gracious, bountiful and aloof as before, she kept the house as she had always kept it, and listened to the troubles of the village as she had always listened to them. She was spacious-minded, even when John took up with Susie Cozens.

Susie was small and pretty—the antithesis in every way of Dora. She was three years older than John, and had been a shop assistant in London before she came back to keep the village stores with her widowed mother. Even Malachi, who was tolerant of all his fellow creatures, could not bring himself to contemplate with any degree of enthusiasm the fact that the shallow, cheaply scented little platinum blonde would be his daughter-in-law. Susie herself looked down on her future relatives. Privately, she would not have been averse to changing her sweetheart had the offer of a better one presented itself. John was young. That in itself was a disadvantage. She fancied she would have preferred the caveman type of lover. John, who was big enough, strong enough, taciturn enough, and sufficiently lacking in any sense of humor to fill the role, was inhibited by his upbringing and by the difference in their ages from treating Susie in the rough, contemptuous manner which she fancied she would have enjoyed. Against the obvious disadvantages of John's youth and courtesy there were, in Susie's opinion, several facts which told fairly heavily in his favor. For one thing, he was, with two exceptions, the only male of her own generation (living in or near the hamlet of Lamkin) who was not a farm laborer. The exceptions were the parson's son, young Eric Greenacre, and the squire's chauffeur, a man of thirty, named Roy. Roy was his surname. His baptismal name was Ham. He earned thirty-five shillings a week and lived rent-free in the room over the squire's garage. He breakfasted free of charge, and paid the cook seven shillings and sixpence a week, inclusive, for the rest of his food. The squire, a bibliophile and a faddist, had curious economic theories, and tried them on his servants. Thus, if Roy were absent from the servants' breakfast for any reason whatsoever, including illness, a sum of tenpence was added to his weekly wage for every breakfast that he missed. Out of the tenpences he was charged accordingly for the breakfasts taken to his bedside during the period his illness lasted. So when Roy contracted influenza he was in pocket over the breakfasts, for he never had any, and once when he broke his leg he was considerably out of pocket, because he found the enforced inactivity so dull that, as he explained to Susie, he had to eat a lot to keep himself from being bored to death.

It took Susie a considerable time to weigh the two young men in opposite sides of the scale, and to make the nice adjustments which were to aid her in making up her mind between them. It is certain that she could have had her choice, for Roy and John were equally blind, foolish and insensitive where women were concerned, and neither was capable of seeing what a cheap little humbug Susie was. John, getting twenty shillings a week from his father and all found, would one day inherit the Swinging Sign. Against this was Roy's extra fifteen shillings, less the seven-and-sixpence for meals and the fact that presumably he would never be his own master. On the other side, again, though, thought Susie, it would be possible for her to be married thirty years at least before John inherited anything, and if those thirty years were to be spent with her husband's parents, who obviously disliked and distrusted her, what would be gained? Roy had no relatives to approve or disapprove of what he did, and he was a good-looking, smart fellow in his trim uniform, whereas John, slouching about the backyard with a couple of buckets, or serving in the bar with his shirtsleeves rolled up, was not nearly as inspiring a spectacle. Lastly, there was the question of the name. Mrs. John Spratt was not exactly a name to aspire to, but then, was Mrs. Ham Roy much better? Roy was good; but *Ham!* John was permissible; but *Spratt!*

It was a pity, thought Susie, that she couldn't take a fancy to the parson's boy, young Mr. Greenacre. Eric . . . Mrs. Eric Greenacre . . . even Mrs. Tom Greenacre . . . even Mrs. Eric Roy. Any of them, and she would have made her choice without difficulty. But as edibles, let alone nomenclature, both Ham and Spratt made her feel slightly bilious. It was too bad that a girl should be bothered, thought Susie. Besides, you could not even refer to your husband by his surname of Roy. It was countrified, and therefore common, to speak of your husband except by his given name; so much she had learned in London. And to talk about Ham! . . . really, it gave her the willies, really it did. Besides, the parents of John Spratt might die. Then there would be the pub and her own motorcar. That would be better than having stolen rides in Roy's employer's automobile. . . .

So, in the end, she plumped for John. Spratt was not such a bad name if one did not visualize it in terms of fish. "And after all," thought Susie, "people do die. I mean, it's the kind of thing that might happen to anyone. . . .'' Fortified by this consideration, she accepted an engagement ring from John, and, suffered by his parents and suffering them in her turn, she used to go to tea and have her weekly bath at the public house every Sunday, and accompany John to Evensong afterwards. They shared a hymn book and a prayer book, held hands during the sermon, walked slowly homeward in the summer gloaming, and for the space of about five months conducted themselves as became two persons who were proposing to spend the rest of their lives in one another's company. John was proud and happy, but Susie was not altogether convinced that she had chosen the right young man.

His parents had nothing to say to John about his choice of a sweetheart. They had learned the futility of attempting to influence his taste. From the age of four onwards, John's likes had been his likes and his dislikes had been his dislikes, and there had been no persuading him into altering his opinion. The father thought that he recognized the mother's characteristic determination coming out in the boy; Dora affected to consider her son's obstinacy a youthful trait which would disappear "as the lad learned sense." As though recognizing his right to choose a mate, however, neither Malachi nor Dora, by word or gesture, gave the slightest indication to John that they disapproved of Susie. Susie knew that they did. She, too, did not mention it to John. She knew that if John thought his parents did not like her, he would leave his home and throw away all his prospects. As she was only prepared to marry John for what she could get, his quarreling with his people would not have suited her at all, so, like a sleek and secretive cat, she made no sign that she observed anything untoward in Dora's manner or in Malachi's silences, and spent a surprising amount of concentrated thought upon the problem of how to make the best of John, Dora, Malachi and the Swinging Sign. Meanwhile she herself was earning a little money for the new home in a new, exciting and very simple way. She was blackmailing a murderer.

One Sunday afternoon in the late fall the weather turned damp and foggy. By half-past two, when Susie and her mother had just finished their Sunday dinner, it was dark. Susie would have decided to forgo her customary walk of just over a mile-and-a-half to the inn had not she quarreled with her mother while they were cooking the dinner. Mrs. Cozens should have been a warning to John—had he been the kind of person to give heed to a warning—of what to expect of Susie at fifty, for she was whining, spiteful and ill-tempered, a disappointed, nagging woman. She had hoped great things of her husband, but when nothing better than the village stores-cum-post-office turned out to be her portion, and when her child turned out to be a girl instead of the son she had set her heart on, and when her husband became paralyzed at the age of thirty, and Susie took herself up to London as soon as she got herself the sack from a most suitable local situation, Mrs. Cozens had grown more and more disagreeable, self-pitying and antagonistic. She suspected that Susie had only come home to live because she had got herself into some sort of trouble in London. Susie could have confirmed this opinion, had she cared to do so, for she had been taken up for shoplifting in a big London store, and was lucky to have had the case dismissed. Not for one moment had the mother ever believed that her daughter had returned home solely on account of the death of Cozens.

Susie knew her mother well enough to realize that if she stayed at home on this particular Sunday, she would have to prepare herself for a most unpleasant afternoon, so, in spite of the weather, she dressed herself in her best and prepared to set out on her usual Sunday afternoon walk to the Swinging Sign. Usually she left the shop at approximately half-past three. By walking briskly she could thus expect to reach the inn round about ten minutes past four. Tea was at five, which gave John roughly thirty minutes, after she had had the promised bath, to sit beside her on the sofa, while Malachi was having his Sunday afternoon sleep and Dora was washing up the dinner things and changing into her Sunday dress and getting the tea ready in the kitchen.

On this particular Sunday, however, Susie was delayed. She was up in her bedroom putting the finishing touches to her hair and wondering whether to tell John about Helm and the funny way he had offered her a sea water bath, when a car drew up. A minute later her mother was calling her downstairs. Roy had come with a message from the squire to request that Mrs. Cozens and Susie would return with Roy to the big house, as the cook had fallen downstairs, and the squire was expecting visitors to dinner.

"You can go, but I shan't," said Susie, decidedly.

As an engaged girl, she felt independent of the squire, whom she disliked. If he had been a little less mean over the question of Roy's wages, she had decided some six days previously, she might not have allowed herself to become engaged to young John Spratt. Privately she considered that her charms were being wasted on John. On the previous Sunday, for instance, he had not even sat beside her on the sofa. He had taken the wireless set to pieces and made her hold small spare parts while he corrected some defect. It had taken him the best part of two hours. She had been intending to tell him about Mr. Helm then, but was so bored and angry that she had not done so.

"Might as well be married already," Susie had thought. She had become sufficiently exasperated to drop a small nut between two gaping boards in the sitting room floor. John had been annoyed and quite unreasonably profane about it. She was going over to make her peace with him as much as for any other reason. Besides, Helm had frightened her.

"All right. If you don't go, our Sue, I shan't go neither," said her mother unreasonably.

"I'll go by myself, but I won't go along with you," said Susie, suddenly changing her mind about the visit to John. "Start her up, Mr. Roy," she added to the chauffeur.

She was quite ready. She had only to slip into hat and coat. Mrs. Cozens, on the other hand, was still in her kitchen garb. Roy was in a hurry, so, with a half-promise flung over his shoulder to Mrs. Cozens that he would return for her later, he started up the engine, and soon the car was lost to sight in the thick white mist which was already blotting out the daylight.

The car crawled along the old main road through the thick mist, and Susie, seriously alarmed at the prospect of an accident, began to suggest to Roy that he should drop her at the crossroads and make some excuse to the squire. Roy, who knew that if Susie and her mother did not come to the rescue, the servants, equally with the squire, would get no evening meal, invited her to think again, and drove on, carefully but steadily, through the white vapor. It was very cold. Hedges would loom suddenly out of the mist. Once they were almost ditched. It was uncomfortable and terrifying. At last they reached the big house, managed the turn at the lodge gates, and the journey was over. It was then, according to Susie's wristwatch, which she had set right that morning by the 10:30 A.M. broadcast time signal from Greenwich, just after half-past four. It had taken an hour for the car to do the three and a half miles which lay between Susie's house and the big house. Once they had stopped while Roy gave directions to a man who had lost himself in the mist.

"You'd better go straight back for Mother," said Susie, as she got out of the car. She stood at the side of the drive and watched while Roy circumnavigated a clump of bushes round which the drive made a circle. The car crawled away. Susie waited until she could hear it no longer, and then went round the house to the side door, where she was admitted by the kitchenmaid. About a quarter of an hour later Roy appeared.

"Didn't you go back for Mother?" asked Susie. He grinned and shrugged.

"Had enough of driving in this fog for one day," he informed her.

"Well, she won't come on her own two legs, not Mother won't," said Susie. "So you better get a move on. I can't manage a dinner by myself."

Roy swore at her.

"Thought you'd parted brass-rags and wouldn't have her come with us," he said.

"Never mind that," said the inconsistent Susie. "You get out that car and go after her. As it is, she'll only be in time to see to the sweet. Get on out of here."

"Start up the dinner and leave Fatty to look after it," suggested Roy, indicating the fifteen-year-old kitchenmaid, "and come along with me, then."

Susie demurred. Roy insisted. The kitchenmaid giggled. In the end, Susie had her way, and remained behind, and Roy, very sulkily, went off alone. He returned at six to find that Susie had disappeared. Susie's mother sniffed, and went on with the dinner, presumably where Susie had left off. The kitchenmaid, questioned by Roy, announced that Susie had gone "out the back" and had not returned. A little later, a man, well-muffled, came to the back door and inquired for Susie.

By ten o'clock that night three of the squire's guests had telephoned to say that their cars were fogbound, the dinner was eaten, and it was declared impossible for Mrs. Cozens to find her way home that night. So she was given a camp-bed in the kitchenmaid's room, and by eleven o'clock all lights in the big house were extinguished and everything was quiet. Later on in the week, Mrs. Cozens told several sympathizers, including the gentlemen of the press, that she did not sleep a wink all night.

"I had them premonitions," she declared, "d'reckly I saw that man. Like a commercial he was, only more so. Asked right out for her as bold as brass, and her engaged to one man and as good as half-promised to

another. I soon sent him off with a flea in his ear. I've got a good eye
for picking out faces, and if he wasn't the very spit and image of that
monster—what was his name, now?—I remember thinking it suited
him right down to the ground!—oh, Cutler. That's it. Cutler. I don't
read the Sunday papers for nothing. Got a regular gallery of murderers,
I have, in the back of me head, and although he was let off with a
caution, I reckon he's a murderer as sure as eggs is eggs. So now!
Some folks can remember figures and dates and things; some can remember the fashions of King Edward's day; it's murderers every time
with me. Kind of an 'obby it is. Poor girl! Ah, well, you never know
what's going to 'appen, do you?"

CHAPTER XIII
FOG

Neither young Spratt nor Roy was moved to vengeance by the discovery of the murdered girl's body. Their attitude was understandable. In
effect, what it amounted to was that she had evidently been deceiving
both of them. What they hated was the thought that she had made fools
of them, not the realization that a scoundrel had done her to death.

The bathrooms at the Swinging Sign were three in number. It was in
the smallest one that the girl was found drowned. Helm was not appre-
hended. Mrs. Cozens, the dead girl's mother, proved to be such an
extremely unreliable witness that the police felt justified in ignoring
her unsupported testimony that she had seen Cutler that day, and the
police inquiry had to proceed along lines other than those which assumed that he was guilty.

The explanation given by the villagers was simple. The inn was
known to be haunted. In some dark manner the powers of evil had
enticed the girl thither, and there, by the agency of the same powers,
she had met her death.

The police, foiled in one direction, soon formulated another theory—
namely, that young John Spratt knew something of the matter. It was
suggestive, they considered, that Susie's death had taken place in the
home of her fiancé. John was questioned, and had to make some damaging admissions. Susie had been invited to the inn and might have

gone to the squire's house very much against her will. It was obvious that she had never had any intention of remaining there longer than the minimum time for preparing the dinner, and it was suggested that she had arrived at the inn without being recognized on the way, owing to the density of the fog, had quarreled with John—although the boy and both his parents strenuously denied this—and the murder had been the result. When it was further shown that Susie was in the habit of taking a bath at the Swinging Sign on Sundays, owing to the fact that her mother's cottage contained no bathroom, further speculation appeared vain. John was arrested and charged with having murdered his sweetheart.

Mrs. Bradley, seated in the pleasant morning room of the Stone House, Wandles Parva, a bright fire burning, breakfast at the toast and marmalade stage, and her young friend, Aubrey Harringay, home for the Christmas holidays, sprawling companionably all over the hearthrug, deep in a detective story, read the account of the murder and the result of the police investigations up to the moment of going to press, and observed, in her rich, full tones:

"Dear, dear, dear, dear, dear! Something more than fiction, something less than fact, makes the poor psychologist wonder how to act!"

She concluded this surprising couplet with an even more surprising hoot of laughter. Aubrey looked up.

"Dry up, love," he said. "You ruin my powers of concentration."

"Put the book aside when you've finished the next chapter, child. I want to tell you a nasty harrowing story," said Mrs. Bradley.

"Honest to God?"

"I am not accustomed to refer my integrity to the Almighty," said Mrs. Bradley solemnly.

"Sorry. Merely a figure of speech." He took a piece of paper out of his pocket and placed it between the pages of his book. "Come on."

"A woman is found drowned at a school," said Mrs. Bradley, "and there seems a possibility that a certain man of her acquaintance was in the neighborhood. This man was once tried for drowning his wife, but was acquitted. Later, a woman escapes from his clutches by the intervention of two perfect strangers, who ought to have made it their business to interfere. There is no actual proof that he intended the woman any harm, but the facts were sufficiently peculiar to be significant. They were as follows: The woman had accepted an invitation to the house, and while she was there, he prepared a bath, ostensibly for himself, for he even went to the lengths of undressing and donning a dressing gown and slippers, and, thus clad, he opened the door to the interfering couple aforesaid. The woman, presumably, was in the bedroom. The bath was in the middle of the living-room floor. These seemingly extraordinary preparations are to be explained by the fact that the dwelling-place was a converted railway-carriage, and therefore not subject to the ordinary customs which govern life in a civilized English home.

"Later, viz., to wit, last Sunday as ever was, a young woman is found drowned in an inn not more than three miles from the railway-carriage, and the dead girl's mother, who appears to be a liar, by the way, swears that this same man called at the house for the girl on the afternoon of the day of her death. What do you make of that?"

"Q.E.D., of course," said the boy. "Is it true?"

"So far as it goes, yes," Mrs. Bradley replied. "At any rate, I think it wants looking at. I have a shrewd suspicion—at least, I hope it's shrewd!—that the young woman of the bungalow and the dead young woman are the same young woman."

"Good," said Aubrey. "May I come with you?"

"No, child. But I will write and ask your opinion on any knotty points which require elucidation."

"Oh, no, I say! Why can't I come?"

"First," said Mrs. Bradley, "your mother wouldn't hear of it. Secondly, you would be in my way."

"Oh, well, if you say so," said Aubrey, resignedly. He turned to his book again and was immediately absorbed in it. Mrs. Bradley grinned like an affectionately maternal alligator at the back of his fair head, and began to make notes, with several references to the newspaper, at the back of a little black book.

Her first action, when she arrived in Bognor, was to seek out the cottage where the dead girl's mother lived, and interview her. The old woman stuck to her story. Helm *had* come to the manor house and he had inquired for Susie. Susie, however, had gone by that time, but her mother was still convinced that the real murderer was Helm (or Cutler, as she called him). On all the evidence, the woman's story appeared unlikely. Helm would have been mad to show his hand so openly if he had really intended to murder the girl. Besides, it was idle to imagine that he could have known Susie was to be at the manor house that afternoon, since she herself had not known it until it was time to start out in the car with Roy. On the other hand, it might well be that Helm *had* murdered the girl at the inn, since it would not have been difficult for him to ascertain that she was in the habit of visiting there every Sunday afternoon. In that case, Mrs. Cozens' story might prove to have been a flight of fancy, and might not, but it would not alter the facts. The fog was certainly an important item. It had been so dense, apparently, that it was possible that under cover of it Helm could have introduced himself into the inn unperceived. If he had taken the trouble to discover the lie of the land, he would know the whereabouts of the various members of the household; this would be especially easy on a Sunday afternoon, when no business was being transacted, for there was no reason to break the peaceful habits of the Sabbath, and thus he could have minimized any risks of running into Malachi, Dora or John. It remained to be seen whether there would have been any way for him to gain admission to the interior of the house without having to announce himself by knocking on the door, and this Mrs. Bradley decided to investigate next.

Dora and Malachi Spratt were both at home. Mrs. Bradley decided to tackle Dora first. The woman was half-crazed with the shock of John's arrest, and at first Mrs. Bradley could get little out of her. As soon as Dora understood, however, that the visitor was convinced of John's innocence, was the mother of a famous lawyer, and was looking for facts to help to clear John's name, she rallied, took herself in hand, and answered Mrs. Bradley's questions with the greatest economy and carefulness.

"She used to come in and out as she liked," was the gist of her testimony, "and I suppose anyone else could have done the same. The door was shut—that door on to the yard is the one we always use for our own private incomings and outgoings—but it's only a case of turning the handle. Malachi never locks it until bedtime. Indeed, it must have been somebody that came into the house who killed her. John didn't drown her, and Malachi and I were together all afternoon and evening, and neither of us had a hand in it, that I do know. My boy is innocent. She was a bad girl, I am sure, and I guess she had bad friends. She was from London, and had been in some trouble there. She left a lady at Bognor through being too busy about other people's affairs. It's like enough she met this man somewhere, and that he murdered her for some reason we shall never know."

Mrs. Bradley began to see daylight. She had thought at the time that Helm had been preparing that rockery for herself, but it was equally likely that he had decided to make away with the girl at his bungalow, and had been foiled. In this case, the rockery would have been designed as a grave for the girl, and not for Mrs. Bradley. It might well be true that the girl in the knitted suit and waterproof, whom Mrs. Bradley had seen leaving Helm's bungalow, was the girl who had been murdered at the Swinging Sign. If she had had any proof whatever that Helm had intended to murder the girl that day when he was interrupted by herself and Noel Wells, she would have gone with her suspicions to the police. But it was Helm himself, apparently, who had been prepared to take a bath that day. The girl had been fully dressed.

She tracked bits of village gossip to their source and learned that John Spratt and Ham Roy had been rivals for Susie's favor. In an interview with the Chief Constable, whom she knew fairly well, she stressed the lack of motive. It would have been more reasonable to apprehend Roy rather than Spratt, she suggested. Roy, however, was fairly well covered by the fact that he had twice covered the distance between Susie's home and the manor house in his employer's car, and that, while he would have had time to get out of the car at the Swinging Sign and murder Susie, the household could scarcely fail to have heard a car draw up at the door; and this Dora, Malachi and John all denied having heard.

CHAPTER XIV
HERO

I

The Reverend Noel Wells was accustomed to think of himself as, if not exactly a coward, at least lacking in that species of virility and insensitiveness which compels human beings to run foolish, unnecessary risks merely for the sake of fame or fortune. He was, however, the troubled possessor of an extremely delicate conscience which compelled him to feats of chivalry against his will and often against his better judgment. His conscience troubled him sorely over the question of Mrs. Bradley and the strange man, Helm.

The most curious thing about Helm was the fact that immediately people learned that he was in reality the renowned Cutler, acquitted of drowning his wife, one and all immediately and irrevocably decided that he was indeed a murderer, and that he had only escaped hanging by some subtle twist of the laws of evidence. Against every instinct for fair play and in direct contravention of everything he had practiced for years with respect to refraining from kicking a man when he is down, Noel Wells was similarly affected by the fellow. He felt as certain that Cutler had murdered his wife for the sake of collecting the insurance money as though he had seen him in the act. The man's behavior with regard to Mrs. Bradley had done nothing to alter his opinion, and the young curate felt that his friend was running ridiculously heavy risks in visiting the man and in arousing his cupidity as she had done.

Wells realized that her reason for tempting Helm to make a murderous attack upon her was, in itself, sound enough. She had explained to the curate her difficulties with regard to the death of Calma Ferris, and he knew that she was determined to demonstrate to the headmaster that nobody connected with the school had been responsible for the crime. Although she had not actually said so, Wells, who was not altogether the fool people sometimes took him for, knew well enough that she had guessed the identity of Calma Ferris' assailant, that it was *not* Helm who was responsible for the murder, and that Mrs. Bradley was determined to keep secret the name of the guilty person. Noel Wells's obstinate, masculine mind refused to accept the reasonable suggestion that Mrs. Bradley was well able to take care of herself, and his sense of chivalry urged him to put himself in her place, provoke a murderous assault from Helm, send a full description of the attack—if he was in a condition to write it!—to Mrs. Bradley, and so prevent her from risking her own life. That he would be risking his own did, of course, occur to him, but he brushed the thought aside.

He went to the garage and took young Tom into his confidence. Young Tom told his father. His father told Police-Constable Alfred Bearden, who was engaged to young Tom's sister, and the plot was laid.

One gray but rainless afternoon, about ten days after Christmas, when Mrs. Bradley, comfortably at home in the Stone House, Wandles Parva, was reading an exceedingly affectionate letter from Helm—the third that had been sent on to her from Miss Lincallow's boardinghouse to the school, and from the school to her home,—three young men set out from Bognor Regis to walk the three miles out to Helm's railway-carriage bungalow. The gray waves, sullen after a gale which had raged for two days and a night, thundered heavily on the gray sand and seethed on to the gray pebbles. The low sky was gray. The road was deserted. About half a mile from the bungalow the curate, his neat clerical dress exchanged (as usual on his visits to Helm in the character of Mrs. Bradley's epileptic son) for gray flannel trousers, a dark crimson pull-over, a tweed jacket and a dark gray overcoat, walked on the damp sand at the margin of the water, climbing the breakwaters as he came to them and occasionally stopping to skim stones on the waves. The young policeman, off duty, walked, with the decided footsteps of the force, along the pavement which bordered the sea road, and young Tom, who had brought an ancient motorcycle with him, bestrode it and rode solemnly and noisily up and down the road until his engine stopped, just about fifty yards from Helm's bungalow, and the motorcyclist, seating himself on his own trench coat on the pavement, began to take off pieces of the antediluvian contraption and strew them about the gutter.

The curate gained the bungalow and knocked at the door. For a moment he fancied that nobody was at home, but slippered feet padded to the door and opened it. Wells experienced an uncomfortable qualm. He was certain in his own mind that this smiling, florid man had committed murder for the basest of all possible motives, that of pecuniary gain, and here was he himself, a man recently married, happy, content, secure in every worldly sense, putting his head into the jaws of death for the chivalrous but idiotic reason that, if he did not risk his life, an old woman with the outward appearance of a macaw, the mind of a psychoanalyst and the morals, so far as he knew, of a tiger shark, would risk hers.

"Ah, it's you," said Mr. Helm. "Come in, my dear boy. Come in. And how is She?"

The little narrow place was very dark inside. All the blinds were drawn. Wells' nebulous fears for his own bodily safety changed, for an instant, to panic terror. Every instinct shrieked to him to fly. Twenty years of subduing instinct to reason stood him in good stead, however, and, with a gulp which was histrionically inspired, he said in a quavering voice:

"Well, of course, you know, that's what I've come to talk about."

II

The first morning of the Easter term was not the best time to choose for a visit to the headmaster, as Mrs. Bradley fully realized, but on the previous evening she had received so extraordinary a letter from Noel Wells that no time, she felt, must be lost in relieving Mr. Cliffordson's mind on the subject of Miss Ferris' murder.

"Dear Mrs. Bradley," the letter began—she reread it in the train— "by the time you get this I trust I shall be with Daphne again. I beg your forgiveness, of course, if I have overstepped the mark, but you knew, I think, how alarmed I have been over your visits to that murderous devil in the railway-carriage hut, so I thought I would take the bull by the horns, and provoke him to make an assault on me.

"To this end I visited him, and, in the course of conversation, I allowed him to infer that the interest in the ten thousand pounds' life insurance you told him of would come to him if anything happened to me after your death. He must be a fool, because he bit it, and, when I was certain he'd taken the bait, I commented on the benefits derived from bathing in sea water, and left him. I behaved throughout the interview as much like a mentally defective person as possible—not a very difficult task, according to my wife, of course!—and then I left him severely alone until I received a letter from him asking after you. I wrote that you had met with an accident and were not expected to live. Later in the day I went to see him, and informed him that you had not the slightest chance of recovery. He managed to lead the conversation on to the subject of the insurance money, and I reassured him as to the clause in your 'will.' The next time I saw him I told him that you were dead.

"In next to no time I was being invited to indulge in the luxury of a sea water bath. You can imagine with what pleasure I watched the evil fellow carrying about a hundred pailfuls of water up to the house. It was a bitterly cold, dark evening. In between his journeys I conversed with him about you and your virtues, and while he was on the job of carrying the water, I conversed with young Tom from the garage, and the policeman who is going to marry Tom's sister.

"It all worked out very nicely. I had the bath, and Helm had got a very pretty and scientific grip on my feet, and my head was right under, when the other three, I suppose, burst in on us. I may say that on my previous visits I had been similarly escorted, so, you see, I took no risks worth mentioning. All the same, when they had overpowered him, I had to be spread out on the floor and artificially respirated; but it was not long before I felt, if not quite myself, near enough so to be glad that

the whole thing had gone off so satisfactorily. Incidentally, I have received inside information that the police now have little doubt that in
some way Cutler is responsible for the death of that poor girl in Lamkin,
the village not far from here, but, unfortunately, nothing can be proved.
They won't charge Cutler with the crime because there is no evidence
at present that he did murder the unfortunate girl Susie Cozens, but he
will be charged with attempting to finish off

> "Your affectionate friend,
> "NOEL WELLS."

"P. S. They are still at work on the Lamkin case, of course. The
difficulty seems to be that they cannot trace any connection between
Cutler and the girl. However, young Tom's future brother-in-law in-
forms me that no pains are to be spared, even if Scotland Yard has to be
called in, so I shall watch my morning newspaper for developments."

Mrs. Bradley folded the letter and replaced it in its envelope. She
laid it on the table. Then she rang the bell for Celestine.

"Madame?"

"You have heard of the legendary Sir Galahad, child?" asked Mrs.
Bradley. Celestine permitted herself to smile beatifically.

"*Parfaitement, Madame. 'Sans peur et sans reproche,'—n'est-ce
pas?*"

"Marvelous," said Mrs. Bradley. "I have the privilege of informing
you that there exists such a person in the flesh."

"In the flesh, Madame?"

"Not in any unpleasing degree," said Mrs. Bradley. "He is young,
thin, deprecating, chivalrous. Incidentally, he has risked his life for
mine."

"*Ah, c'est Monsieur le curé?*" cried Celestine, clasping her hands.
"Oh, but he is the tiger of bravery, that one! Always I have understood
that!"

III

When Mrs. Bradley reached the school, she sought the school keeper's
house before she went to interview Mr. Cliffordson.

The school keeper was not on duty, and Mrs. Bradley produced a
snapshot of Helm and requested him to examine it.

"Do you recognize this man?" she asked. The caretaker scrutinized it closely, but was compelled to acknowledge that he did not, "without it's the gent whose picture 'angs in the 'eadmaster's room." Mrs. Bradley was determined not to give him a clue to the identity of the original, but took the photograph straight away to Mr. Kemball. Mr. Kemball was superintending the distribution of school stock to his form, and was in a bad temper. He had found Christmas a time of great expense; he was in possession of a brand-new daughter whom he neither liked nor wanted; her birth had cost him dear; he had had to pay a term's school fees for his other children; he had had to pay his income tax; he had received thirty-one letters all pointing out the same small error in his monograph on the Renaissance popes, the monograph of which Mrs. Bradley had purchased fifty copies; he had three new girls in his form and did not want them; and he was quite certain, he told Mrs. Bradley bitterly, that the headmaster thought his teaching methods old-fashioned and his class management weak.

He could not identify the man in the photograph, unless by any chance it was the original of the portrait in the headmaster's room.

Mrs. Bradley thanked him, sighed heavily, and went in search of the headmaster.

"Ah!" said Mr. Cliffordson when he saw her. "Any news?"

"Yes," replied Mrs. Bradley. "You've read your newspaper lately?"

"Yes," replied the headmaster. Mrs. Bradley handed him Noel Wells' letter.

"Does it surprise you to hear that the Cutler who is suspected of the Lamkin murder and the Helm with whom Miss Ferris became acquainted at her aunt's boardinghouse are one and the same?"

The headmaster, having perused the letter, handed it back, and then shook Mrs. Bradley's skinny claw. He looked ten years younger.

"You think that this monster was responsible for Miss Ferris' death? That is the best news I've heard for weeks," he said. "But why should he have wanted to kill poor Miss Ferris, I wonder?"

"That," said Mrs. Bradley solemnly, "I'm afraid we shall never know." She thought of the photograph of Helm which was in her handbag. It seemed impossible that the elusive electrician who had visited the school and robbed the school keeper could have been Helm. He must have been a common thief, with neither interest in nor knowledge of the existence of the inoffensive Calma. But her object, that of persuading the headmaster to let the inquiry drop, was apparently gained. Mr. Cliffordson, after clearing his throat and moving the inkstand and a couple of pens from one side of the desk to the other, said suddenly:

"I wish I could tell you what it means to me to know for certain that none of the staff, nor the boys and girls here, were involved in that dreadful affair. I shan't carry the inquiry any further. It would be impossible to prove the crime against this wretched fellow, and so I would sooner let the whole matter drop. After all, poor woman, it can't make any difference now, and perhaps it is kinder, from every point of view, to let things remain as they are."

Mrs. Bradley agreed. Negligently she took the photograph of Helm from her handbag, tore it across and dropped the pieces on to the pleasant little fire which was burning in the headmaster's grate. It seemed unreasonable to inform him that to the best of her knowledge Helm had been nowhere near the school on the night when Calma Ferris was murdered. She herself, however, was determined to solve the problem to her own satisfaction. Before she had gone to Bognor Regis she had felt fairly certain of the identity of the murderer, but to psychological she was anxious to add tangible proof. To this end she suggested to Mr. Cliffordson that she should stay on at the school and give a series of talks on matters of public interest. The headmaster, who thought that he saw in this a desire on Mrs. Bradley's part to make a study of a coeducational system, gladly assented, and a list of subjects for the talks was drawn up there and then. Mrs. Bradley, whose interests were varied, suggested a lecture on Roman sports and pastimes as the first of the series, and this drew from Mr. Cliffordson the reference to Miss Camden which she had hoped to evoke.

"That girl looks ill. I saw her for about two minutes this morning. You know more about these things than I do, but, you know, I believe she works too hard. Your suggestion regarding a lecture on sports made me think of her," he said.

"Miss Camden?" said Mrs. Bradley. "I think she does work far too hard. But you can't prevent that. She's of the type that always works because it can't bear to sit still and think. She ought to be in a girls' school."

"Why?" said Mr. Cliffordson, who, like most headmasters and headmistresses, held, unconsciously but tenaciously, the opinion that the assistant masters and mistresses in his school were easily the most fortunately placed teachers in the whole of the profession.

"She would be allowed full scope for her activities. She might even," added Mrs. Bradley, eyeing the headmaster with semi-humorous gravity, "receive a little encouragement and a little praise for what she accomplished. Even the devil likes to receive his due, you know."

The headmaster rubbed his chin.

"I don't agree with all these compulsory games and sports," he said. "She ought to have some help, though. I'll see about it, I think. Now, look here, how would you like to start? I owe you something for finding such a—ahem!—convenient murderer for us."

"I should like to sit in the staff room, if I may, and make out a few headings and subheadings," said Mrs. Bradley. "It is very good of you."

The headmaster opened the door for her. The staff room was deserted. Mrs. Bradley, consciously thankful that she had not to give out stock, examine health certificates, make polite, insincere inquiries about the holidays, keep sports' accounts, answer questions, read and initial the headmaster's beginning-of-term notices, collect subscriptions, inspect lockers, allot cloakroom pegs, supervise the writing of labels, grumble about unmarked shoes, tunics, school hats and caps, blazers and hockey sticks, settled herself with a sigh of relief in the most comfortable chair she could find, took out her notebook and pencil and wrote on a clean page:

"1. Moira Malley.

"2. Hurstwood.

"3. Mr. Smith, art master.

"4. Miss Camden, games mistress."

Having made this neat list, she studied it with knitted brows.

At this moment Alceste Boyle came into the staff room. She did not see Mrs. Bradley at first. Her eyes were downcast and she walked slowly and heavily, as though she were laboring under an extraordinary burden of years.

"Oh, I beg your pardon," she said, when she noticed Mrs. Bradley. "I didn't know anyone was in here."

Mrs. Bradley smiled.

"Are you busy?" she said. Alceste lifted her right shoulder, and her mouth twisted oddly.

"Not since last Saturday fortnight," she said. Enlightenment came to Mrs. Bradley.

"Not—?" she said. Mrs. Boyle nodded.

"She died the day before you went to Bognor," she said. "The funeral was last Saturday fortnight. Fred hasn't . . ." She fought with herself for a moment, and then continued steadily, "Fred hasn't been near me since. I can't . . . you know what it was like. We were . . . I mean . . ."

She floundered. Mrs. Bradley came to the rescue.

"The man thinks the conventions ought to be observed," she said soothingly. "Men are queer people. Don't worry. Leave him alone for a bit."

But to herself she said, "Ho, ho! What have we here?"

"By the way," said Alceste, changing the subject, "I ought to let Mr. Cliffordson know that Moira Malley has not turned up this morning. I don't know whether he has received any message about her, but *I* haven't heard anything. I do hope the poor child isn't ill, because there's the scholarship examination in about six weeks' time, and, according to her place in form last term, she isn't nearly ready for it."

"Is Hurstwood back?" asked Mrs. Bradley.

"Hurstwood? Oh, yes; he's here. That boy ought to do well, but I wanted Moira to do well also. If I *have* a weak spot, it is for the girls," confessed Alceste. "But I can't understand Moira. She was doing no work at all during the last part of the term. Just sat there staring into space. I used to get rather angry with her."

"She found Miss Ferris' body," Mrs. Bradley reminded her. Alceste nodded, and sat down.

"Oh, yes, I know. And I make all due allowance for shock and so on. But a girl of that age shouldn't brood like this. After all, she didn't actually see her dead. She only just touched her. I don't mean to be callous, but I do think she might have got over it a little sooner than she did. Of course I blame Donald for the girl's state of mind. It was very wrong of him. I don't think he'll ask one of the girls to sit to him again without mentioning it first to me!"

"I am glad you remonstrated with him," said Mrs. Bradley. "He and the girl would see the thing from two very different points of view."

"I can't think why she ever thought of doing it, the little idiot!" said Alceste. "But I wish I knew why she hasn't come back to school. It's very foolish, but since Miss Ferris' death I'm nervous about unexplained absences. Ridiculous, isn't it?"

"Is it?" said Mrs. Bradley. Without a pause she added abruptly, "What was the cause of Mrs. Hampstead's death?"

"She fell into the ornamental lake and was drowned," replied Alceste. "Didn't you see the announcement in the papers? She had been drinking again."

"Curious," said Mrs. Bradley meditatively, but the word conveyed a different meaning from the one which Alceste attached to it.

"You mean it is curious that she should have been able to obtain the drink?" said Alceste, flushing.

"No, not that. The thing I find curious is this—epidemic of drowning," replied Mrs. Bradley quietly. "Yes, I mean it," she added, without giving Alceste time to interpolate any remark whatever. "It is strange. First, Calma Ferris. Secondly, or rather, thirdly, that wretched girl at Lamkin near Bognor. Thirdly, or rather secondly, Mrs. Hampstead. It's a nightmare." She had risen while she was speaking. Alceste rose too, and they confronted each other.

"What are you saying?" demanded Mrs. Boyle hotly. "What *are* you saying? You don't mean . . . you can't believe . . ."

"I am remarking," replied Mrs. Bradley, her rich, deep, quiet tones in marked contrast to Alceste's stormy voice, "on certain curious facts which are not necessarily interdependent. Sit down, dear child. Let us discuss the matter quietly." Suddenly Alceste began to laugh.

"I beg your pardon," she said. "I—yes, do let's talk. Are you any nearer a solution of our mystery?"

Mrs. Bradley sighed.

"I have allowed Mr. Cliffordson to believe that I think a man named Helm drowned Miss Ferris," she said. She told Mrs. Boyle the story of the infamous Cutler at some length, ending with the attempt on the life of Noel Wells.

"It sounds only too likely that he killed Miss Ferris, then," Alceste said.

"Unfortunately for the maintenance of any such convenient theory," Mrs. Bradley pointed out, "it is not yet at all certain that Helm was within miles of the school that night. The only evidence that Helm knew Miss Ferris' school address rests on the word of a woman whom I believe to be thoroughly untruthful. In addition to that, no stranger was seen on or about the school premises on the night of the murder except a man—the electrician, you know—who cannot be proved to have been Helm. He may have been Helm—an unreasonable belief assails me that he *was* Helm—but it can't be proved."

"How do you mean?" Alceste inquired.

"Well, I showed a recognizable newspaper photograph of Helm to the school keeper and to Mr. Kemball, both of whom saw and spoke to the bogus electrician, and neither can identify the man in the photograph. As a matter of fact, I never really felt that Helm had murdered Miss Ferris. His specialty is murder in a bathtub. He would have gone to Miss Ferris' lodging to murder her, or else he would have met her here and persuaded her to return with him."

"Does Mr. Cliffordson believe that Helm killed Miss Ferris?" Alceste inquired.

"I don't know. He pretends to accept my suggestion that Helm was the murderer because he wants the inquiry dropped. I don't think he believes that Helm is guilty."

Alceste looked uncomfortable.

"I suppose, then, that you know who did it, and that it was—one of us," she said. Mrs. Bradley took out her notebook and showed Alceste the four names she had written down. The senior English mistress looked distressed.

"But surely—Moira Malley! She *couldn't* have done such a thing. You don't know the child as I do. It is quite, *quite* impossible to suspect her of an awful crime like *murder!*" she said. Mrs. Bradley nodded.

"I agree! I agree! But consider the facts: The girl had opportunity. She had motive—"

"Miss Ferris may have known about the sittings, you mean? She may have warned the girl she was going to report her? Oh, but that's nonsense. Moira knows Mr. Cliffordson well enough to realize that Donald would be blamed, not she."

"Don't you see," said Mrs. Bradley, "that that may have been the motive?"

Alceste went white.

"I hadn't thought of that," she said. "These poor, idiotic children! There's that ridiculous boy Hurstwood making a fool of himself over Gretta Cliffordson, who isn't worth a second thought by anybody. I see you've got him down."

"Motive and opportunity," said Mrs. Bradley solemnly. "The same words, in all their sinister significance"—she cackled harshly—"apply equally in the case of the other suspects, Miss Camden and Mr. Smith."

"Of course, Camden,—I can imagine that," said Alceste slowly. "Overworked, strung-up, extravagant with money and energy and bad temper—an explosive sort of person altogether. And Miss Ferris had certainly got the wrong side of her."

"Yes," said Mrs. Bradley, smoothing a crease out of the sleeve of her raspberry-colored jumper. "And Mr. Smith is an artist, and there-fore—according to the ideas of the ordinary citizen, who regards art as expensive, and not even as a luxury at that!—a person who does not hold human life sacred. I know, too, that Miss Ferris damaged the Psyche and generally behaved in a Philistine manner. But what of it?"

She turned upon Alceste Boyle and said firmly:

"When I went away from here last term I was convinced—abso-lutely convinced—that Miss Camden was the murderer of Miss Ferris. Then I found out about Moira Malley and the sittings, and I became uncertain. So I also reconsidered the case of the boy Hurstwood, and it seemed to me that there was more than a possibility that he was guilty. Mr. Smith—I will be frank with you—I don't suspect at all of the mur-der of Calma Ferris."

She ran a pencil through his name in confirmation of what she was saying.

"But there's something wrong," she said vigorously. "There's some-thing behind all this which I don't yet understand. If it *was* one of these three, and I can prove it to my own satisfaction, the matter will rest there. I shall take it no further. But——" She pursed her thin lips into a little beak and shook her head vigorously for a moment.

"But I *can't* believe it was one of those three," said Alceste. "At least—" she hesitated, and then added: "I believe any one of them could have committed the murder, but not for any of the given reasons."

"My difficulty entirely," confessed Mrs. Bradley. "And yet," she said, as though she were thinking aloud rather than addressing Mrs. Boyle, "I don't know. What might appear to me, or to you, as a God-given and sufficient reason to eliminate a fellow-creature might seem airy, casual and of no importance to anyone else. On the other hand, you see, although it would not occur to me to murder anybody for the sake of gain, to a man like Helm it appears to be the obvious, natu-ral thing to do. This motive business is very difficult. Nobody can say without fear of contradiction that any motive for murder is too trivial. My difficulty is that, if I read these three people right, their spirits may have been willing, but I'm certain their wills would have been too weak, when it came to the point, to hold Calma Ferris' head down in that basin of water until she died. There is only one person who was behind the scenes that night who is capable of visualizing and performing such an action, and on that person I cannot pin the faintest shadow of a motive. Opportunity in plenty, but motive—none whatever!"

"And who is that?" inquired Alceste, interested but unbelieving.

"Suppose I said that it was the headmaster?" replied Mrs. Bradley, with one of her unnerving hoots of laughter. Alceste laughed too.

"Simply and briefly, I shouldn't believe you," she said. "If he committed the murder, why should he call you in to investigate the matter, when the coroner and his people had already most obligingly called it suicide? Besides, I thought he had no opportunity."

"True, child, true," said Mrs. Bradley, sighing. "The one thing above all others which is clear in my mind is that somebody very closely connected with the opera committed the murder. The time so carefully chosen, for instance, and—"

"The clay in the waste pipe," said Mrs. Boyle. "I have been puzzled over that. Who, besides Donald Smith, would have been thinking about clay from the art room? Yes, you'd like to say Moira Malley——"

Mrs. Bradley shook her head.

"Moira Malley wasn't thinking about clay," she said. "I'll tell you something else. I don't believe that child committed the murder, but I believe she suspects Mr. Smith, and that is what is upsetting her."

"Who do you think tampered with the electric light switch?" inquired Alceste.

"I believe it was Hurstwood. And I believe he did it because he suspects Miss Cliffordson. Aren't they funny children? I certainly think it was he who disconnected that switch. Incidentally, Miss Cliffordson thinks that the method employed—that basin full of water—was an easy way to kill anybody."

Alceste shuddered.

"I don't," she said. She shuddered again, and her lips twitched. Mrs. Bradley watched her closely for a moment, and then she said:

"Ah, well! It's all very interesting and mysterious. I don't know that I've ever had a similar case."

"There is one comfort," said Alceste slowly, after a pause, "no foul play can be suspected with regard to the death of Mrs. Hampstead. I can assure you that that was an accident. They didn't think the pond was deep enough to be dangerous, but she tripped and went on her head. It stunned her, and so she was drowned."

"I know," said Mrs. Bradley. "I have written to the doctor who was called upon to examine the body. I know all about it. I did nothing but remark upon the coincidence. There seems to be an epidemic of drowning lately. You know," she added, "I wish I could imagine any reason, other than the fact of her guilt, which caused Miss Camden to refrain from confiding to me that she had been called out of the audience to attend to Miss Ferris' injury that night."

Alceste shrugged.

"Send for her and ask her," she said. "There's never any drill on the first day of term, so she's sure to be free. I'll go and find her, if you like."

Without waiting for an answer, off she went, and returned in about five minutes' time with a very reluctant physical training mistress.

"Enjoyed your holiday?" asked Mrs. Boyle. Miss Camden glowered at her own black walking shoes and said that she had not.

"Oh, well, you're not going to enjoy yourself now," Alceste continued. "Mrs. Bradley is very much annoyed with you."

"Not at all," said Mrs. Bradley in her most soothing tones. "I am not anything but puzzled. Tell me, why did you hide the fact that you were called out of the audience to attend to Miss Ferris when she hurt herself on the night of the opera?"

"But I wasn't!" said Miss Camden, flushing and looking extremely frightened.

"Well, I'm bothered!" said Alceste, before Mrs. Bradley could speak. "Here, wait a minute."

She was out of the room and halfway down the staff room stairs before Miss Camden had a word to say. Then she ejaculated:

"What lies have they been telling about me?"

"I don't know, my dear," said Mrs. Bradley. She looked at the frightened girl shrewdly and added, "I was told that you are the person sent for whenever anybody is injured, and that, knowing this, one of the children went to fetch you when Miss Ferris cut her eye."

Miss Camden said nothing more until Alceste Boyle returned with the fourth-form girl who had acted as callboy and messenger on the night of the opera.

"Now, Maisie," said Mrs. Boyle, "did you ask Miss Camden to attend to Miss Ferris' eye, or didn't you?"

"Oh, yes, Mrs. Boyle," the child answered unhesitatingly. "And Miss Camden came."

"You must be mad, Maisie!" cried Miss Camden. "You never came near me the whole evening!"

"Please, Miss Camden, I did," the girl reiterated. "It was dark, and Miss Galloway guided me to where you were sitting, and I began asking you, and you said, 'Don't bellow, you little idiot. All right. I'll come.' And you followed me out into the corridor and then you said, 'Where is she?' and I showed you where she was sitting on a chair in the water lobby, and you said, 'All right. Cut along. I'll see to it.' So I went."

"Oh, yes. I remember," said Miss Camden savagely.

"That's all, Maisie," said Alceste Boyle, and the girl disappeared. When she had gone Miss Camden rose to her feet. She was like a cornered animal turning on its pursuers.

"Now take me away and hang me! Go on! Send for the police!" she screamed. She wrenched at the front of her dress and pulled out a whistle attached to a length of silk cord. "Here you are! Here, take it!" she yelled hysterically. She tore and tugged at the whistle to detach it. Alceste Boyle stepped up to her and coolly unfastened the clip which held the whistle on to the cord.

"And now stop being ridiculous, my poor child," said Mrs. Bradley. "Nobody is going to send for the police. Here, sit down. That's better. Now, then. *Did* you murder Calma Ferris?" she went on in a conversational tone. The girl, quieted by the attitude of the two older women, shook her head defiantly.

"What is the use of my saying anything?" she demanded. "You both know that I'm a thief and a liar. Why shouldn't I be a murderer as well?"

Mrs. Bradley shrugged her thin shoulders. "It would be a most unusual combination of criminal characteristics if you were," she said, "and very interesting. So interesting that I should not dream of sending for the police. Tell us all you know, and let me see what I can make of it."

"There isn't anything more," Miss Camden said. "I was with her less than five minutes. I was afraid to tell you before. I made certain you would think I'd murdered her. Maisie came for me, as she said, and I went along with her to the water lobby. But, upon my honor, Miss Ferris left the lobby with me, and the light was as usual, and the—the water ran away. Please believe me! *Please* believe me!"

Mrs. Bradley cackled suddenly, as though she had seen a joke.

"I do believe you, dear child," she said. "I perceive that if you had been Calma Ferris' murderer you would have given the game away long ago."

CHAPTER XV
DEDUCTION

I

It was Miss Sooley who made the momentous discovery. She took the newspaper to Miss Lincallow and, pointing to the photograph of the drowned girl at Lamkin, said excitedly:

"Surely that's the maid we used to have?" It was. Miss Lincallow verified it, and, what was more, went round to the police station with the newspaper under her arm, a stout ash plant in her right hand, "in case I am set upon by that wretch in the street," and triumph in her heart.

Names, dates and descriptions were compared and checked, the girl's mother was interrogated afresh, and it was established beyond doubt that the girl had been in Miss Lincallow's service at the beginning of the summer holiday.

"Dismissed for making herself too free with the gentlemen guests," Miss Lincallow explained, "and with that Cutler in particular."

It was a valuable clue. Following it up, it proved that the girl had been discovered tampering with property belonging to some of the visitors at the boardinghouse, and particularly that of Helm, and that for this reason she had been dismissed, and had gone home to live, after she lost another situation in London for dishonesty and for having been arrested for shoplifting. Unfortunately, although it could be proved that the dead girl and Cutler had been to some extent acquainted with one another, the police were as far as ever from being able to put their fingers on a motive substantial enough to be regarded as Helm's reason for murdering the girl.

"H'm! What about her putting the screw on Cutler some way until he got fed up with her?" suggested Detective-Sergeant Ross to Detective-Inspector Breardon, when every scrap of information they could wangle or frighten out of Miss Sooley and Miss Lincallow had been vouchsafed them.

"Sounds all right," said his superior. "The trouble is to prove it. Besides, I don't see what she could put the screw on about. He didn't harm those two funny old dames, where she was in service. I don't see any reason for blackmailing Cutler. In any case, motive or no motive, there's the question of tracing him to that inn on that particular Sunday, you know. That beastly fog has about done for us, I reckon. Even Spratt's father and mother, who would do anything, up to sticking their own necks in the hangman's noose, to get their son released, can no more explain the drowning of that girl in their bathroom than I can. They saw nobody; they heard nobody. The public bar wasn't open, but the side entrance was unlocked as usual, for the girl to come in to have her bath. Both of them were having a lie-down upstairs. We're up against a blank wall," said Breardon morosely. "We can fake up a charge against young Spratt all right, because, although he says he was out in the garage, there's nobody to swear to it. But a good lawyer will make mincemeat of our case against him, especially the jealousy motive. Besides, between ourselves, I'm certain the lad didn't do it. I reckon he *was* in the garage and never saw them come into the inn. We're holding him because he had the opportunity for the crime; but, come to that, so had his father and mother. Neither of 'em liked the idea of having the girl for their daughter-in-law, you know. What about *them?*"

"Oh, Cutler did it, all right," said Ross. "But we'll not be able to fix it on him, I'm thinking, sir."

"Well, we'll have a jolly good try," said Breardon, who was red-haired and very resentful of newspaper comment on the methods of the police. "I shall have another talk with that chauffeur, What's-his-name. He used to take the girl out in his employer's car, I'll bet. Perhaps they met Cutler some time, and things got said. You never know, and a nod's as good as a wink in some of these murder cases, my lad."

Accordingly Roy was again questioned, but he was certain that on their very infrequent joyrides they had never met anybody with whom his companion entered into conversation. He gave it as his opinion, which the police could take or leave as they chose, that if Cutler and the girl had met on the Sunday afternoon, they had met by accident and the drowning had been an unpremeditated crime. His difficulty, he said, was to imagine why Susie had ever taken the fellow into the inn with her. The inspector listened patiently, but passed no comment, and Roy was allowed to go. But when he had departed:

"Why shouldn't *he* be the murderer?" inquired Breardon suddenly of the sergeant.

"Because he's got an alibi, sir. He went back to fetch the old woman, the girl's mother, and he *did* fetch her. Besides, where's the motive?"

"Sweet on the girl, wasn't he? Weren't he and young Spratt rivals or something at one time?"

"Jealousy crime? Won't do, sir. He'd more likely to have killed the other fellow—the arrested man—than the girl."

"Not necessarily. He could have killed her to make sure the other bloke didn't get her. They do it in Spain, don't they?"

"Yes, but not in England, sir. It wouldn't be decent, Inspector!"

"All right, Sergeant. You know," said his superior, grinning. Ross, unperturbed, smiled dutifully, and then remarked:

"You know that inquest last fall, sir, at Hillmaston School?"

"The teacher who committed suicide? Yes."

"I wouldn't mind betting that was murder, sir, if the coroner had known his job. She was the niece of that woman who told us about this girl being in her service in the summer. The niece could have met Cutler, sir. She spent her summer holiday with her aunt."

The inspector smiled ironically and patted him on the back.

"Tell me when you feel better, my boy," he said paternally. The sergeant said doggedly:

"I can see that's how it would strike anybody, sir, but, all the same . . ." His voice trailed off, but he shook his head as one who had his own convictions and meant to abide by them.

II

Mrs. Bradley, seated in the room which had once been rented by Calma Ferris, was pitting reason against instinct, to the obstinate but ultimate defeat of the former.

"The woman was and is a liar born and bred," she told herself, referring to the mother of Susie Cozens. "But, on the other hand, she may, just for once, have been telling the truth, and, if she was, there are solid grounds for believing in Cutler's guilt."

The point at issue was the story told by Mrs. Cozens of the visit of Cutler to the manor house on the afternoon of the girl's death. If Cutler had visited Mrs. Cozens at the manor house instead of at her own cottage in order to inquire after Susie, there were strong reasons for assuming that he had already met Susie and learned from her where her mother was to be found. If this were so, his reason for visiting the mother could have been nothing but an attempt to create an alibi *after* he had murdered the girl. It was merely fortuitous that Susie and her mother had gone to the squire's house that afternoon. Cutler could not by any possible combination of circumstances have known that they would be there unless he had encountered Susie and learned the facts from her. He could not have learned the facts from her until after about half-past three on the day of her death, and he could not have met her between that hour and the time she reached the squire's house in the car driven by the chauffeur Roy unless the car had stopped somewhere on the way. The time taken to drive the distance of three and a half miles between the Cozens' cottage and the manor house—an hour all told—was certainly long enough to have allowed for stops, but, on the other hand, the density and dangers of the fog had made it imperative that Roy should proceed at something less than a walking pace along a road unlighted except for the big outside light and the lighted windows of the Swinging Sign. The inn was, roughly speaking, halfway between the cottage and the manor house.

Mrs. Bradley decided to interview Roy.

"You aren't going back to Bognor again, surely to goodness!" exclaimed the landlady, who had once been Calma Ferris' friend. Mrs. Bradley cackled happily.

"Oh, but I am!" she said, and at lunchtime on the following day she was seated at a table in the window of Malachi Spratt's public dining room, placidly eating cold beef and pickles, and potatoes boiled in their jackets. She was waited on by Malachi Spratt in person, and to him she reopened the subject of the murder. Malachi was inclined to shy away from all mention of the topic, but Mrs. Bradley gradually led him back to the subject. All that resulted, however, was his reiteration of the fact that he and his wife and son had neither seen nor heard Susie Cozens' arrival at the inn. This was the utmost that she could get out of him, so she went to the manor house not very much the wiser for her talk. She had informed Malachi that John would certainly be released. She was surprised, in fact, that the magistrates had committed him for trial, but she supposed that the police had pressed for it in the absence of all other suspects.

Ham Roy was off duty. He willingly described the drive in the dense fog from Susie Cozens' home to the house of his employer, but denied emphatically that they had met anyone on the road except a man who had lost his way in the fog and had asked to be directed. Roy was unable to direct him and had not seen his face clearly enough to be able to recognize him again, for he was wearing a waterproof coat and a check cap, the one with the collar turned up and the other with the peak pulled down. He had offered the man a lift as far as the squire's house, but this had been refused. Susie, according to Roy, had given no sign that she knew the man, but the chauffeur admitted that he had not taken much notice of Susie at the time, never for one moment imagining the possibility that Susie and the stranger might be acquainted.

There remained, then, Mrs. Bradley noted, the following possibilities:

First, that the "lost" man had been Helm (otherwise Cutler) and that his inquiry might have been a genuine one, or, more likely, in view of what had happened, he had followed up the car—not at all a difficult matter, since, in a fog so dense, he could probably manage to walk more quickly than the car could travel—from Susie's home. This meant he knew that she was in it, but did not know where she was going. In other words, he did not know where to find her when he wanted her. At some point on the journey he must have managed to pass the car, turn about, and accost it.

The second point was in the nature of a query. Had Helm and Susie walked or driven back to the Swinging Sign? This would have been immaterial from the point of view of the time taken over the journey, since walking or driving would be equally slow, and, on a country road, almost equally dangerous on such a day, but it would be important if anyone had seen them together between the manor house and the inn. It seemed reasonably certain to Mrs. Bradley that, as no sound had been heard by Malachi, Dora or John, the two had walked.

The chief difficulty in the way of proving Helm's guilt was the apparent absence of motive. Blackmail by Susie on the strength of what she had learned from rummaging among his possessions at the boardinghouse was not at all likely, Mrs. Bradley thought. What was required was that Susie should have discovered somebody whom he had actually done to death without having been discovered. There might be such a person, and Susie Cozens might have found out the details; but how had this been accomplished? What evidence could she have found?

Mrs. Bradley went to interview Mrs. Cozens. Nothing could shake the mother's story that Cutler had come to her and had asked to be allowed to speak to Susie.

"Ever so cut up he seemed when I said she had gone," Mrs. Cozens explained. "He didn't stop long. Said it was just his luck. All the nice girls loved a sailor, or some such rubbidge, ma'am, and him a commercial if ever I set eyes on one. Handsome in a bold, popeyed sort of way, ma'am, if you like them like that. Well, everyone to their fancy, and if he got my Susie into trouble in Bognor or up in London, or anywhere else, she'd ask for it, that's one thing about our Sue. Bold and daring, though I'm her mother that says it. But if it *should* turn out to be him, well, my picture in the papers, that I do expect, and no odds whatever to no one that I know of."

Mrs. Bradley came away absolutely convinced in her own mind that the woman really had seen Cutler. If this could be proved, Cutler had made a terrible blunder.

There remained the extraordinary coincidence of Mrs. Hampstead's death in the ornamental lake. Over this problem Mrs. Bradley spent hours and hours of thought. Several conclusions, but none different in essence from the rest, came to her mind, but she dismissed them as the result of softening of the brain.

"If only I could solve the mystery of Calma Ferris' death to my own satisfaction," she said to Alceste Boyle when next they met, "I believe the other affairs would solve themselves. No, I'm not being forgetful or tactless, dear child," she went on, as Alceste flushed and drew back at the reference to the recent death of Mrs. Hampstead.

Alceste did not reply immediately, and when next she spoke she volunteered the information that, during Mrs. Bradley's absence at Lamkin, Moira Malley had returned to school.

"Influenza," she replied in response to Mrs. Bradley's next inquiry. "Child looks terribly ill."

"I want to see her," said Mrs. Bradley. Alceste began to protest, but the little old woman cut her short with unusual abruptness.

"It is necessary. I shan't upset her."

"When do you wish to interview her?" said Alceste, who was angry.

"Now, at once," said Mrs. Bradley, returning to her usual manner, which was that of a well-disposed alligator.

"I shall remain in the room," announced Alceste.

"Very well. I would very much prefer, for your own sake, that you did not, but if you have made up your mind, that settles it."

"Moira shall settle it," said Alceste. To her surprise, the girl, who was looking exceedingly ill, begged her to go and leave Mrs. Bradley to conduct the interview.

"So I'm right," thought Mrs. Bradley. Aloud she said, "Tell me everything about it, Moira."

The girl looked frightened.

"Do you—know?" she asked. Mrs. Bradley pursed up her thin lips into a little beak and shook her head.

"I know, in one sense," she said. "In fact, I know, in the only sense that matters. But——"

"Will anyone be hanged?" said the girl, in a suddenly loud and very hard voice. Mrs. Bradley shrugged her shoulders, and waited patiently. At last the story came.

III

"I'm telling you in confidence," began the girl, "because I must tell somebody, and Mrs. Boyle wouldn't understand."

Mrs. Bradley accepted the implied compliment with a wave of her skinny claw.

"It was on the night of the opera. Oh, well, perhaps I'd better tell you everything. Mr. Smith called me back after drawing, one day—we have it last period on Thursday afternoon: it's mad, because of the light, but Mr. Cliffordson doesn't like the Sixth to spend time on anything except examination subjects and music—and asked me to sit to him. I have always liked Mr. Smith, and I said I'd like to, and asked what it was I had to do. He said:

" 'I saw you at the swimming gala. I want to model you. You have just the body I've been looking for.'

"I was embarrassed. We don't talk about bodies in Ireland. I did not know, either, that I was to be naked, but that was what he wanted. He teased me when I didn't want to, and told me that, anyway, I would have another girl or one of the mistresses to sit in the room. I did not want that. He tried to insist, but I said I could not bear that, but I would sit to him if he would promise not to tell anyone. He promised, and he kept his promise. I minded badly the first two times, but after that I did not mind. He told me I had a beautiful body, and I was glad that he liked me, even if it was only for something I could not alter and had not made.

"Then Miss Ferris damaged the clay model. It was almost finished, and it had to be cast in plaster later. It was no good to anyone when she had dropped it, and Mr. Smith was very angry. I heard afterwards that he had stamped on the clay in his anger, and that Miss Ferris was afraid and went for Mrs. Boyle to comfort the man.

"I was angry, too. I was terribly angry. I was afraid, too. I had become used to the shape of me growing and growing under his hands, and, although it was not my head and face that he was putting on the clay girl, I imagined that everyone who saw it would know it was my body. I thought Miss Ferris would know. Yet, how could she know? But I did not think of that. I was afraid Mr. Cliffordson would be very angry, and I was afraid that he would shame me before all the school when he was after telling them that I had sat naked before a grown man and he after making the shape of me with his hands."

Moira's carefully acquired schoolgirl speech was deserting her for her native idiom. Mrs. Bradley noted the change, and smiled. The girl, after a pause, continued:

"It was then she was killed. The night of the opera I found her dead in the water lobby the first time I came off the stage. I was terrified. I could not think what to do. I told Harry Hurstwood; he has the clever head on him and will not betray secrets. He said he would disconnect the light so that she should not be found until later. I did not tell him what I thought. I thought it was Mr. Smith had done it for love of the little clay girl she had damaged. Harry believed it was someone else. He would not tell me who.

"At the end of the opera they had not found her, and I thought to myself that it was a terrible thing indeed to leave her by herself in that empty place with her head in the cold water and herself not shriven at all.

"Then Mr. Smith came round to my aunt's house and begged me to say nothing about the accident he had had, knocking off Miss Ferris' glasses and cutting her face so that she had been obliged to go into the water lobby to bathe it and had died there. When he asked me would I not mention the accident, I was quite certain that he had murdered her, and it made me ill. I have thought of nothing else, and it was her voice wailing like a lost thing round our house that made me tell you what I never thought to tell anyone, for I love him, God help me, so I do."

She broke down and sobbed. Mrs. Bradley comforted her. Later, she let her go, and sent for Hurstwood.

"Whatever made you think Miss Cliffordson had murdered Miss

Ferris, child?" asked Mrs. Bradley. The boy flushed and grinned.

"I say, please don't tell her!" he said. "I don't think so now. Haven't for a long time."

"I promise," said Mrs. Bradley. "Have you done any boxing during the holidays?"

"Rather. Nearly every morning. Gretta—Miss Cliffordson—doesn't like it—thinks it's brutal; but I can't help that. Mr. Poole is going to enter me for the public school championship at Aldershot, I think."

Mrs. Bradley dismissed him and sighed with relief. He and Moira, at any rate, were clear of the wretched affair. Remained—she grinned as the title came into her head—"The Adventure of the Kind Mr. Smith."

She consulted her notebook before sending for Mr. Smith, and re-read the entry relating to Miss Sooley's having given the school address to Helm. The entry interested her. She reread it. The fact appeared to be that Helm had known the school address. What he had not known was that Calma Ferris was a mistress there. Mrs. Bradley re-read the entries relating to the murder of Calma Ferris from beginning to end. Two of them stood out as particularly important. The first read:

"Smith, Donald, senior art master.

"Motive for murdering Calma Ferris:

"Calma Ferris had damaged irretrievably a small clay figure of Psyche, the property and creation of Smith.

"N.B. Smith apparently expected to receive two hundred and fifty pounds for the completed plaster figure. That seems a good deal of money for a work by an unknown (?) artist. I deduce the fact from the remark Alceste Boyle volunteered when I was talking to her on the occasion of our first meeting, i. e., she said, without being asked, 'Smith isn't the man' (who was her lover). 'Oh, and I lent him two hundred and fifty pounds for the loss of the little Psyche.'

"See Page Fifteen," Mrs. Bradley had appended.

Page Fifteen, when she turned it up, informed her that Donald Smith had said, when she was questioning him:

"Yes, I was angry." (About the statuette.) "But it was all right. Alceste lent me the money to pay Atkinson."

Mrs. Bradley clicked her tongue. Then she sent for Mr. Smith.

"I have to warn you," she said, when he came in, "that anything you say may be used in evidence."

Smith lowered himself carefully into a chair, propped his left elbow on the back of it, leaned his head on his hand and said nonchalantly:

"I see."

"First," said Mrs. Bradley, "can you tell me how much I ought to pay for a plaster statuette sixteen inches high? It is a nice little thing by a living but entirely unknown artist."

"Dunno," said Smith simply. "Anything the artist liked to ask, if you really wanted it, I suppose. *Do* you really want it?"

"To the extent and limit of about thirty pounds, yes," said Mrs. Bradley.

"Oh? Well, I should make him the offer. Has it been exhibited yet?"

"No. It was done to order, but something went wrong. The artist told a friend of mine that he hoped to get two hundred pounds or more for it."

"Humorist," said Mr. Smith concisely.

"You think so? But I understood that you allowed Mrs. Boyle to think that that was the value of your Psyche which was damaged by Miss Ferris."

Smith brushed a hand across his brow.

"Did I? I can't remember," he said. "I must have been tight, mustn't I?"

"You know, Donald," said Mrs. Bradley, "you provoke my unwilling but sincere admiration over the whole of this business. I suppose it was you whom Cutler came to see on the night of the opera?"

Smith blinked at her. He seemed about to go to sleep. Suddenly he said:

"You can't touch me, you know. I've taken legal advice. If I say to a bloke that it would be worth two hundred and fifty pounds to me to know that a certain woman was dead, and suddenly, several weeks afterwards, she dies, and the bloke claims the money and *doesn't get it*, it seems that I'm untouchable."

"You certainly are," said Mrs. Bradley, grinning hungrily. She began to turn over the leaves of her notebook, and, in doing so, came upon the following entry:

"Sooley, Miss, partner to Miss Lincallow, the aunt of the dead schoolmistress. This woman may be under the influence of Helm. I suspect that he is after her savings."

Mrs. Bradley skipped a couple of hundred words relating to Miss Sooley's psychological peculiarities, and then read: "This woman gave Helm the address of Hillmaston School. But did she? She actually said that Helm informed her he was going to Hillmaston School to see his nephew. Miss Sooley then appears to have exclaimed, 'Why, that's where Miss Lincallow's niece is a teacher! You know—the one that was staying here and got so friendly with you over the burglars.' "

"I suppose Cutler saw you here by appointment on the night of the opera?" said Mrs. Bradley.

Smith shook his head.

"Can't remember," he said. "Who is Cutler?"

"The man to whom you offered the two hundred and fifty pounds if he would drown Mrs. Hampstead," said Mrs. Bradley pleasantly.

"Oh, is he? Well, what would you have had me do? There were those two charming people, Hampstead and Alceste, and there was that poor demented creature in a mental home which is surrounded by a hedge that a child of three could have broken through. I knew she was an inebriate. The thing was how to get her doped sufficiently. Mind, I had nothing whatever to do with the proceedings, but I think the gin did it. Cutler had no trouble. In she went, dead to the world, and he held her head down with a forked twig, or so he said. Very neat. I can't think why they let these poor creatures out without an attendant. It gives murderers like Cutler such a lot to think about."

"How did you come to think of engaging Cutler for the delicate task?" inquired Mrs. Bradley, geniality itself.

"I advertised," said Smith, grinning. "You know the sort of thing: 'Acquitted man wanted to earn two hundred pounds. Only ex-murderers need apply.'

"The papers thought it was a code or a silly joke. Anyway, they inserted it in the Personal column, and it brought home the bacon in the form of Corporal Nym, otherwise Cutler."

"Suppose the police had made it their business to investigate the details that led to the insertion of such an advertisement in the newspapers?" said Mrs. Bradley.

"I should have said it was a joke. The police will believe anything of a public schoolboy," replied Smith. "I should have said it was for a bet. Besides, I chose the right papers. No lowbrow rags. All the important dailies every morning, for a fortnight, printed that brightly worded paragraph, and no questions asked."

"But what happened when you did not pay the man?" inquired Mrs. Bradley. "He was the electrician who came here on the night of the opera, of course?"

"Yes. He was disguised a bit. Not enough to see through, but just enough to prevent a casual observer from recognizing him. Very clever. Alone I did it. He kicked up a fuss, I believe. I don't quite remember. Anyway, I told him I'd fix the murder of Calma Ferris on him if he gave any trouble. He was on the premises, you see, and he admitted that he knew her."

"You admit, then, that Miss Ferris *was* murdered?" said Mrs. Bradley.

"I admitted it at the time, if you remember," said Smith, still speaking in the same sleepy, noncommittal tone. "But *I* didn't murder her, if that's what you're still getting at. I admit I was responsible for Mrs. Hampstead's death, but I'm not a bit perturbed about that. How came you to know that she had been murdered, though?"

"I deduced it from the fact that Mr. Hampstead is no longer desirous of marrying Mrs. Boyle," said Mrs. Bradley. "I assume that he is troubled by the kind of scruples which would scarcely affect *you*, for instance."

"Oh, I know Hampstead suspects foul play. He said as much to me," admitted Smith, with cool effrontery. "But that feeling will wear off. He and Alceste are made for one another, and why should an insane creature stand in their way? Luckily, some purblind idiot of a doctor wrote a certificate all right, and the coroner made a quick job of the inquest. The only thing on my conscience is that I didn't get this idea of finishing her off ten years ago."

"And what about that girl at Lamkin?" said Mrs. Bradley.

"She meddled with Cutler's correspondence. Must have been a fairly quick-witted baggage to piece out enough to hang blackmail on, mustn't she? Of course, Cutler's yellow. She'd got him cold. So he finished her. That's all about that."

"I see," said Mrs. Bradley. "Yes. Thank you, child."

Smith rose. Mrs. Bradley, absorbed in her notes, did not even watch him as he went leisurely out at the door and shut it behind him. Suddenly he opened it again.

"And still the mystery of Calma Ferris remains unsolved," he said. Then he went away. Mrs. Bradley pursed her thin lips into a little beak and nodded her head very slowly like a Chinese mandarin. Then she took up a volume of modern poetry and began to read.

Members of the staff came in at intervals, deposited or collected their belongings, and went out again. Mrs. Bradley, absorbed in her reading, took no notice of anybody. At last she put down the little book.

"He had the opportunity and some sort of motive," she said to herself. "He is responsible for the death of Mrs. Hampstead and, indirectly, for the death of Susie Cozens. But I don't believe for one instant that he had anything whatever to do with the death of Calma Ferris, because, first, he wanted the time for that interview with Cutler, to whom he had to give the most detailed, exact and reiterated instructions for the murder of Mrs. Hampstead; and because, secondly, the motive would not be *his* motive. He's a perverted philanthropist; a kind of amoral public benefactor. In short, he's God. Most artists are! It's the effect of the creative instinct on undisciplined intelligences. There was no reason, from his point of view, for killing Calma Ferris. It would not benefit anybody. The destruction of his statuette angered him at the moment, but the anger passed. Besides, the point is that he wouldn't kill for a purely personal reason like that. And if it wasn't Mr. Smith it must have been—" She took out her notebook and scowled at the three names—"Miss Camden, Moira Malley or Hurstwood. I don't believe it! I've cleared the two children— or they've cleared themselves. And I've decided that Miss Camden would have given herself away if she'd done it. Well, if the people with motives didn't do it, the people with opportunity *did*. That's clear. But, oh! how tiresome of them!"

CHAPTER XVI
SOLUTION

Mrs. Bradley went to the lodgings where Calma Ferris had once lived, and spent an hour and a half in writing a detailed account of the case, as she saw it, against Cutler, in connection with the murder of Susie Cozens. She sent the statement to the Chief Constable of the county, who passed it on to Inspector Breardon. The charge of murdering Susie Cozens was preferred, and the charge of attempted murder of Noel Wells was dropped. At the trial, an underhousemaid was called who was prepared to back up Mrs. Cozens' statement that Cutler had called at the manor house that evening and had asked to see Susie. As it was shown that, unless he had met Susie earlier in the day, he could not possibly have known that she would be at the squire's house that afternoon, the jury found him guilty of the murder, and his subsequent appeal failed.

Having despatched the letter, Mrs. Bradley took out the small cards and played three varieties of Patience; then she took out a scribbling-block and began to write on it every characteristic of Calma Ferris which had impressed itself upon her mind.

"She was inoffensive.

She had financed the production of *The Mikado*.

She had damaged Mr. Smith's Psyche.

She had annoyed Miss Camden by keeping a girl in instead of allowing her to play in the school netball team.

She had been given a chief part in the opera, and, in consequence, Miss Camden had been left out of the cast.

She was conscientious.

She was hard working.

She was painstaking.

She was so colorless herself that she expected other people to be much more colorful than they were.

She knew that Alceste Boyle and Frederick Hampstead were lovers.

She had seen Hurstwood embracing Miss Cliffordson.

It does not appear that she knew of the sittings which Moira Malley gave Mr. Smith for the Psyche.

Nobody gained anything by her death, except certain persons above-mentioned, who were relieved from immediate embarrassment, perhaps, but who cannot have thought that they would suffer indefinitely if they were betrayed to the headmaster by Miss Ferris.

Apart from the persons above-mentioned she had no enemies so far as I can discover.

She was killed during the first act of the opera, before she had made any appearance on the stage.

She was a failure at the dress rehearsal.

She greatly improved at a subsequent rehearsal.

At this subsequent rehearsal the actors were not in costume.

At the dress rehearsal Alceste Boyle demonstrated how the part of Katisha should be played. On the night of the opera Alceste Boyle took the part which Calma Ferris should have taken.

Therefore, in two respects, the dress rehearsal and the actual performance were alike: i.e., Both were done in costume and complete makeup.

Therefore, in the same two respects, the dress rehearsal was unlike any other rehearsal.

Both the dress rehearsal and the final show were performed with Alceste Boyle instead of Calma Ferris in the part of Katisha.

But at the dress rehearsal Alceste Boyle took the part over when Calma Ferris had done it badly, because she wished to help and instruct her.

Whereas, at the final performance, Alceste Boyle took the part because Calma Ferris was not there to take it.

And Calma Ferris was not there to take it because Calma Ferris was dead."

Mrs. Bradley reread what she had written, tore off the last sheet, which was still attached to the scribbling block, clipped the sheets together, and put them on one side. Then she addressed herself to the virgin sheet on the block and began again:

"Calma Ferris was drowned.

The people who knew she went to the water lobby the first time to bathe her face are:

Hurstwood,

Miss Camden,

Little Maisie Something, the callboy,

Mr. Smith (perhaps. He may not have known which water lobby she used, as there is another on the same side of the building),

Alceste Boyle (perhaps. She does not admit it).

The people who knew she went to the water lobby a second (?) time to bathe her face were (?)

But she *must* have gone a second time."

Mrs. Bradley tore the sheet off, laid it with the others, and began again:

"The murderer must be

1. Prompt to act. This would be so in the case of Hurstwood, Moira Malley, Miss Camden. This would not be so in the case of Mr. Smith.

2. Somebody who was offering to render assistance, i.e., first aid, to Miss Ferris. This could have been Moira Malley; Miss Camden;

possibly, but not probably, Hurstwood; possibly, but most improbably, Mr. Smith.

3. A conversationalist. Something had to be done to distract Miss Ferris' attention from the fact that the bowl was filling up. Of all the people who appear to be most nearly concerned, I cannot imagine Hurstwood, Moira Malley nor Mr. Smith producing a flow of prattle. Miss Camden *might*, but somehow I cannot imagine it from what I know of her.

4. Somebody who can act a part and preserve a face of brass. There was that dreadful interval to get through. Calma Ferris, dead. The possibility that at any moment the body might be discovered. It must have been a time of dreadful strain. Moira Malley and Hurstwood were both upset. Mr. Smith did not appear to be—at least, nobody has suggested that he was. Miss Camden was in the audience.

It looks like Miss Camden, except that, evidence or no evidence, I feel *certain* she would have given herself away. Smith, of course, is an artist. 'Art for art's sake' and so on. Oh . . .?"

Light had come.

Mrs. Bradley tore the sheet off, and laid it with the others. Then she rang for milk and biscuits, and began to write a letter.

"My dear friend," she wrote, "I should like to come and see you if I may. I have solved the mystery of Calma Ferris' death, and I think you might be interested to hear my conclusions. As I know your motive for removing the poor woman from the cast of *The Mikado*, I am convinced that you have committed your last crime against society in the interests of your art. I admire an artist, and one who is so consistently and integrally on the side of the Muses as to commit murder in their defense seems to me worthy to have been born in a less decadent and squeamish age than this in which we live. I admit myself to be decadent and squeamish in that, while I appreciate your motive, I deprecate the cruelty of robbing that inoffensive woman of her life.

"My difficulty in finding a solution to the problem has been the fact that one person besides yourself possesses most of the characteristics necessary for the commission of this particular—I was about to say 'crime,' but, perhaps, I had better say 'wilful act.' The murderer, it seemed to me, had to possess courage, willpower, initiative and tremendous self-control. I ought to have seen sooner that Miss Camden, whom I suspected for weeks, did not sufficiently possess this last characteristic.

She is not particularly self-controlled. She is reckless, extravagant, unstable, and would have given herself away to everybody if she had committed the deed. No. Everything points to you. You killed Miss Ferris—I see it more clearly every minute—because you are essentially an artist. You saw Alceste Boyle perform the part of Katisha at the dress rehearsal. You observed that she is a particularly fine actress. You had already seen poor Calma Ferris bungle the part hopelessly. You are an old woman, and you wanted to see the part played once more—perfectly. You removed Calma. Alceste, as you foresaw, had to take the part. You had not premeditated the crime. Nobody could have foreseen that Mr. Smith was going to charge down the corridor, break Miss Ferris' glasses and cut her face. You went into the water lobby after her, I think—nobody appears to have seen you—to see whether you could be of any assistance. You saw her bending over the basin. Then Miss Camden came along the corridor, and you slipped into the nearest doorway, I suppose, and left her to render first aid. But the little cut was deep, and when Miss Ferris had been attended to, she had to return to the dressing room so that her makeup could be replaced. You took care to reopen that small, deep cut. She had to go again to the water lobby to bathe it. This time you went along with her. You had a lump of modeling clay for the purpose of broadening Mr. Smith's nose, when you made him up as the Mikado. This lump of clay you thrust into the waste pipe. Poor Miss Ferris, blind as a bat without her glasses, did not notice what you were doing. Then you pressed the tap with one hand, dabbed her face (with Hurstwood's handkerchief) with the other, and kept up a flow of easy, interesting, amusing chatter. Oh, that chatter! How it bothered me to think who, among those teachers or those children, could so easily have held the victim enthralled—so enthralled that she did not heed the basin filling . . . filling. . . .

"It was beautifully done. And I congratulate you. You slipped into your seat—your nice seat in the middle of the third row—and you saw the first entrance of Katisha. You felt justified in what you had lately come from doing. During the interval you touched up faces, adjusted wigs, chattered and laughed, an actress in every sense of the word. Then you returned to the auditorium for the second act, while that inoffensive woman—you told me yourself that she was an inoffensive woman!—do you remember?—lay out in the lobby dead. But to murder her *because* she was an inoffensive woman seems to me almost a divine gesture. She was too inoffensive to play the part as you felt it should be played, and so you murdered her, and had Alceste Boyle instead to entertain you in the character of Katisha.

"I remain for always your sincere admirer,

"BEATRICE A. L. BRADLEY."

She addressed the letter to Madame V. Berotti.

APPENDIX

Editors' note to reader: *It is not necessary to read this through unless you're interested in Mrs. Bradley's thought processes while working out the solution to the puzzle. Question: do you think she was justified in letting the murderer off the hook as she did?*

MRS. BRADLEY'S CONCLUSIONS

1. SMITH, DONALD.

Capable of murder.

Is a teacher.

Is an artist.

Loves Alceste Boyle.

Does not hate Calma Ferris.

Relieved his feelings by stamping on his ruined clay model.

Spent a considerable amount of time during Act One of *The Mikado* in conversing with the electrician.

The electrician was a bogus electrician.

He was not sent by the firm.

He did not understand electrical appliances.

He may have been Cutler.

Mrs. Hampstead, a dipsomaniac, is drowned. As soon as Mrs. Hampstead died, Hampstead was free to marry Alceste Boyle.

Was Mrs. Hampstead murdered?

Did Cutler murder her?

If Cutler murdered her, it was for gain.

Would Cutler consider a promise of £250 sufficient inducement to commit murder?

If he thought it worth while to steal a watch and a small sum from the school caretaker—yes.

THE ARTIST: Smith borrowed the money from Alceste Boyle to pay the price of her freedom.

THE TEACHER: Smith deputed another person to perform the messy manual labor of murder.

Proof presumptive but not proof absolute that Mrs. Hampstead was murdered by Cutler at the instigation of Smith.

THE MURDER OF SUSIE COZENS

Cutler murdered Cozens.

He did not murder her for pecuniary gain.

This is extraordinary, therefore she must have been a menace to his safety.

How could she be?

When she worked for Miss Lincallow she could have found correspondence relating to the proposed killing of Mrs. Hampstead.

Was she smart enough to read between the lines of such correspondence?

Apparently she was, if she had to be murdered to shut her mouth.

She, then, could have proved that Cutler murdered Mrs. Hampstead. If it could have been proved by Susie Cozens, it must have been a fact.

Proof.

Therefore, Cutler did murder Mrs. Hampstead, and, since he could have had no reason for disliking her, since he did not know her, he murdered her for money. The money would have been promised by

Hampstead,

Alceste Boyle or

Smith.

Which of them could have known where to write to Cutler? (For the silly story of the advertisement inserted in the newspapers cannot be true.)

Smith, since he had painted his portrait. I wonder why he presented the portrait to the headmaster?

2. BEROTTI, MADAME V.

Capable of murder. (We all are!)

Knew of the accident.

Knew that Calma Ferris went a second time to the water lobby.

Was the only person, probably, who *did* know this, since she and Calma would have been in the dressing room together until it was time for Calma to get ready at the side of the stage for her first entrance.

She had the modeling clay in her possession, since she used some of it in making-up Smith's nose.

She was an actress.

She was the most likely person, therefore, to retain her composure and *sang froid* under difficult circumstances. This would account for the fact that not one of the suspected persons gave himself or herself away under interrogation.

True, Smith was ill at ease, but then he had the Cutler-Mrs.. Hampstead-murder on his mind. True, so was Miss Camden, but she had a guilt-complex over the forgery, connected with the headmaster's check.

True, Moira Malley was nerve-ridden and hysterical, but then she thought Smith had committed the murder.

Motive.

Mrs. Berotti is an artist. Everyone insisted on it.

She had seen Calma Ferris act very badly.

She had seen Alceste Boyle act superlatively well.

She risked her neck to get the part of Katisha performed as she knew it could be and ought to be performed.

I recognize that this motive would be more easily credible if the piece had been grand opera or great tragedy. It seems a slight motive when the piece was comic opera.

But

Mrs. Berotti is a very old woman. She may not see many more pieces performed.

Besides

The murder was a gesture. "Away with incompetents!" she said. "Let us have the thing done as it might be done by the angels."

Proof.

But the proof of her guilt is that she was the only person who must have known *for certain* that Calma Ferris went to the water lobby a second time.

THE END

If you enjoyed *Death at the Opera* ask your bookseller for the other mystery by Gladys Mitchell available from The Rue Morgue Press: *When Last I Died* (0-915230-85-2, $14.95).

About the Rue Morgue Press

"Rue Morgue Press is the old-mystery lover's best friend, reprinting high quality books from the 1930s and '40s."
—*Ellery Queen's Mystery Magazine*

Since 1997, the Rue Morgue Press has reprinted scores of traditional mysteries, the kind of books that were the hallmark of the Golden Age of detective fiction. Authors reprinted or to be reprinted by the Rue Morgue include Dorothy Bowers, Pamela Branch, Joanna Cannan, Glyn Carr, Torrey Chanslor, Clyde B. Clason, Joan Coggin, Manning Coles, Lucy Cores, Frances Crane, Norbert Davis, Elizabeth Dean, Katherine Farrer, Constance & Gwenyth Little, John Mersereau, Marlys Millhiser, Gladys Mitchell, James Norman, Stuart Palmer, Sheila Pim, Craig Rice, Kelley Roos, Charlotte Murray Russell, Maureen Sarsfield, Margaret Scherf, and Juanita Sheridan.

To suggest titles or to receive a catalog of Rue Morgue Press books write P.O. Box 4119, Boulder, CO 80306, telephone 800-699-6214, or check ourwebsite, www.ruemorguepress.com, which features complete descriptions of all of our titles, along with lengthy biographies of our writers.